RED ANGEL

BO BLACKMAN
BOOK FOUR

HELEN HARPER

FROM HIGH STAKES

The world is full of crazy unsolved mysteries. The humans have them in abundance with things like the *Marie Celeste*, Lord Lucan and the grassy knoll. The Families have them with the second Lady Stuart and Jack the Ripper. The witches have Moll Dyer and Alex Sanders. Kakos daemons, well, they're enough of a mystery themselves without any extra help. But the Agathos daemons have Tobias Renfrew. He might just top them all.

It's said that Renfrew was conceived the night the *Titanic* went down. His mother, a young Agathos noblewoman, was scandalously travelling alone on the ill-fated ship to make a new life for herself across the Pond. She certainly did that, although given that it's been suggested it was a highly placed crew member who she was making that new life with, it's possible that hundreds of other lives were also lost in the process. Renfrew's alleged father had been on duty the night they hit the iceberg; he was mysteriously absent during the initial collision, however, and reportedly unkempt and dishevelled when he finally did appear - with Toby's mother in tow. Still, even if it had been his negligence that had contributed to the disaster, and he went down with the ship himself, he did manage to see his lover safely onto a lifeboat, saving the tiny embryo that was to become Tobias Renfrew in the process.

Devastated by what happened, and with a growing belly, she holed up in a corner of Brooklyn and sent tearful letters back to her family in England. Not long before Tobias was born, her father turned up on her doorstep and dragged her back home. I'm not sure whether he actually had to drag her, though; it can't have been a lot of fun being single, pregnant and penniless. Unfortunately for her, things didn't really improve back on home soil. She was hidden away in some godforsaken corner of the country to preserve the family honour. When she finally went into labour, the midwife wasn't called until it was too late. Little Toby was breech and was eventually cut from his mother's womb, apparently wide-eyed but entirely silent. She, meanwhile, bled out.

It would be safe to say that the Renfrew family suffered Tobias's childhood rather than enjoyed it. He was, after all, a bastard son. There were whispered tales of savage beatings and bloodstained dungeons. I suspect the truth is that he was simply ignored. Whatever, by the time he was a teenager, he had been incriminated in a number of local crimes and had run away at least three times from his spartan boarding school. His one champion was his aunt Molly, who tried her best to do right by him. But she was only a female daemon and the worse Tobias's behaviour, the more her pleas to help him fell on deaf ears. Eventually the rest of his relatives had had enough. Tobias was thrown out with only five pounds to give him a head start. Molly, in a fit of desperation, gave him her favourite ruby earrings, thinking that he could pawn them. He never did.

He joined the army, signing up just in time to get involved in the civil war in Afghanistan. He rose quickly through the ranks, even though daemons were viewed with as much suspicion in those days as any human who wasn't white skinned,

God-fearing and male. He tripped from conflict to conflict, growing more bloodthirsty with each one until, inexplicably, he bowed out not long before the advent of the Second World War. He got involved in munitions manufacturing instead.

Whether it was from ill-gotten gains during his time fighting around the world, or from black market sales in the weapons' trade, by the time the 1950s rolled around, Tobias Renfrew had enough money to buy his ancestral home. He did to his relatives what they'd done to him: tossed them out with a barely civil farewell. Molly was long dead, killed during the Blitz and, despite his wealth, Tobias was still completely alone.

Instead of warmongering, he filled his days with politics. He schmoozed all the right people and feathered all the right pockets. His coffers grew and his sticky fingers dabbled in all manner of pots. And he did it all while wearing Molly's ruby earrings. If anyone ever teased him for such a girlish affectation, there is no record of it. He was not the kind of man you wanted to insult. Indeed, it was said that if he ever came across another daemon wearing similar jewellery, even if it was for reasons of flattery via imitation, he ripped it from their flesh no matter who they were.

At one point, Tobias seemed to take on a veneer of respectability. He started withdrawing from his more dodgy – as well as lucrative – dealings. My grandfather met him briefly during this time; unsurprisingly he dismissed him as a 'rough amongst diamonds'. It's been whispered Tobias was on course to become the first daemon Prime Minister. But that was before one cold night in January, 1963.

Tobias flung open the doors of his mansion to all and sundry. He didn't just invite politicians: there were film stars, powerful witches and the five Family Heads – apparently one of whom was the reigning Lord Gully. Champagne flowed, opium abounded and everyone had a merry old time. Despite his history, Tobias was a congenial host. His family had taught him how to hobnob with the rich and he'd taught himself how to mix with everyone else. Prior to a breathtakingly expensive fireworks' display, he gave a speech. There's an old recording of it somewhere that has been pored over by historians and conspiracy theorists for years. He made reference to 'hidden wealth' and 'mysterious saboteurs'. Then, just as he invited the entire gathering to raise their glasses and toast their own health, there was a flash of light and he disappeared.

His guests were amused, believing it to be some kind of clever trick – until someone went searching and discovered several body parts in an upstairs bathroom, along with copious amounts of blood. They came from at least five different corpses: one human, two witches, one vampire and one Agathos daemon. Tobias Renfrew was never seen again.

In the absence of any other suspects, he was indicted for murder. His surviving family members, all of whom had fallen on hard times, demanded that his wealth and properties revert to them. As a suspected, albeit not confirmed, murderer, the state and the increasingly powerful Agathos court wanted to confiscate everything for themselves. Tobias's will, meanwhile, left everything to a defunct children's charity. However, a very clever lawyer argued that in the absence of a body, his death could not be confirmed.

No traces of him were left behind. Because he was an Agathos daemon, Tobias's disappearance couldn't be explained away by him being turned into a vampire. The public nature of his departure also suggests that he wasn't attacked by a Kakos daemon. (There are, of course, those who suspect that in a fit of Sleeping Beauty-esque jealousy at not being invited to the lavish party, a Kakos *was* involved but then there are always conspiracy theorists.) The witches were equally discounted, as invisibility spells are nigh on impossible to maintain. Furthermore, to add to the mystery, to this day not even the more talkative ghosts will discuss it.

So, to all legal intents and purposes Tobias Renfrew is still alive. Nobody gets his money: not the descendants of his fickle family, nor the charity, nor the government. Every so often, another legal challenge is made and thanks to the intricacies of daemon law and the bitter greed of the parties involved, it always fails. It doesn't help that each interested party advertises large rewards for information regarding Tobias's whereabouts. They're each determined to get the jump on the other.

If he is still alive, Tobias would be well over a hundred years old – not unheard of for a daemon but not all that likely either. His wealth continues to grow and estate managers continue to be hired. The Agathos community, by some strange unspoken agreement, never wear rubies in their ears. Whether it's out of deference or fear, I don't know, but it's one of those weird foibles that people have that continues to linger.

CHAPTER I

SAVING THE DAY

I stare glumly at my reflection in the mirror. While I imagine the make-up girl has done the best job she can as far as television is concerned, here, in real life, my skin itches and my pores feel clogged and heavy. I suppose I should be happy that the huge spot on my chin has been masterfully concealed under several layers of foundation, powder and skin toned gloop. At least the midnight blue trouser suit I'm wearing is well tailored. In fact, open as it is to reveal flashes of cleavage which surely can't be appropriate for breakfast television, it's even sexy. My old Montserrat buddies will no doubt be less than impressed to see me sporting their house colours. But this isn't about pleasing them or me. It's about continuing to improve human-vampire relations. And anyway, it's my own bloody fault for getting caught on camera in an apparent act of heroism when the Agathos court was attacked last month.

"Well, well, well," drawls a smooth voice next to me, "the Red Angel herself."

I glance over to see a man sit himself in the chair beside me. He looks vaguely familiar, with a chiseled jaw and all over tan which is so perfect it can only be fake.

1

"Marcus Lanscombe," he says, holding out a hand in my direction.

I take it, muttering, "Bo Blackman," back at him.

He holds onto my hand for a fraction too long. "It's a pleasure. Although," he says as he frowns into his own mirror at some invisible blemish, "it's really quite uncivilised to be here so early in the morning. Not that I imagine five am is difficult for you, of course."

I do what I can to appear ambivalent. "Well, I am a young vampire. Being awake at this time comes with the territory."

"Indeed, indeed." His eyes drift down to my chest and linger there. "How on earth are you going to get home though? Sunrise is less than an hour away and we won't be finished until well after that."

"I have my ways," I say stiffly. I stand up, getting one of my suit buttons caught in the fabric of the chair as I do so I'm forced to awkwardly yank at my arm to free myself. Lanscombe looks on with an air of amusement. "Excuse me."

I stride out into the corridor. Various harried looking people trot past me in various difference directions. Few of them notice me. Even those who do simply flash brief perfunctory smiles in my direction and continue on their way. I'm more used to being given a wide berth by humans. This lot don't seem to care that I'm higher up in the food chain than them and a theoretical danger to their lives. The world of television is clearly as far removed from the rest of society as the world of bloodguzzlers.

I walk along until I find an emergency exit at the far end. Although there's a ripped sign on it stating that it's to be kept closed at all times, it's been propped ajar by what looks like an old shoe. I push it open so the gap is wide enough that I can squeeze out and get some fresh air. There's already someone out there, puffing away on a cigarette. I move as far away from him as I can get and dig out my phone.

It's answered within three rings. "Good morning, Bo," says my grandfather, sounding as if he's been awake for hours. "You do realise how incredibly rude it is to call at such an ungodly hour, don't you?"

"It's almost dawn. Besides, it couldn't wait."

"Let me guess. You don't think you should be on television and you want me to find a way to get you out of there."

"Doing this is a stupid idea! I shouldn't be here."

"We've spoken about it. Several times. It's for the good of the firm. Not just the firm, in fact. It's for the good of mankind."

I roll my eyes. "Since when did you become best mates with hyperbole? All this is going to do is keep the spotlight on me. We should be focused on the Families and all their vampires. I'm not the one who needs better PR. They are."

"Which is why you're the one who's there and who is going to provide it. As distasteful as the media are, we need them. You have to take one for the team."

I scowl to myself. "People know who you are," I point out. "You should be the one doing this."

"My dear, the public need to see the softer, more feminine side of the bloodguzzlers. I'm human. And you're the heroine. You're the one they want."

I scratch my nose, realising only too late that I've probably just messed up the caked on make-up. "I should have just spoken to one of the tabloids. It would have made far more sense."

"We have more control this way. As long as you manage to fool the watching public into thinking you're a charming young lady, then we're onto a winner."

"You don't think I'm normally a charming young lady?" I ask sardonically.

"Well," he answers with a sniff, "you're certainly young."

I sigh in exasperation, stuffing the phone away again while I gaze out at the rooftops in front of me. I could just run away and leave now. I'd be leaving Breakfast UK in the lurch but they're probably used to it. I'm sure guests do it all the time.

"You'll be fine."

I flick a look over at the smoker. He's smiling at me in reassurance. "Yeah."

"I mean it." He sounds earnest. "A lot of people get scared when they're about to go live on air. Once the cameras start rolling, you'll feel much better."

"I've faced down a pair of psychotic serial killers," I tell him. "I'm not scared of being on television. I just don't want to do it, that's all."

He chuckles. "Sure." He leans in towards me. "I'll give you a tip. Keep your hands folded neatly in your lap instead of waving them around. You'll look much more confident that way." He stubs out his cigarette and walks back inside.

I watch him go, slightly open-mouthed. I'm confident enough. I exhale loudly and straighten my shoulders. I'll show him; Bo Blackman isn't afraid of anything.

Stalking back into the make-up room to get my face patched up, I'm just in time to see Marcus Lanscombe make a grab for the breast of a fresh-faced looking girl holding a powder puff. She jerks away.

"Come on," he leers, "what are you? Frigid? Don't you know who I am?"

I suddenly realise where I've seen him before. He's the head of a new online bank which is apparently doing a brisk trade in offering loans and mortgages to people who can't afford them, not to mention that there have been various rumours in the press of drug-taking and sex parties. I step in front of the girl and bare my fangs.

"Oh, I see." Lanscombe raises his eyebrows. "You're after a

threesome. I've never had a vampire before. Promise to bite me and I'm all yours."

I eye him up and down, assessing where I can hit him to do the most damage. I think about slamming the base of my hand into his nose. Unfortunately, the idea that such a move will force someone's nasal bone into their brain and kill them is nothing more than a myth. It'd still hurt a damn lot, however. Despite my constant bemoaning of the way that many humans are terrified of vampires these days, Lanscombe's lack of fear is only serving to rile me up further. The man thinks he's sodding untouchable. Combine good looks, power and money and you'll often find darkness. I cock my head and let my gaze drift to his jugular. Then I lick my lips. There's just the slightest flicker of uncertainty in his expression.

"I could end this for you right now," I say, dropping my voice to a low purr.

His body goes rigid. "You wouldn't dare."

Telling myself that I'm here to make the vampires look less like rabid bloodthirsty monsters and more like friendly keepers of the peace, I reach into my pocket, my fingers curling round the cool smooth pebble from Doctor Love that sits there to remind me of my humanity. Maybe I could just knee him in the groin.

"We're ready for you, Ms. Blackman!" trills out a guy from behind.

Lanscombe rushes towards him for safety, making sure his body doesn't so much as brush past mine. "Keep that … thing away from me," he snarls.

I simply smile. It's a shame that the make-up girl in the corner now appears more afraid of me than of him though.

I'm LED out to the main studio area. When you see it on the screen, it looks like a vast, comfortable living room, with huge sofas, a designer coffee table and all manner of sponsored accoutrements. The reality is actually far different. It's more like a barn composed of dark walls and complicated technical equipment with a tiny colourful couch oasis in the centre.

The incident with Lanscombe may have diverted my attention for a few minutes, but now I'm wholly focused on what's about to happen. As I sit down opposite Joyce and Jim, the beaming hosts whose heads are bent towards one of the producers, I realise my hands are genuinely trembling. I clutch at the fabric on my trousers in panic. A huge bright light swings in my direction, half blinding me, and I blink rapidly. From behind the cameras and their gaping lenses, someone gesticulates towards me. With a dry mouth, I gape in stupid confusion while someone else starts counting down from the end of the ad break. I only just manage to adjust my vision in time to register it's the smoker. He mimes clasping his hands together. In sudden understanding, I knit my fingers together in my lap, while my heart thuds almost painfully against my ribcage and the intro music kicks in. Oh God. Give me an army of vicious tribers out to destroy me any day over this.

The producer glides away as the music comes to a halt. As if they're one, both Joyce and Jim turn towards me, their wide-mouthed grins broad and fixed.

"Ladies and gentleman, we are thrilled to welcome our first guest for the day. She was captured on camera saving the life of a woman in during the recent terrorist attack on the esteemed Agathos court and, even though she's a vampire, she has assured us that she will keep those lethal fangs of hers safely hidden away. Welcome to the Red Angel, Miss Bo Blackman."

There's a smattering of backstage applause. I smile weakly. "Hi."

"So," Jim booms, "how does it feel to be a real life hero?"

I stare at him. My tongue is cloven to the roof of my mouth and my mind is utterly blank. "Uh..." I stammer.

Joyce smoothly steps in to cover my sudden ability to form a single word. "We really are so lucky to have you here. Why don't we see that footage first before we start the interrogation?" Her eyes are kind but the sentiment doesn't stop my nausea.

"Let's!" Jim agrees, turning towards a screen where images suddenly appear of my stooped figure carrying Meg, the Agathos court receptionist, safely away from the inferno in the building behind us. He hisses at me under his breath, "what the hell's wrong with you?"

I turn to the bank of cameras, as if they'll provide me with some aid. The helpful smoker nods towards me in encouragement. I glance to his left and see that Marcus Lanscombe has joined us while he waits for his turn to shine. The banker's oily amusement at my obvious fear does the trick. Something in my belly hardens and, as the footage ends and the camera turns back to me, I finally find my voice. Anything to avoid that wanker feeling superior.

"It seems strange looking back at it," I admit, with a girlish giggle to hide the tremor in my voice. "I hadn't realised I was being filmed at the time. I was just focused on getting everyone out of the building as quickly as possible."

Joyce, palpably relieved that I've recovered the power of speech, beams. "Yes, because after you rescued that woman, you went back in, didn't you?"

"I only did what anyone would," I answer meekly.

"I'm sure that's not true."

"I was in the right place at the right time," I say. "But I know for a fact that any vampire would have done the same in my position."

Jim leans forward. "But fire can still kill a bloodguzzler..." he clamps a hand to his mouth for a second, "I'm sorry. I mean vampire, of course."

"You can call me bloodguzzler," I grin, even though his 'embarrassment' is obviously a calculated gesture. "I don't mind. And, you're right. Vampires aren't immortal like some people think. We live for longer and we are stronger but we can still die. Just a few days ago, one of my colleagues was almost flattened by a bus while trying to rescue a boy who'd run out in front of it. If he'd been hit, then he wouldn't still be with us."

"This is one of your colleagues at New Order? The firm that's been described as a conduit between the Families and us humans?"

I nod. "Yes. We started out with just a few of us from the Montserrat Family." I gesture down at my suit to draw attention to its colour. "Now we have investigators from Gully, Bancroft and Stuart as well."

"But not Medici?" Jim probes.

I smile pleasantly. "Not right now." Dahlia doesn't count – at least not as far as I'm concerned anyway.

"It's fascinating that all this began with one severed ear. Do we have a picture of it?"

The screen next to us dutifully flashes up the shrivelled piece of flesh. The ruby is still there, winking away in the dark lobe. Both Jim and Joyce shudder.

"That's the one," I say calmly. "The presence of the ruby suggested it belonged to Tobias Renfrew, the billionaire who disappeared back in the sixties. DNA testing, however, has proven otherwise. But we believe it was because the ear was at the Agathos court that caused the terrorists to attack." And try to kill Rogu3 too although I refrain from bringing him into the conversation.

"And these terrorists? The police know they are in

Venezuela which has no extradition treaty with the United Kingdom?"

"A few of them. Probably not the ones who were actually in charge, however. We're still looking for them."

"Have you had any luck?"

I open my mouth to answer him when, all of a sudden, there's a shriek. It pierces across the room. Joyce jerks her chin up in confusion while Jim freezes. Clearly, screams don't often interrupt the show.

"Kakos daemon!" someone yells.

I spring to my feet. Well, it's one way to get out of an awkward interview. I'm not sure I'd have wished up a Kakos daemon appearance, however. Out of every triber in the damned world, they're the most dangerous and the most unpredictable. Most people don't survive encounters with them. Fortunately, I'm not most people. I may not have the strength to match one, but I do have a fairly good idea about what to expect even if it makes no logical sense for one to randomly show up on early morning breakfast television.

I lunge forward, grabbing Jim with one hand and Joyce with the other, then fling them behind me. "Get out of here," I snarl. "Get everyone out of here!"

For a second, no-one reacts. Then a door to the far right of the studio slams open and a huge shadowy figure appears. People scatter. I empty my mind of every coherent thought and instead start counting. As I discovered not too long ago, Kakos daemons possess the unpleasant ability of mind-reading. As long as I can keep my nonsensical counting at the forefront of my thoughts, the daemon won't know what I'm going to do next.

I search around for a weapon. This is daytime television though – it's hardly teeming with useful items. In the end, I snatch a boom mike from where it's hovering above the sofas. It's not like I have much of a choice.

The daemon glides into the room. I can't see its face, obscured as it is via some kind of samurai-styled helmet but its head twists from side to side as if it's searching for something. From its size, it's definitely Kakos. When its gaze lands on me, ice slides through my veins. It's actually less scary than the sofa with Joyce and Jim though.

There's a squeak from the opposite side of the room. The daemon turns to look. I don't bother. My attention is focused in one place. As long as I can keep it occupied long enough for everyone to get out of the building then I'll deem this a success. I'll probably get my heart eaten in the process. With any luck, the cameras won't still be rolling.

Even though I'm the only one not hiding, the damn thing decides to leave me alone for now and focus on whoever is in the corner. It marches forward while two pale faces bob up from behind some fragile looking wooden crates. I recognise both Lanscombe and my Samaritan-esque smoker. Bugger it.

Gripping the boom in my hands, I race forward to intercept the daemon. Before I can take a swing, however, it casually thrusts out one arm. Its large hand slams into my chest, knocking me backwards. Winded, although curiously not in much pain, I leap back up to my feet. It's too late, however. The daemon has already kicked away the crates and is lifting Lanscombe up by his throat. It drags him over to the nearest sofa as I catch a glimpse of black, glittering eyes.

"Let me go!" Lanscombe stutters. "I'll give you money! Girls! Anything!"

The daemon throws back its head and laughs. Then, with its one free hand, it thrusts into his chest. Blood spurts everywhere, decorating the once cream sofa with vivid splashes of red. Lanscombe's body slumps forward. Still counting, I rush at the daemon again.

I know I need to keep well out of the way of those powerful hands. As inevitable as it may be, I don't particularly want my heart ripped from my chest too. My palms are sweaty and it's difficult to maintain my grip on the mike. I just about manage it, however, swinging it as hard as I can and this time catching the daemon in the side of its head.

It roars in pain, spinning round in my direction. Out of the corner of my eye, I spy the smoker scrambling up to his feet. He throws an anxious look in my direction as if he's keen to help out. I shake my head minutely. Thankfully, he takes my silent advice and decides to run instead, sprinting for the nearest door. It clangs shut behind him. Now it's just me and the daemon left. There are already sirens screaming outside as the emergency services arrive. By the time they get up to this floor, it'll all be over though. I swallow hard.

"Come on then," I spit.

It rushes me, head down and body barreling into mine. We both fall backwards and I'm forced to drop the mike. Then the daemon curls one steel arm around my waist and lifts me up into the air like I'm nothing more than a ragdoll. The position is awkward. Its grip is so tight that I have no possible room to manoeuvre. All it needs to do is fling me against the wall and I'll be out for the count. Instead, however, the daemon adjusts its hold ever so slightly and throws me in the opposite direction. I end up landing this time on the cushioned sofa. It could have already killed me by now. The damn thing is playing with me, like a cat would with a mouse. It's galling but it might just give me enough wiggle room to come up with a way out of this.

I jump back to my feet and let my fangs elongate. Most tribers would see this as a sign of aggressive danger and consider fleeing.

Unfortunately this is a Kakos daemon. I can't see its expression but I have the definite impression that it's grinning at me. Leaping upwards, I throw out a scissor kick. It's only meant as a feint to allow me to get into a better position but, much to my surprise, my feet smash into its chest and it staggers back. I take advantage of the situation and launch a series of fast punches at its exposed neck. It moves further and further back until we're beyond the now useless cameras. There's a faint snarl from underneath the helmet and it abruptly vaults upwards, landing behind me and back in between the two couches. It doesn't so much as flick a look downwards at Lanscombe's corpse.

I tilt my head to the side, permitting myself one fleeting glance to my left. The light on one of the cameras is blinking green. That has to mean it's still broadcasting live – and for some reason the daemon wants this to be filmed. I grit my teeth. It's not just playing with me; it's playing for the millions of people watching too. I'm not in the mood for that kind of show.

I shuffle back, swiftly yanking up a length of electrical cord. This will serve two purposes. Before the daemon can make another move to stop me, I sprint forward, using the edge of the nearest sofa as a step up so I can fling my body upwards. Then I loop the cord round the daemon's neck and twist it hard. I kick it in the stomach, forcing it to stumble backwards so that the cord is pulled tight. It's not enough. I launch myself at its body as it makes a slight choking sound. Its fingers claw at its neck but it's too late – the plug behind us is pulled out of the socket, the sudden movement making the daemon crash down. I reach down and wind the now loose cord round my hands.

"You're not being filmed now, you bastard!" I sneer, as I pull it upwards to try and choke the thing to death.

The daemon's deep black eyes regard me steadily for a moment. Then its hands abandon its own bid to free its throat and simply yank the cord apart, freeing it from the binds completely. My stomach drops. I toss the now useless wire to one side and start backing away as it gets to its feet. It shakes its head then, with both hands, grabs its own helmet and slides it off.

"Not bad," X says mildly, "although I think we could have dragged it out for longer."

I gape. "What...?"

He laughs. "Come on, Bo. You didn't really think you'd be able to fight a Kakos daemon, did you? Even with all that ridiculous counting, I still knew what you were going to do before even you did."

"But you ... you ..."

"Me." He smiles lazily.

"Why?" I gasp. "Why would you do this? I thought we had an understanding."

"But we do." He throws the helmet to one side and takes a moment or two to adjust his hair. "I just hate hat hair, don't you?" he murmurs. He glances in my direction, registering my continued open-mouthed horror, and sighs as if I'm an idiot. "I am trying to help," he says calmly.

"Help?" I half shriek. "Help how? I might not have wanted to be on television but bringing the place down around our ears and killing someone is hardly helping!"

"The camera was recording," he says mildly. "Now the whole world will have even more reason to believe that you're a national hero. What's the term I should use?" He frowns. "Kickass?"

"You're crazy," I whisper.

X tosses me a look of frank derision. "I have plans for you. I need you to be a hero, Bo. I need the world to believe you're a hero. And what better way to achieve it by having you beat up a Kakos daemon live on TV?"

I drop my head, connecting with Lanscombe's dead, staring eyes. "You killed someone. For a bit of fucking PR, you actually killed someone!"

X shrugs. "He deserved it. Check his dressing room."

I back further away. "You're nuts."

"No, I'm not." He lifts up the corner of his mouth into a half smile. "You'll understand later when I ask you for that favour you still owe me."

"Stay away from me, you freak!"

He tuts. "And to think you were once so terrified in my presence that you could barely speak." Before I can react, he steps over and chucks me under the chin. "Now you're almost all grown up."

I jerk away, folding my arms across my chest. X leans his head to one side as if listening. "Interesting," he murmurs. He raises his eyebrows in my direction. "I should go. Tell them that you stabbed me in the chest and I disintegrated."

"Huh?" I stare at him stupidly.

He reaches into his inside pocket and takes out a baggie filled with what looks like ash. He tips it upside down onto the floor and points down. "Me."

"I'm not lying! You're a homicidal maniac! You need to be stopped!" There's an edge of obvious hysteria to my tone.

"Suggesting that I'm still alive will serve no purpose, Bo. Even if you want it to happen, I can't be caught."

"You're a visible face. You work for Streets of Fire. And you've been seen at the Agathos Court."

"Not me. My alter ego." He smiles. "Tell the public at large who I really am and all you'll do is create a panic. They'll imagine Kakos daemons hiding round every corner. If you want more blood in the streets then go for it. But do nothing and I will stay out of the way - for now." He takes my hands in his. I can't repress a shudder. "Do the smart thing." He leans over and gives me a peck on the cheek. Then he's gone.

It's a pointless effort but I still crouch down and check on Lanscombe. I'm just closing his eyes when the door bursts open and Michael's familiar figure appears. His gaze immediately falls on me then he runs forward and envelops me in a huge hug. He squeezes me so tightly that it feels as if my ribs are about to crack.

"Uh, Michael? Can you let me go?" I squeak.

He releases me and pulls away. "I was watching. I thought..." his voice trails away and he scans my face. "Are you alright? Where's the daemon?"

"Gone," I mutter.

"Where?"

I desperately want to tell him the truth. I meet his anxious eyes, however, and know I can't. He'd launch into a full blown daemon hunt. Even with every Family behind him, X still might win. Kakos daemons are just too damn strong. I swallow hard, inwardly praying for forgiveness for the lie. Then I point down at the tiny mountain of ash.

Michael follows my finger and pales. "You killed him?"

I shrug uneasily. Fortunately, he doesn't notice and instead bends down to inspect the pile of ash. "No-one's ever done that," he mutters. "Not on their own."

"I got lucky," I say unnecessarily. Bile rises in my throat and I realise I'm about to retch. I rush out and down the now empty corridor, flinging myself into a nearby bathroom. I only just reach the toilet in time.

When I'm done, I wipe my mouth on the back of my hand. Michael, who'd been enough a gentleman to keep back until I'd recovered on my own, puts an arm round my shoulder and gently brushes away the tendrils of sweat dampened hair. "You're a hero, Bo," he whispers.

I squeeze my eyes shut. No, I'm not. I'm just a fucking liar.

There's a sudden thud from nearby and my eyes fly back open. I stare at Michael. "Stay here," he says grimly, turning on his heel.

There's no bloody way I'm about to do that. I follow right after him. He edges down the corridor then, when he reaches a nondescript door with a paper sign proclaiming simply 'Marcus Lanscombe', he puts his ear against it. He looks at me and nods. I bite my lip.

Michael takes a step back. I blink in agreement, tensing my muscles. When he kicks the door open with one fell swoop, I'm right by his side. Rather than leaping in, however, his body relaxes. I peer round his muscular frame. Hiding behind a clothes rack is a young girl.

I gently nudge Michael out of the way. "Hello," I say softly. "It's okay. You're safe now."

For a moment, I don't think she's going to move. Then she shakily stands up. I realise she's painfully young – probably not much older than Rogu3. There's a purple bruise across her cheek and I suck in a breath. Marcus fucking Lanscombe, I think. X had been right. A brief flicker of satisfaction at the fact that he won't hurt her – or anyone like her again – fills me before my fingers fumble in my pocket and tightly squeeze my little white pebble. I tell myself that he deserved to be put in prison, not to be killed.

I reach out for her just as there's the sudden sound of heavy footsteps and hushed voices from outside. The girl flinches.

"Cavalry's arrived," Michael says softly.

CHAPTER 2
SPIKING YOUR DRINKS

I had initially been planning to make my own way home via London's underground network of tunnels. In the end, I spend so long going over my story with the police and Special Branch officers, not to mention being thanked a million times by every damn person in the building from Joyce and Jim to the tea lady, that there's no need to bother – it's already dark again by the time I leave. Michael had vanished hours earlier, his dark eyes glittering in my direction as he'd gestured goodbye.

I sidle out of the back exit to avoid having to face the gauntlet of flashing cameras and shouting journalists. Connor is already there, seated on my motorbike. He holds out his wrist.

"I know you're drinking from others these days but I thought you might be hungry."

I beam at him in gratitude. "Thank you, Connor. You're amazing."

The tips of his ears turn pink. "I'm glad you're alright, Bo. Taking down a Kakos daemon like that…" he whistles.

I try to smile then take his proferred hand and sink my

teeth into his vein to avoid having to respond further. At least the familiar taste of his blood helps to soothe me. When we're done, we switch positions on the bike and drive to Covent Garden. There is a line of journalists here too. My heart sinks.

"I can take you back to my place," Connor offers.

I sigh and push back my hair. "No. I'm going to have to face them sooner or later. If I give them what they want now, they'll leave me alone later."

Connor doesn't question this but I see the doubt in his eyes. "Okay. Shall I park the bike round the corner?"

"Yes. There's no need for you to be eaten alive by them too." He looks so relieved that I almost laugh. "Go home, Connor. It's late and I'm in the mood for doing nothing more than having a few drinks and collapsing. You deserve some time off anyway."

He smiles at me, gunning the engine. A few of the journalists' heads turn in our direction. It takes them less time to react than it would for Kimchi upon sight of a squirrel. Somehow I feel even more like prey than I did when I had been fighting X.

It's a good thirty minutes before I manage to extricate myself from the hordes. When I finally escape into the sanctity of the building, all I'm craving is some peace and quiet. At least Drechlin, the dentist we share the building with, has apparently gone home. It's a good thing too – I've barely put my foot on the first step up to the New Order offices when I hear Kimchi's exuberant barking. Unless he acts this happy when everyone arrives at the door of New Order – which I've yet to see – I can only wonder how on earth he knows it's me. He almost bowls me over when I open the door, leaping up and placing his paws on my chest. He tries to lick my nose but, alas, I pull back so he can't quite reach it.

"Down!" I order.

He licks my neck instead. I sigh in mock exasperation and

fondle his ears. That's when I realise that the office is packed and everyone is staring at me.

Even when we first moved into these premises, there wasn't a great deal of space to go around. Now that New Order includes two representatives from the Gully, Bancroft and Stuart Families too, it's definitely a tight squeeze. I lift my hand up somewhat awkwardly in greeting. They all just continue to stare. Unfortunately it's Dahlia who breaks the silence.

"Bo!" She picks her way over to me in a manner which can only be designed to make everyone remember what a delicate, fragile thing she is. "I'm so glad you're alright!"

I bite back my sarcastic response and force a smile. "I'm glad to be back. How are things here?"

Arzo raises his eyebrows at me. "Not as busy as they have been with you. Although part of that might be because we've had to leave the phone off the hook."

"Journalists?"

"And then some," he agrees. He looks up at me from the confines of his wheelchair. "How did you do it?"

I deliberately misunderstand his question. "I answered some of their questions to keep them happy for now. Hopefully they'll stop calling quite so much. We do have other business to attend to after all." I give everyone in the room a pointed look. The only possible reason why they're all here rather than at home or out helping clients is because they want to gawk at me.

Arzo frowns but doesn't comment. Since Dahlia's first uninvited appearance, he's been much more relaxed and content. I wish I could be happy about it. As his ex-fiancee who betrayed him in every way possible, I personally think she should be hung, drawn and quartered. Her history with Arzo isn't actually even the most troubling part although I'd be more likely to trust bloody Lord Medici himself than I would Dahlia - even if her vampire Lord hasn't once made inquiries as to her whereabouts. He's the only Family Head who thinks that New Order, set up to build bridges between the human and vampire communities, is an abhorrence, along with the fact that newbies like Matt and myself who have been allowed 'out' to participate in it should be kept under lock and key instead. Notwithstanding her human age, Dahlia is an even younger vampire than I am. His lack of contact can only mean that she is here with his full blessing, which suggests he's not finished trying to screw us all up. I just can't seem to persuade anyone else of this rather salient point yet.

Kimchi settles at my feet, immediately slobbering over my shoelaces. I'm saved from enduring that particular indignity for long, however, when the door to my grandfather's office opens and he beckons me inside.

I ignore the desperate glances of curiosity from the others and do what I'm told. "Good evening, grandfather," I say, when I close the door behind me. "How are you?"

"Very well, thank you." He looks me up and down. "Why did that Kakos daemon throw the fight?"

I stiffen. "What? You're not going to ask me how I am?" He's normally fastidious about manners. Considering his question, however, I guess recent events are superseding his natural instincts.

"I've had reports every hour on the hour from one of my contacts. And I can see how you are for myself anyway. Not that it matters. You were clearly never in any danger."

I try not to fidget. "I don't know what you mean."

"Everyone else might have been fooled, Bo. I know what I saw. Are you in cahoots with this daemon?"

"Cahoots? We're not in the nineteenth century any longer, you know." His astute understanding is putting me on edge.

His bushy white eyebrows lower and he seems to be studying the blank space on his desk. "Are you in trouble?"

I wonder if he's avoiding my eyes because he doesn't want to see a lie written there. I walk over, forcing him to look up. "No. Everything is fine. I didn't plan this and I didn't want it to happen. You know how desperate I was to get out of the damn interview in the first place." I take a deep breath. "I can't tell you the truth about the Kakos daemon because he's a bloody Kakos daemon. But it's not as bad as it looks. I promise."

He regards me steadily. "He killed a man."

"He might have deserved it."

My grandfather's shoulders slump ever so slightly. "What happened to your once vehement disapproval of capital punishment?"

"It wasn't me who murdered Marcus Lanscombe," I remind him gently.

"All the same," he grunts.

I rub my forehead. "How many other people noticed?"

"That you won an unwinnable fight? No-one. I've even been in touch with MI7." There's a faint hint of disgust in his tone. "Clearly their standards have dropped. In my day there would have been a full scale investigation if such a thing had happened."

I shouldn't feel relieved but I do. "Well," I say briskly, "I'm sure all this will blow over soon enough."

IN THE END, it takes three days – and considerable effort on my part in answering inane questions – before the crowd of paparazzi leaves the street outside New Order. Drechlin spent the time making almost hourly complaints. He's sent us a bill for loss of income due to all the customers who've suddenly avoided getting their root canal ops done with him. I offer to pay it although I'll admit I'm hoping it doesn't come to that.

Keeping a dog who'll eat just about anything is costing me more money than I'd have thought possible.

It's with some relief that I finally make it outside with a real assignment to complete. I'm even paired with Matt. It almost feels like old times. It's unfortunate that he took my instructions to 'dress for a night on the town' so seriously. He's wearing a velvet mauve suit complete with skinny tie and paisley shirt. He looks more like a walking nineteenth century drawing room than a sexy twenty-first century vampire. Before he'd been affected by O'Shea's warped spell, he'd been arrogant enough to probably possess a vast trendy wardrobe. Where this has come from, I have no idea.

Choosing to opt against a long discussion about the merits of velvet, I don't comment on his attire. Instead, I simply take his arm when we park round the corner from the exclusive nightclub we're targeting and point him in the direction of the snaking queue.

"You need to do what you can to get inside," I instruct.

"Why can't you come with me?"

"I can't afford to be recognised. I'll wait here on the off chance that Bergman comes out. We need to cover all our bases."

"Okay, Bo." He nods vigorously. "Are you sure they'll let a vampire in?"

"They let Bergman in." I toss him a small camera. "If you see anything even vaguely suspicious going on, take some shots of him with this. We'll need proof that he's dealing for Stuart to act."

I give him a gentle nudge, watching him amble to the back of the line. He immediately starts engaging a pretty blonde girl in front of him in conversation. Despite his weird get up, she seems amenable to his advances. I smile in grim satisfaction then quickly cross the road and make my own way up to the top of the building opposite.

It was one of the bartenders who clued us into Bergman Stuart's activities. It had been a brave thing to do considering the vampire frequents this club on an almost daily basis – and is treated by the management as a favoured guest. Spiking the drinks of humans and potentially selling illegal drugs is not a matter to be taken lightly. Not in these troubled times anyway. All Matt and I have to do is get proof.

From my vantage point, I have a clear view of not only the club's entrance but also the alleyway to the left where the deals apparently take place. I set up a camera of my own, albeit with a long range lens to get the best possible angles, and take a few test shots. Once I'm happy, I sit back and wait.

It's not long before Matt and his new companion are ushered inside. Judging that it'll take him some time more to locate Bergman and get back to me with what's happening, I sit back and scan the line of waiting people. Some look impatient while others seem merely bored. It's still fairly early to be hitting a club but this place is apparently popular, both with tribers and with humans. To pass the time, I gaze at each person in turn, trying to decide whether their main motives for coming out are to dance, drink or pull. It's not until my eyes land on a stiffly upright young woman that I see anything out of the ordinary.

She seems to be alone. That in itself isn't unusual. I could pick out several other women who are. I've already mentally dropped all of them into my 'pulling' category. She's also dressed in the typical nightclub camouflage of short skirt, high heels and pretty top. But she's carrying no purse or bag and I'd be amazed if there are any beauty pockets to be found in her skin tight clothes. Equally, despite her straight back, her right hand is braced against the wall as if she's already got so much alcohol in her system that she's afraid she'll topple over.

When the line moves forward, she takes tiny shuffling steps. Her head seems to be swaying and, while I can't tell for sure from this distance, I'm betting that her pupils are wide and dilated. I make a quick decision and swing the camera from its fixed position so that I can focus on her instead. Before I can snap her face, however, one of the bouncers wanders down the queue and nods in her direction.

My eyes narrow. Someone in the state that she's in should be put in a taxi and sent home, not given preferential access. The burly doorman also seems to be well aware of her condition. Without saying a word, he takes her arm to help her walk to the front. When I crane my neck back to get a better view, I can see that he's virtually dragging her. Interesting.

I press my comm button. "Matt, where are you right now?"

"Pardon?"

"Where are you?"

"Pardon?"

I roll my eyes in exasperation and try again. "Where. Are. You?" I enunciate as loudly as I dare.

"Oh, sorry, it's kind of loud in here. I'm watching Bergman. He's sitting at a table with a few others."

"Vampires?"

"No, humans. Should I start taking some photos?"

It would be good to know who Bergman's companions actually are. I can't get rid of my gut instinct that there's something up with the girl, however. "Actually, can you head out towards the front? There's a young woman coming in wearing a black mini skirt and a pink top. Brunette. Find out where she goes."

"Pardon?"

I grit my teeth. "I said, there's a..."

"Wait," Matt interrupts. "There's a woman walking up to Bergman. Brown hair, pink top. She seems a bit unsteady on her feet."

I hiss softly. "Watch her."

"Pardon?"

I curl my fingernails into my palms. It's not Matt's fault that it's so loud in the club. Neither is it his fault that thanks to my minor celebrity status, this will be easier on both of us if I stay outside. It's still sodding frustrating though.

"Watch the woman," I repeat.

My earpiece crackles. I can only hope that Matt got the message. I re-adjust the camera and anxiously scan both the entrance and the alleyway. Unfortunately – or I suppose fortunately - there's nothing untoward happening in either. I stretch out my muscles and try to keep focused.

There's another crackle. "Hey!" I hear Matt yell. "Let go of me! I didn't do anything!"

Shit. Whatever he's done or whoever's noticed him, at least he's had the foresight to tune me into the communications. Barely five seconds later, there's a kerfuffle in the doorway and he's thrown unceremoniously out on his arse. The line of people stare at him wide-eyed. He blinks up in my direction.

"Don't look this way!" I mutter in a warning undertone.

Matt abruptly glances downwards, then gets to his feet and brushes himself off. His tie is askew and there's a rip in the shoulder of seam of his jacket.

"What happened?"

He walks a few feet away to disguise the fact that he's talking. "I don't know. I wasn't near to Bergman, I promise. I only did what you asked."

"Watch the woman?"

"That's what I did."

I bite down on my bottom lip. Matt takes every instruction

absolutely literally. He probably stared wide-eyed at the brunette, not taking his eyes off of her. Although the fact that he got himself physically thrown out for such an action only serves to solidify my suspicions. She's got something to do with Bergman. I just don't know what yet.

"Best thing you can do now is get out of there," I tell him. "They'll already be on high alert. If you leave now, they might just think you had the hots for her."

"She was pretty cute," he replies. "Even if she did have VPL."

"You really were staring at her, weren't you?"

"I only did what you told me to. I think her knickers are edged in lace."

I roll my eyes. Talk about unnecessary information. "You're disgusting. Go on. I'll meet you by the bike when I'm done."

He gives me a slight nod and shoves his hands in his pockets, walking away and whistling. He's so obvious about it that I'm amazed the bouncer frowning at his back doesn't try to follow him. Matt can look after himself in a fight though. He is ex-army, after all. I turn my attention back to the club. I still can't see anything happening.

I really hate sitting around and waiting for things to happen. It doesn't suit me. If Arzo and my grandfather had wanted someone to simply stake out Bergman and the club, I decide, then they'd have picked someone else for this job. I'm still not quite stupid enough to enter the club myself but I can, however, get a little closer.

I switch the camera to video mode and ensure it's recording. It means I'm forced to make a final choice between the front door and the alley but, frankly, if Bergman comes out of the main entrance, I'll be able to follow him with ease. If any action is going to happen here, it will be down the little side street. I abandon my post and climb quickly back down, skirting round to the left of the now even longer queue to avoid anyone spotting me. Taking a circuitous route, I make it to the far end of the alley. It's open at both ends – the street by the club entrance and the quieter one behind it. I've yet to see a single person use it as a shortcut though so I reckon as long as I keep to the shadows I'll be safe.

I sidle up as far as I dare and then duck down behind a wheelie bin. It's surprisingly clean and, when I flip up the lid to peek inside, it smells of nothing more than plastic. I'd swear it's never so much as seen a rubbish bag. I'm just musing over this as the side door to the club opens and I'm forced to quickly hide behind it again.

"I don't see why we always have to come out here. It's far more comfortable inside."

"Bergman, Bergman. You have to remember that vampires aren't what they used to be. People are scared. If you start chomping down on them in the middle of the dance floor, then we'll lose a lot of our human customers."

"I spend a great deal more money than they do."

"True. But you come to us because we provide the best merchandise. It would hardly suit any of our purposes if that merchandise decided to go to Stringfellow's instead."

"I suppose it'll mean I drink less. Honestly, I don't know what happened to me last time," Bergman snorts.

I shuffle forward ever so slightly so I can see what's going on. There are two men, not including Bergman himself. As far as I can tell from my awkward position, they're both human. I narrow my eyes. Is he selling to them?

The door opens yet again. This time the woman I'd spotted out the front stumbles down the steps.

Bergman frowns at her, catching her arm just before she falls. "Is she drunk? You know I like my meat clean."

My lip curls. This bloodguzzler is an affront to his Family.

"She's had a few too martinis, that's all."

I scratch my head. From what I've seen so far, she's had more than a few martinis. This isn't just a simple drug deal.

"Oh my God!"

I freeze, realising the excited shout came from behind me. I slowly turn my head, my stomach sinking when I see two women pointing at me.

"You're the Red Angel! Guys! Come look! It's that vampire that killed the Kakos daemon! The one who must have superpowers!"

Two men appear as well. Their jaws drop as all four of them gaze at me as if I'm a damn exhibit in a zoo. I wave my hand frantically in a bid to get them to shut the hell up. It's already too late though – the damage is done.

"What's going on over there?"

One of the shady club guys breaks away and starts striding down towards me. Between the civilians at one end and Bergman and his buddies at the other, I'm out of options. I curse to myself and step out from behind the bin.

"Hey!" I say cheerily, "how's it going?"

The man looks almost as surprised as the women did. "You're... you're..."

I nod. "I'm the Red Angel." The words sound stupid in my own mouth but I roll with them. "I was in the neighbourhood and saw your club and thought I could really do with a drink. I wanted to use the side entrance to avoid all the crowds though." I smile pleasantly.

"She killed a freaking Kakos daemon," Bergman breathes. He starts towards me. "Miss Blackman! I'm a huge fan."

The second guy's face twists and he starts to turn away. "Kill them now," I hear him mutter.

Bergman goes blank with confusion, momentarily halting his steps. "What...?"

I rush towards the group. There's a flash of silver and I gasp as I see a long stiletto blade sink into the woman's throat. Suddenly comprehending, I shout.

"Run, Bergman!"

I've barely even finished the sentence when the second man twirls and throws something at him. As soon as it's left his hand, he starts to sprint away. I fly past Bergman, who's clutching what can only be a wooden stake jutting out of his chest, and leap over the body of the woman. I'll run those bastards down in about three seconds flat.

They disappear round the corner and into the main street. Using the far wall as leverage, I twist upwards and run my feet a few steps across the brick in order to spin left and reach them even faster. The one in front is already shouting towards the waiting queue, however.

"The Red Angel! Look!"

The crowd turns in my direction. Several people break away and start heading towards me.

"Can I have your autograph?"

"How about a photo?"

I ignore them, running after the men who have now been swallowed up by the queue. I spot their two bobbing heads, pushing their way past the people, and try to sprint down the far side. It's no good, however. Too many of the wannabe clubbers are too taken by my presence. They abandon the pavement and flood out towards me.

"Get out of my way!"

It was the worst possible thing I could have said. Instead of shifting out of my path, they freeze, making it even harder for me to get past them. I curse again, weaving in and out and shoving people to the side where I need to. By the time I manage to pull away from them all, I hear a screech of tyres and only just see the back end of a shiny red car as it takes off down the street.

I hurriedly press my comm button. "Matt! Red sports car heading straight down Blair Street. You need to follow it. Now!"

I hear the bike's engine rev. Matt swears in my ear. Then he emerges from the side street up ahead and accelerates after the car. I stare after them helplessly.

Someone pats me cautiously on the shoulder. I look round to see a young guy, inexplicably with tears in his eyes. "You're my hero," he bleats. "You're amazing."

I can only shake my head in disgust.

I sit on the edge of the pavement, some distance away from the still gawking crowds. They've abandoned the apparent allure of the nightclub in favour of the outstanding thrill of watching me breathe. At least now the police have arrived, they're being kept well back.

"What happened, Bo?"

I glance up at Foxworthy. His eyes are kind, although worried. I can't say the same about Nicholls behind him.

"I was acting for New Order," I say. "We'd had a tip off that one of the Stuart vampires, a guy called Bergman, was dealing in drugs."

"Is that the guzzler whose corpse is down that street?"

I nod. "That's the one. I think we got it wrong, however. I'm betting that the postmortem will find the drugs in the system of the woman who's dead. The guys in this club were probably drugging vampettes and giving them to Bergman. He'd drink from them so then the drugs would be in his system too. They were using him as a front for their own business. He was probably so out of it most of the time he had no idea what was happening."

"Did you kill her?"

I throw him a dirty look. "No, I bloody didn't."

"Are there any witnesses?" Nicholls demands. "How can you prove it?"

"There were four people behind me…" I begin.

"They told us they run off when things started getting nasty."

I narrow my eyes. "There's also a camera that's been recording everything." I point up at the building where I'd initially been camped out. "You'll find it up there."

She seems only faintly mollified. "You really screwed up this time, didn't you, Blackman?"

The worst thing is that I can do nothing but agree.

CHAPTER 3
NEGOTIATIONS

"How about this?" I say, pointing at a slim file. "It's a simple vampire abduction case. All I'll have to do is find out whether..." I crane my neck, "...Alan Tims is with the Bancroft family or not and how he was recruited. I won't even need to speak to a single member of the public."

My grandfather barely even twitches. "Lars from the Gully Family is taking care of it."

I grit my teeth. "Well, this one then. Investigating whether there's an affair going on between this woman and a vampire. I'm pretty good at that kind of stuff, you know. I did a lot of it at Dire Straits."

"I've assigned it to Peter."

I count to ten in my head. "Arzo aside, I'm the most experienced investigator we've got."

"You also can't step outside without being set upon by adoring fans." The tone of his voice leaves nothing to the imagination as far as what he thinks of those 'fans'.

"I can! I went out for a walk with Kimchi last night. We managed fine. Not a single person came up to us!"

He fixes me with a steady look. "What time did you go out?"

"Does it matter?" He doesn't answer, merely raises his eyebrows. I sigh. "Fine," I snap. "It was about three." He makes a gesture to indicate fait accompli. "Oh come on! This isn't fair!"

"You're not six years old, Bo. Get over it."

"I can't sit here twiddling my thumbs. It's not my fault things got screwed up the other night! You saw the camera footage. I did everything I could!"

"I'm well aware of that," he says mildly. "In fact, it's not even your fault that Bergman and his vampette died. The post-mortem results came back and the drugs she had in her system would have killed both of them anyway."

"They *were* taking him out," I breathe. "He'd served his purpose."

"Indeed. At least the drugs account for why he had been straying from the Stuart fold. We can pin the entire thing on miscreant humans rather than dodgy vampires."

"Has anyone found these humans yet?" I demand.

He shakes his head. "No. Matt on that ridiculous contraption you call a vehicle was the best shot we had. They had too much of a lead on him though. They've not been back to the club and even the police can't locate them."

I bunch up my fists. "I could go and..."

"No."

"But..."

"You'll just get yourself into more bother. We need to find alternative assignments to suit your new," he pauses, "skill set."

My eyes narrow. "What skill set is that?"

"Looking pretty in front of the cameras."

"What?" I splutter.

My grandfather pulls out his fob watch and begins polishing it. "Bo, you will do more good in that role than a hundred investigations into alleged abductions and seedy affairs ever could."

"I think I've already proven that interviews aren't my thing. Besides, I've spent days answering every damn question that's been thrown at me. I've got nothing else to say."

"I wasn't thinking of another interview," he says mildly.

I'm instantly suspicious. "Then what?"

"Things started getting really bad for the Families when your friend Nicky got involved."

"I wouldn't exactly call her my friend."

He ignores me. "And the fact she was with the Montserrat Family means that they are having a harder time than all the others put together."

"I'm aware of that. So?"

He shrugs. "The public love you. The last time someone got the better of a Kakos daemon was over a century ago. And even then, they still died three days later. You run into burning buildings to save humans. Your lack of height makes you appear cute. Despite those ridiculous clothes and grubby leather jacket, you're becoming the pin up girl for 2015."

"I don't think pin up girls exist any more." I start to raise up my hands and gesticulate wildly to emphasise my irritation.

"Stop flapping, Bo. You look ridiculous."

"What then?" I demand. "What's the damn assignment?"

"You might find you enjoy it more than you expect."

I bare my teeth. "Out with it."

He recoils slightly. "If you think a show of bloodguzzler aggression is going to sway me, then you don't know me as well as you think you do. It's Lord Montserrat."

"Huh? What does Michael have to do with this?"

My grandfather offers me a smile. I could swear there's an edge of glee to it. "We need the human majority to view him in a better light. He's the most lenient and liberal of all the Family Heads and yet he has the worst reputation. You're going to become his very visible girlfriend."

My mouth drops open. "You're kidding me? That's my assignment? To be pretend to be Michael's latest squeeze?"

"Will it be pretending?" my grandfather inquires. I simply glare. "Either way," he continues, "it's the absolute optimum path to take."

"He won't agree to it," I declare.

"He already has."

"What?" I screech. "You've been discussing this behind my back?"

There's a knock on the door. My grandfather holds up his hand to forestall any further protests. "Come in," he calls out.

Dahlia appears. I watch her entry, silently seething. "Good evening, Mr. Blackman."

"Dahlia." He opens up a nearby drawer and pulls out another file. "Here you go. You'll find everything you need."

She smiles prettily, taking it and flipping open the front cover. Her eyes go wide. "I'm going to help Lord Gully with his recruitment?"

"You'll offer assistance and double check each of his short-listed candidates."

"Thank you so much! I won't let you down!" She looks at me. "Can you believe it, Bo? I'm so excited!"

I watch her leave then turn back to my grandfather, putting my hands on my hips. "Actually," I spit, "I can't believe it at all. Her? She gets a real assignment?"

"Arzo will be checking her work."

"We can't trust her though! Don't tell me you swallow that tale she spun about escaping from Medici through an open sodding window!"

He sighs. "It might be a cliché, Bo, but you need to learn to keep your friends close and your enemies closer. Until we really know why she's here, we need to make her think we believe she's on our side."

"Let me do that," I plead. "I'm not cut out for fake girlfriend stuff."

"You can't keep the snarl off your face when you look at her."

"Well, let me go to Venezuela then! I still need to find those bastards who tried to kill Rogu3!"

"It's too complicated for a new vampire like you to avoid the sun on such a journey. Plus, it's a large country and no-one has been able to pinpoint their exact location." He picks up a fountain pen, indicating that our conversation is coming to an end. "I sincerely hope you've not been in touch with that child."

"No," I answer shortly. Rogu3 has suffered enough thanks to our relationship. "I've not."

"Good. You should go now. Lord Montserrat is waiting for your call."

He bends his head and starts scribbling something on a notepad. I stay where I am for a moment, staring at him. Then I shake my head and stalk out.

WHAT'S galling is that it's actually not a bad plan. Despite my best efforts, I do appear to be the media darling of the moment while Michael remains the devil incarnate. It doesn't help that it's also a well known fact that I absconded from the Montserrat Family embrace. I've read various articles opining that the only reason could be that they're all monsters and I couldn't stand to be around them any longer. Those articles don't mention that the reality is I'm as much of a 'monster' as they are. It still doesn't mean I want to pretend to be his latest love though. For one thing, I'm not sure I trust myself.

I drum my fingers impatiently on the chair rest as I wait for him. I can't help wondering whether he's deliberately keeping me cooling my heels. It would make sense. He came to my aid at the television studio and arrived too late to be of any use. He's going to want to remind me who's really got all the power, even if right now he happens to be accepting my help.

"Good evening, Bo."

I glance up, stiffening slightly. He's wearing one of his Montserrat blue suits, with a crisp white shirt underneath. There's no tie, however, and the first few buttons are undone, revealing smooth tanned skin that no self-respecting vampire should be allowed to have. He looks more like a bloody model than a leading member of the bloodguzzling fraternity. I resist the urge to look down at my own attire. My grandfather's comments about appearing grubby are already making me feel inferior enough.

I get to my feet, awkwardly holding out my hand in a bid to keep things formal. "Good evening."

Instead of shaking it, he takes hold of my fingers and brings them to his mouth, his lips gently brushing against them. From almost any other man, the gesture would be sleazy. Unfortunately, from him, it has the opposite effect. My heart starts to race and my mouth goes suddenly dry. I snatch my hand away.

"That's not necessary," I blurt out.

His face remains impassive. "You gave me your hand."

"To shake! Not to slobber over!"

He quirks up an eyebrow. "Slobber?"

"You don't kiss Ursus's hand, do you?"

Michael simply looks amused. "No, I don't. But I'm not trying to pretend that Ursus and I are involved."

"We're alone. You don't need to put on a show for the damn walls."

He leans his head to the side. "You're really annoyed about this."

I sniff. "Are you surprised?"

"If you don't want to do it..."

"You know I don't want to do it." I lift up my chin. "But I will. We just need to set some ground rules first, that's all."

He folds his arms. "Go on then."

"We keep the displays of affection to when we're out in public. Otherwise there's no point."

"It'll look awkward if we don't normally..." I narrow my eyes. He holds up his hands. "Okay."

I tick off my fingers. "We only meet in public when there are definitely going to be lots of press around."

"From what I hear that won't be a problem for you."

I scowl. "No more than one date a week."

"Four." He regards me steadily. "The world needs to believe we're in love, Bo."

"Fine. Two dates."

Michael shakes his head. "Three." I hiss through my teeth. He merely gives me an amiable shrug.

"If you see someone else on the side, you make sure no-one finds out. I don't want to look like an idiot."

"I'm not going to see anyone else." He rolls his tongue across his teeth. "Neither should you."

"Chance would be a fine thing," I mutter. "How long are we going to have to keep this up for?"

"A few months perhaps? It's not going to be as bad as you think, Bo. We do get along." His eyes gleam, dropping momentarily to my mouth. "Most of the time."

I swallow. "I don't like lying," I mumble. Even though it's all I seem to do.

"It's not lying." I gaze at him in sudden shock. He smiles. "We'll just be acting ... affectionately towards each other. The world can draw its own conclusions."

"Semantics."

"If you say so."

We remain like that for what it is probably only a few seconds, staring at each other. It feels like forever.

"I should go," I mutter eventually.

"Tomorrow night then? I'll pick you up around nine."

"I can hardly wait."

As my new 'assignment' will take up a mere fraction of my time – and New Order won't allow to take on any more jobs – I decide to go freelance. I'm not going to sit on my thumbs until this stupid media furore dies down. I'll just be a bit more careful, that's all. Besides, I do actually have things of my own that I want to investigate.

I jog from the Montserrat mansion to the nearest Underground entrance. It's already late and there's a guy pulling across the barrier to close it just as I approach.

"No more trains, Miss," he says, barely glancing in my direction.

"I'm not after a train," I tell him. "I just want to get inside."

"Why would you want to do that? You don't look homeless. Only the…" his voice trails off as he finally recognises me. "Only the Red Angel uses the tunnels," he finishes weakly.

I give him a small curtsey. "As you see."

"Of course, ma'am. Of course!" He scrambles to re-open the gate. "Are you going after a bad guy?"

"I have some business to take care of," I prevaricate. I'm still technically breaking the law by entering, even if the station's caretaker doesn't seem to care. Not to mention that in theory I don't need to use the vast tunnel system to travel around when it's dark. I don't want to end up being followed by a posse of journalists and fans, however. "It's really important," I say softly, "that no-one finds out where I've gone."

He nods his head vigorously. "I won't tell a soul."

I scan his face. I reckon he's telling the truth. "Thank you."

He bites his lip and looks at me anxiously. He obviously wants to say something else. I give him an encouraging glance and he breaks out into a huge beaming smile. "Can I have your autograph? It's not for me, you understand. But my daughter…"

"Of course. Do you have a pen and paper?"

He fumbles in his pocket, handing me over a small pad and chewed pen. He looks embarrassed. "Sorry, I should find you something better."

"This is fine. Who do I make it out to?"

"Lisa. And Jonesy."

"That's you?" He nods. I scrawl out my signature and pass it back. "You ever need some help, Jonesy, you just get in touch with me. Alright?"

He looks like he's about to pass out. "Yes, Miss! I mean the Red Angel! Ms Blackman!"

"Bo is fine." I clap him on the shoulder. The offer of a favour is the least I can do if he's going to let me sneak in here. Maybe being famous does have its advantages after all. The hero worship is more than slightly awkward, however so I quickly take my leave, darting down the steps to the train tracks.

"Bye Bo!" he shouts out enthusiastically from behind me.

I wave in return and hastily jog away.

It doesn't take me long to reach the exit I require. There are naturally no trains running at this hour and I've spent enough time recently studying the network of tunnels that I know exactly which route to take. It helps that I think I'm finally starting to come into my own as far as my vampiric skills are concerned. I sprint at breakneck speed, barely breaking a sweat.

When I emerge back onto the street, I fill my lungs with fresh air and make the last few yards to the pub. No longer wishing to be recognised, I keep my head down as I enter.

Fortunately, D'Argneau has had the foresight to sit in the dark corner at the back rather than at his usual spot at the bar. I sidle over towards him, grabbing a stool and positioning it so my back is to the door. It makes it harder to react in the event of danger but at least I'll be able to keep my face turned away from the other punters.

Unfortunately D'Argneau has other ideas. He grins at me, holding up his phone and snapping a photo before I can react.

"Sodding hell! What did you do that for?"

"It's pretty obvious, isn't it? People will be flocking to my door when they hear that the Red Angel is one of my clients."

I grit my teeth. "I'm not your client. I just need a little help, that's all."

"Same same." He waves a hand in the air. "Let me do a selfie of the pair of us and I'll keep this consult free of charge."

I eye him warily. "Where are you going to put the photo?"

"In my office. It'll impress new clients who walk in." He gives me a pleading hangdog look.

I sigh. "Fine."

In a flash, he's by my side, holding the phone out at arm's length. After five shots of him trying out different angles, I eventually push him away. "How is business anyway?"

"Great!" he grins. There's a smarmy edge to his voice that I choose to ignore. "You are looking at the official human legal representative for the Stuart Family. It's only in name right now, of course. They've decided to go all out with the whole pretending to be friendly to humans thing. But I reckon I can persuade them to actually make use of me in reality."

"Don't they have plenty of lawyers of their own?"

"Sure. None of them have my skills though." He flips back his tawny hair.

"Speaking of those skills…"

"Of course, of course. What can I do for you, Bo? No request is too great."

"I need a time bubble."

D'Argneau visibly deflates. "It can't be done."

"You just said no request was too great."

"I didn't know that's what you wanted! I thought you were after a media lawyer! Book rights, publicity contracts, that kind of thing."

"Time bubble," I repeat firmly. "That's what I need."

"I have contacts at Penguin. I'm sure they'd be thrilled…"

"Harry," I say warningly.

He rolls his eyes. "They're illegal, Bo. You must know that. The government rushed through legislation after Matheson did his thing."

I raise my eyebrows. "Did his thing? You mean rape and murder several daemons, vampires, witches and humans? That thing?" I'm starting to remember why I find D'Argneau so annoying sometimes.

"You know what I mean." He dismisses it with a wave of his hand. "No-one can get hold of time bubbles. Not any more. Even those live forever companies have had to give theirs up. They've all gone bust as a result."

I lean forward. "But it's thanks to me that Matheson was caught. Perhaps they'll make an exception."

"I'm sure they'd love to. But they can't and they won't." He looks at me shrewdly. "Fame won't buy you everything."

"You're sure about this?"

He nods. "Positive."

I shrug. "Okay." I stand up to go.

"Hey! Wait! How about a drink for old times' sake?"

"Sorry, Harry. I'm busy."

I leave him blustering away and dig into my pocket for my phone. My fingers brush against my little white pebble, the gift from Dr. Love that's meant to remind me of my humanity, and I feel a slight twinge of guilt for veering from the straight and narrow legal path. Then I shrug. It's not like I'm going to hurt anyone. I need a time bubble for the greater good. I search through my contacts until I find the right one.

"O'Shea? We need to catch up."

CHAPTER 4

SHOPPING FOR ANSWERS

O'Shea refuses to meet somewhere quiet. He is, he says, working so I'm forced to buy a pair of fake Gucci sunglasses along with a Prada scarf to cover my head in order to remain incognito. I don't mind the disguise part. It'll be a good test to prove to my grandfather – and everyone else at New Order – that I'm still capable of working undercover. The only slightly galling part is that the scarf is emblazoned with the word 'Prata'. Wearing it, I do indeed feel like a prat.

Still, it seems to work. No-one stops me in the street to ask for my autograph and there are no delighted screams to deal with. I even make it through the doors of Magix without being stopped by a security guard. Considering I've long been labeled as public enemy number one by the large magical wares firm, that's no mean feat. I don't blame them for the way they feel. At least it's a damn sight more honest than all those celebrity stalkers I seem to attract these days.

I spot O'Shea in amongst a section selling love potions. My heart sinks. I really hope he's not reverted to his old ways. I'd hate to have to ask Foxworthy to arrest him.

"Since when did this place start opening so late?" I offer as a relaxed opening gambit instead of 'are you planning to meddle with spells in a manner that will result in several deaths?'

He turns and blinks at me, his orange pupils slitted and focused. "We're not supposed to communicate!" he hisses in a low undertone.

"Uh..."

O'Shea tuts loudly and grabs my hand, pressing hard on the fleshy part of my palm and twisting. I yank away. "What the hell?"

He freezes. "Bo?"

"Of course it's bloody Bo, you moron! Who did you think it was?"

"Never mind."

"Devlin..."

"I thought you were another mystery shopper, alright?"

I'm beyond confused. "What do you mean?"

"It's the gig I've currently got," he explains, exasperated. "I told you I was working."

"As a mystery shopper?"

"Well, yeah. I hit all the criteria. I know about magic. I'm a quarter daemon so if any of the floor staff are racist then I'll be the first one they'll show it to... I'm the perfect candidate." He leans back with a self-satisfied smile.

"And you thought I was a mystery shopper too?"

"Look at you! Dark glasses, strange headscarf. You fit the mold."

I shake my head. "Preposterous." Then I frown. "Was that some kind of secret mystery shopper handshake you were trying to give me?"

"Shhhh!" He darts his head from side to side as if someone is listening in. The reality is, of course, that apart from a few strung out potion-heads, the shop is empty. It is the middle of the sodding night. "Besides," he adds, "if I were you I'd be more concerned that you're starting to sound more and more like your grandfather."

"What do you mean?"

"Preposterous? Is that even a real word?"

I roll my eyes. "You know very well it is. Although," I concede, "I have been shut away with the old man for the last few days. Perhaps he is rubbing off on me."

"Mmm." O'Shea doesn't appear impressed. He picks up a pretty glass vial filled with swirling purple liquid and pockets it.

"What are you doing?"

He shrugs. "They don't pay me very much. I think I deserve a bonus."

"I am not hanging around with a shoplifter," I say firmly. "Put it back."

O'Shea flicks me a disdainful look. "Worried about Magix's bottom line are you? I would have thought you'd be happy to see them lose a few quid."

"Perhaps but I'm not a thief. Put the bloody thing back."

He scowls at me. He does at least, however, return it back to the shelf. He selects another bottle and starts strolling in the direction of the till. "So, what do you want anyway?"

"That's it? That's the greeting I'm going to get? What happened to 'hi Bo, how are you?'"

He stops in his tracks, his head slowly turning towards me and his eyebrows shooting up.

"Okay," I mumble, "I guess I am starting to sound like my grandfather."

"At least you admit it. How are things anyway? How's Connor?"

I frown. That's an odd question. "He's fine. I'm fine. We're all fine."

"Great." He places the bottle in front of the cashier. "I couldn't find any Valentine's vials."

She smiles politely. "We only stock those in February, sir. If you'd like to make a special request…"

"No, no," O'Shea says airily. "That's fine."

She starts wrapping up the bottle. "Would you like a bag to go with that?"

"Yes, please."

She bends down, pulling one out from underneath a shelf. O'Shea nudges me. "What?" I ask baffled.

His nose wrinkles in irritation. He hands over some money and pays for the potion then starts to walk out. "Did you see that?" he says. "It'll be going straight into my report."

"Um, see what?"

"Her attitude! It was patently rude."

I stare at him as we exit the shop. "No, it wasn't."

"Her tone of voice, the way she rolled her eyes…"

"O'Shea, she was perfectly nice. You're taking this way too seriously."

"It's my job."

"One you're prepared to lose by stealing?"

I simply receive a disgusted look in return. "What do you want, Bo? Clearly, I'm very busy." He licks his lips. "Is it Michael? Is he feeling lonely?"

I punch him in the arm. "Don't be ridiculous. I need some help getting hold of a time bubble."

There's a moment of silence. Then, in a funny tone of voice, O'Shea says, "But Bo, surely you know that all the time bubbles are being kept under lock and key and away from dangerous serial killers and the like. The fact that you're here asking me to help you obtain one means you must want me to steal it. And here was me thinking you weren't a thief."

Er… "It's completely different. I just want to borrow it."

"Really," he says flatly.

"Really!"

"Well, in that case..." he drawls with an exaggerated wink in my direction. "Let's do it! This will be fun!" He chucks the Magix bag with the potion inside into a nearby bin. "Thank goodness! I couldn't cope with much more shopping."

For some reason I already have a sinking feeling deep in the pit of my stomach.

THE GATES to the Black Market are, well, black. Gazing up at them looming over us, I can only barely manage to repress a shudder. The collection of suspicious characters loitering out the front doesn't help.

"Are you sure this is the best place?" I ask O'Shea doubtfully.

"It's the only place," he replies firmly. "All the time bubble orbs we know of have been appropriated by the army. If we want to find where they are, then we need information. The sort of information that can only be bought and paid for here." He glances at me sidelong. "You're not trying to tell me that badass Bo, aka the Red Angel, has never been to the Black Market?"

I lift my shoulders in an uncomfortable shrug. "You forget that until recently I was very human. Even the best and most experienced PIs from Dire Straits avoided this place. It's not exactly ... safe for non-tribers."

"Pshaw!" he says, snorting. "All propaganda."

Just at that moment one of the shadier looking black witches grabs another by the throat and forces him to kneel. He slides out a long curved blade from under his coat and holds it against his hapless victim's cheek, pressing into the skin at the exact centre of the black magic tattoo pulsating there.

I start forward but O'Shea moves quickly, his hand encircling my arm. "It's only safe if you don't involve yourself in other matters, of course."

A drop of blood squeezes out from underneath the blade's edge while the crouching witch whimpers. I desperately want to get involved and stop whatever is going on but I know it's neither my place to interfere nor the time to make a spectacle of myself. Unfortunately, the dodgy witch holding the knife has already spotted me.

"Well, well, well," he drawls. Rather than being rough and stereotypically East End, his accent is smooth, with the sort of nasal quality that implies upper class. Somehow that makes him scarier. "The Red Angel herself is darkening our door. Do you know, boys, that she's a Blackman?"

Every single one of them, even the witch on the ground, turns to look at me. I process the situation as quickly as I can. I don't think that logical reasoning is going to be my ally in this particular situation. I'm going to have to use the 'gift' that X gave me instead.

In an exaggerated move, I adjust the collar on my leather jacket and swagger over. "If you have a problem with my family," I say with a little smile that I pray is more dangerous than it is girlish, "then be upfront about it. We can sort it out right now. I'll be more than happy to oblige." I ignore O'Shea's sudden indrawn breath from behind. "I'm still a bit sore from a little brawl I had the other night but I think I can rise to a challenge. Perhaps you saw it? I believe it was broadcast live on television." I turn casually to O'Shea who I swear is virtually cowering. "Is that right, Devlin?"

He coughs. "Yeah. Yes. It was on TV."

The black witch regards me for a moment. "I thought you'd be taller."

"Oh," I purr, "size really isn't everything." My eyes travel down the witch's body, resting for longer than would be deemed polite on his groin, "although…" I add thoughtfully, without finishing my sentence. I look back up and smile.

I'd never normally dare to taunt a black witch so openly, even now I'm becoming more confident in my vampire skin. The opportunity to slide by unnoticed into the Market has gone, however. Besides, sometimes, you have to fight fire with fire. As long as my reputation precedes me, I might just get away with it.

One of the bolder witches hovering in the background snarls and steps forward. "I'm betting she's not as tough as she makes out. An itty bitty thing like her? I'll take you on, Blackman."

Damn. I try to look vaguely amused and beckon him on. The leader merely watches while his henchman, filled with obvious braggadocio, makes a show of taking off his jacket and handing it someone else. He holds out his palm and another witch drops a brass knuckle into it. Sliding it onto his fist and adjusting it, he bares his teeth in my direction. I return the favour – at least my fangs are better than his. Despite my own display of bravado, the knotted tension in my stomach increases. Unless I dispatch this idiot quickly, it's going to become very quickly apparent that I'm not as tough as X tried to pretend.

He swipes forward. Although there's a great deal of force behind his punch, my reflexes are better than that and I duck to avoid him with relative ease. His mouth twists and he tries again. Once more I escape. It occurs to me that there's a better way out of this than trying to hurt the witch back and laying him out. It'll be humiliating for him but it'll mean neither of us get hurt – and, as irritating as it is, I'll get to keep my Red Angel reputation.

I keep my toes light and wait for him to make another move. He jabs towards my stomach with the brass knuckles. I duck again but this time, instead of simply waiting for the next punch, I dive forward and through the gap in between his legs, finishing with a little forward roll. I leap back up to my feet and twist round. It takes him a moment or two to recover from his confusion and spin to face me.

"I was really good at gymnastics when I was in primary school," I comment lightly.

He balls up both fists, feinting right but kicking with his left leg immediately after. I vault upwards, somersaulting in the air and landing behind him. I tap him on the shoulder and, when he looks back at me, I wiggle my fingers in the semblance of little wave.

"Stop playing, bitch, and fight!"

I grin. He rushes me so I sidestep away, my feet dancing in a vague approximation of a Bavarian two step. No prizes for guessing who made me learn formal dancing. The witch is enraged even further but his watching companions, who are keeping well away from us, chuckle slightly. It doesn't help his mood. His hand twitches, jerking towards his back pocket where, no doubt there's a more lethal weapon concealed. Rather than wait for him to take the opportunity to play dirty, I spring up from the balls of my feet, grabbing the top of the street lamp above. I swing in the air for a brief second and then drop down onto the witch's shoulders as if he's giving me a piggy back ride.

He roars in anger, twisting first one way then another in a bid to try and shake me off. I cling tightly on with my legs, however, dropping my hands down to cover his eyes. Blinded, his movements become even more frantic. He stumbles forward, his head down. Rather unfortunately for him, his crown crashes into the nearby wall encircling the Market. He collapses to the ground, groaning, while I free myself and dust off my jeans. I hadn't actually intended for that to happen.

The leader, still holding his knife to his captive's face, raises his eyebrows and looks mildly impressed. "I suppose what they say about you is true. I did wonder whether the fight with the Kakos daemon had been staged, you know."

I do what I can not to react. I guess my grandfather isn't the only wholly naïve being in London after all. "If you'd like I can try again with a different witch?" I inquire. "In case you're still not sure, that is." I cross my fingers tightly, inwardly praying that the fallen witch's embarrassment is enough for the others to leave me alone.

"I'm sure that won't be necessary." He holds out his free hand for me to shake.

I eye it for a moment. He's still a black witch and I'm still a Blackman. "If you don't mind," I say, "I won't shake hands with you just now. You never know what spell traces might be clinging to your skin."

From the flash in his eyes, I know I was right. For all that I sometimes leap before I look, caution can do wonders. He withdraws his hand. "I hope we have not offended you with this silly little confrontation."

"I am feeling a little, well, irked." I smile unpleasantly. "Why don't you appease me and let him go?" I gesture down towards the terrified witch at his feet.

"This is nothing to do with you. He deserves to be punished."

I take a step forward. "You're obviously the leader of this little gang. Perhaps you deserve to be punished for making me late for my appointment inside."

His lips thin. He's obviously weighing up the odds of all of them being able take me on compared to losing face at releasing the witch. I'm pretty sure I know what he'll do but I still feel a bit nervous.

"He's not that important," he shrugs. There's a still a

dangerous darkness in his eyes that suggests otherwise though. "Have him." He virtually throws the witch at me.

"I already have a pet of my own." I curve my mouth into a wide smile. "But thanks." I help the witch back up to his feet. He stares at me then at his captor. A second later he sprints away off down the street. I nod towards O'Shea and the pair of us stroll through the Black Market gates.

The moment we're out of earshot, O'Shea sags. "Did that really just happen? Bo, you're crazy! I know you killed that Kakos daemon but what if one of them had used a spell?"

I think about the leader's proffered handshake. "One of them almost did." I wipe the sweat off my brow. "We got lucky."

"Don't ever do that to me again!" He wags his finger in my face. "It's not like I have a chance against eleven witches. If you go down, I'm dead meat."

"I'll do my best," I say weakly.

"Why did you make them let that other witch go?"

I shrug. "I don't know, to be honest. It just seemed like the right thing to do." I stand up on my tiptoes and spy a sign for the bathroom. "Wait here."

"Where are you going now?"

I grimace. "I really have to pee. And throw up." It's unfortunately becoming a rather bad habit.

O'Shea still looks pale when, feeling slightly less nauseous, I finally return. "You know you've thrown down the gauntlet, right?"

I check my breath. It doesn't seem too bad. "What do you mean?"

"You're a four foot woman who's apparently a superhero.

There's going to be a lot more of that. Everyone's going to want to see if they can best you."

"I'm five foot," I return in mock irritation. "And I had hoped that most people – tribers included – would be too scared to take me on now. All I seem to get are starry-eyed autograph hunters. Not black witches with decades old vendettas. He was the exception to the rule."

O'Shea rolls his eyes. "You don't get it. Of course there will be a lot of people who think you're the best thing since bottled spells. But you're also presenting a challenge. If you're famous, imagine how famous the person will be who takes you down."

I swallow. He actually has a point. Yet another reason to stay out of the public eye. Bugger it.

"By the way," O'Shea continues, "how *did* you kill that Kakos daemon?"

I offer him a weak grunt as an answer and change the subject. "Dawn's only a few hours away. Let's search this place and be done with it." I look around and jerk in surprise, then point over at a nearby stall. "Look, she's selling orbs."

He clicks his teeth. "They're snow globes. Good for enemies."

"What do you..." I blink as I put two and two together. "You mean you can spell people inside them?"

"And make them freeze in swirling blizzards whenever you take the fancy," he adds cheerfully. "Don't worry. They almost never work."

All the same, I still give the stall a wide berth. "Which way then? Shall we try down here?"

"No, Bo, darling. There's only one person we need to see. Merlin."

"Merlin? You have to be kidding me."

"Obviously not the real one," O'Shea says. Then he

scratches his cheek. "Well, probably not anyway. But that's what he likes to be called." He takes my hand. "This way."

I let O'Shea lead me through the claustrophobic winding pathways. I try not to gawk at the sights on offer but shrunken heads that blink and chameleons the colour of a tropical sky make it hard not to. The only saving grace about the place is that everyone around here is so weird, I'm left in peace as another unremarkable oddity, despite one or two surprised stares here and there.

We eventually come to a halt outside a small tent. From the outside it looks shabby and unappealing, not to mention not much larger than a child's playhouse. O'Shea gestures at me to enter. Frowning, I do as I'm told.

One of things I've learnt over the years is not to judge people by appearances. Patently, I should apply the same to places as well. Despite the tent's exterior, inside is a vast opulent space with intricate Turkish carpets, ornate wooden chests and what appear to be several rooms leading off from the main entrance.

O'Shea, watching my expression, is delighted. "It's like the Tardis, isn't it?" he asks gleefully.

"And then some," I breathe.

Just then, an old man shuffles out from towards the back. His white bushy eyebrows snap together when he spots O'Shea.

"Devlin! What a joy!" His eyes flick to me. "Surely, you're not switching teams?"

O'Shea doesn't take the slightest umbrage. "Hardly, Merlin. You know me better than that. Anyway, if I were to change my very nature, I doubt I'd go for someone like her. I'd probably end up murdered in my bed. Or worse."

I throw him a nasty look but, unsurprisingly, it slides off him. "I'm Bo," I say firmly, interjecting myself into the conversation.

"Of course you are, my dear. I've been hearing a lot about you. I am Merlin." He dips his head.

"Nice to meet you." I try to smile. Merlin looks as old as Methuselah, with pure white hair which reaches beyond his shoulders. If he weren't dressed as a hippy with tie-dyed t-shirt and bright bell bottom trousers, I'd be inclined to believe he really is the Merlin of yore. His bright blue eyes certainly look sharp enough. "I'm looking for…"

"Some incense," O'Shea interrupts, elbowing me in the ribs.

Merlin's eyes crinkle. "Something fruity or more floral?"

"Surprise me."

Merlin walks through a nearby door, closing it behind him. I turn to O'Shea. "What are you doing? I don't want any bloody incense!"

The daemon sighs. "I'm playing the game, Bo. Just try to keep quiet."

"But…" I splutter.

He places a finger against my lips. "Shhh."

I subside. I don't like this at all. I fold my arms and take a few steps forward. There's a pretty doll sitting on top of a shelf that catches my attention. I reach out to touch her but O'Shea pulls me back.

"Don't touch anything," he hisses. "I mean it."

I glare at him but take his advice. I'm in the unknown here and I need to act more sensibly. Instead I simply look around. Merlin appears to be quite the collector. His tent is strewn with all manner of objects. Some are obviously magical while others, like a battered coffee pot, appear far more mundane. I gaze at a painting hanging from the canvas wall. There's something not quite right about it. Several small figures stare out from underneath a smoky sky. It's oddly reminiscent of Lowry. I peer more closely and one of the figures winks. I draw back with a hiss.

"What the hell…?"

O'Shea joins me. "It's like the snow globes we saw earlier," he tells me quietly.

I stare aghast at the artwork. "Those are real people? Every single one of them? Trapped in there?" Revulsion ripples through me.

"Yup."

"There are so many of them."

O'Shea shrugs awkwardly. I turn and look at him, "Why are there so many?"

There's a creak and Merlin reappears behind us. "Because, my dear, it's a very clever spell. Not one of mine, alas." He permits himself a tiny smile. "I do wish I'd thought of it, however. You see, whenever someone decides to free one of the painting's occupants and they cast the spell to do so, they fail. They end up inside the painting too."

My stomach turns. "So they think they're doing someone a favour and saving them from a life trapped in pain and instead they ruin their own life too?"

Merlin's smile grows. "Genius, isn't it?"

I flick a look at O'Shea but he's pointedly ignoring me. Just where exactly has he brought me? This place is evil.

"Your incense?" Merlin asks, jolting me back into the reason we're here.

I realise he's holding a simple box. He beckons us closer. Reluctantly, I edge a bit nearer. I don't want to get too close to him. He makes my flesh creep. With a flourish, Merlin pulls off the lid. Expecting to see some heavily scented candles or something of that ilk, I'm astonished when I see a familiar orb containing blue swirling light nestled amongst some tissue paper. I even momentarily forget how creeped out I am.

My mouth drops open. "How..."

O'Shea interrupts yet again. "What a fabulous smell," he murmurs.

"Indeed." Merlin beams.

"I take it the high quality is reflected in the price?"

"It is. One thousand pounds."

I stiffen. It's a lot of money. But a time bubble orb even before the vast majority were seized by the government should cost considerably more. Something else is going on here. I cast another look at the painting. I don't trust Merlin one little bit.

O'Shea lifts an eyebrow. He's less concerned about the price tag than I am. Neither does he appear particularly bothered by the witch's less than seemly joy at other people's misery. "I don't suppose there's any room for manouevre on that figure?"

Merlin doesn't even blink. He just smiles pleasantly at the both of us. Apparently not then. I reach into my jacket for my wallet, deciding I want to get out of here as quickly as possible. Something tells me that annoying Merlin would not be a wise move. I can't think why. "Do you take plastic?"

"I've got this," O'Shea says. He takes out a grubby roll of notes and peels off ten. All of a sudden I feel like I've walked onto a gangster film set. I'm almost tempted to look around for Al Pacino.

Merlin lowers his head again, performing some sleight of hand and magicking the money away. He passes the box over. It's surprisingly light.

"Do come again," he twinkles. "And don't lose sight of that stone, Ms. Blackman."

I start. "Pardon?"

"The human world may have decided that angels are a force for good," Merlin says, without repeating his freaky little aside about my white pebble, "but don't forget that not every religion originally saw them that way. Some of the most powerful celestial beings were known as tools of vengeance. And there is nothing more bloody than that. You might be better off sticking to the daemons." He jerks his head at O'Shea. "Even this one."

I glance at O'Shea. He meets my eyes, trouble mirrored in both our expressions. When I turn back to Merlin for clarification however, he's already gone.

"What did he mean by stone?"

I tug at my earlobe. "Who knows? Let's just get out of here." Merlin's tent and its creepy interior is leaving me cold.

"He's a criminal, Devlin," I say flatly, when we're several metres away. "That painting..."

"Of course he's a criminal, Bo. This is the Black Market. What did you expect?"

I hug my arms round myself. I'm just glad to be escaping while I still can. I don't ever want to come back here again.

The only good thing about this entire visit is that the cluster of shady black witches outside the Black Market's gates have scuttled back to whichever hole they sprung from. I still wait until we're some distance away, however, before I trust myself to speak again. I don't want to talk about Merlin any more.

"Mystery shopping must pay well," I say to O'Shea.

There's a glimmer of a cheeky smile. "It's not my only gig."

I dread to think. "I'll pay you back," I promise. "At least we have an orb now though. I hadn't realised it would be so easy."

O'Shea throws back his head and laughs. I stare at him. "What?"

He only laughs harder, bending double and clutching his stomach. Growing irritated, I put my hands on my hips. "What?" I repeat.

He straightens up and wipes away genuine tears from his eyes. "Bo, you're a funny girl. How did you ever survive before I came along?"

I'm slightly offended. "Hey, I'm the one who helped you to survive! You'd be dead without me!"

"I guess we'll never know if that's true or not." He winks. "That's not a time bubble orb."

"It looks like one."

"Because it's a Trace. A semi-sentient object, Bo. It knows what you're searching for so it's taken on that aspect. For you. Merlin wouldn't have seen what you did."

"Oh." I feel stupid. O'Shea's request for 'incense' makes more sense now. And I have actually heard of Traces. I'd known some PIs who used them at Dire Straits. They are, however, notoriously unreliable. Try using one to find a bunch of lost keys and it'll attempt to direct you to whichever set it deems is closest. In a city the size of London, that's like looking for a specific needle in a haystack filled with a million other needles. Besides which, even an only semi-effective Trace would cost a damn sight more than a grand. "Is it going to work?"

"Yes."

"Is Merlin really that good?"

O'Shea laughs again. "No. He's an absolute charlatan. But we're in the rather fortunate situation of knowing that almost all time bubble orbs, if not every single one, are being held in the same place. Their combined signatures will mean that this little thing," he gestures at the box, "will have no trouble locating them."

I absorb this information. O'Shea is correct. Except I already know where all the damn orbs are being kept. So does anyone who reads a newspaper. Have I just placed myself in debt to the most unreliable Agathos daemon in the city for nothing? Along with meeting quite possibly the most unsavoury witch I've ever had the misfortune to come across? "I know where the orbs are."

He merely nods. "Brigstone Army Base."

I wait for the penny to drop. When it doesn't, I throw up my hands in despair. "Why do we need a Trace to show us where the Army Base is? The internet will give us more reliable directions."

O'Shea pats me on the shoulder in a patronising manner. "Have you ever been inside an army base?"

"No."

"Anthony Davis." He rubs his thumb along his bottom lip and gazes dreamily off into the distance. "Lance Corporal Davis to you. A muscular hunk with enough sex appeal to drown a kitten in to me."

"Devlin," I begin warningly.

"He used to sneak me into his base," O'Shea explains. "Not because we couldn't find an alternative spot for a tryst of course. But the thrill of being interrupted by a group of soldiers was too delicious to pass up. In fact, one time..."

"Get to the point."

"It's a good story!"

I make a show of looking at my watch. O'Shea sighs. "If you insist. Anyway, I learnt from those little experiences that army bases aren't exactly compact and bijou. It's one thing to know that the time bubble orbs are being kept at Brigstone. It's another to find out exactly where. I made the assumption that you wouldn't want to wander around the largest army base in the country asking for directions. I know you women like to do that but I'm not sure bloodguzzlers are welcome in the middle of the night with Her Majesty's finest."

"I hate it when you're smarter than I am," I mutter.

He laughs. "Don't worry about it, little Bo."

"You've not asked me yet why I'm so keen to get hold of an orb."

He taps his temple. "Smarter than you, remember?"

I growl. "Not all the time."

O'Shea smirks. "It's pretty obvious. I've been waiting for you to get around to it. You're going to find Tobias Renfrew. And I'm going to help you. Solving the biggest mystery the Agathos daemons have ever experienced by finding a reclusive billionaire who may or may not be a serial killer will be a piece of cake for my brains and your...” he looks me up and down, “um, your … your …”

I thump him on the arm. “Idiot.”

He sweeps out a bow. “I aim to please.”

“Even though that wasn’t his ear, he has to have something to do with those attacks. If we investigate Renfrew we might find the pricks who hurt Rogu3.”

“I’m with you all the way, Bo. That kid didn’t deserve that. In fact, he’s lucky to still be alive.”

I refrain from mentioning that I turned Rogu3 into a vampire to save his life and then used X’s daemon blood to turn him back to human. I know several people have their suspicions around what I did but to mention X’s existence would be to seal their fate.

O’Shea flicks a glance up at the sky. “Dawn isn’t far off. Shall we reconvene tomorrow evening?”

I start to agree before belatedly remembering I already have a prior engagement. Bugger. “As long it’s after eleven.” I’ll just need to come up with a good excuse to finish up my date with Michael early. Telling him the truth isn’t going to work. He would only get pissed off if he knew I was planning on breaking the law and doing something this daft. But he’s only the Head of the most powerful vampire Family in the country. It’ll be easy to tell him that I’m far busier than he is and have to leave. No problemo.

CHAPTER 5
CAUSE CELEBRE

Matt and Connor perch uncomfortably on my little sofa. I'm not entirely sure whether their awkward position is because they're unhappy with the job I've tasked them with or whether it's because they're too afraid to move Kimchi out of the way. The dog is sprawled out behind them, giving off every impression of being fast asleep. From the way he keeps opening one eye to peek out at the action, I know better.

"What do you think of this one?" I give them a twirl.

"It's lovely, Bo," Connor answers, deadpanned.

"You said that about the last dress."

"It was lovely too. They both kind of look the same to me though."

"It was long! This one is short." I frown down. "Too much cleavage?"

Matt stares thoughtfully at my breasts. "Definitely not enough." I roll my eyes.

"Bo," Connor interjects, "you'd be better off getting a woman to do this. Dahlia is downstairs. She can..."

"I'm going on a date with a man. Not a woman," I say

firmly. The last thing I want is her inside my flat. "I need a male perspective. Let me try just one more."

He groans. "Please no." Holding out both his wrists, he pleads with me. "Drink me dry, Bo. Take every drop of blood I have. Just don't subject me to any more."

I point at him. "Stay."

Connor looks desperately at Matt who simply shrugs. "I can only do what I'm told."

"This is for the good of all vampires," I tell them both sternly.

"And it's about time you had some sex," Matt agrees.

"There will be no sex!" My voice is shrill. "It's for show."

"Of course, Bo. You're always right."

"Damn straight I am," I grumble. I half turn towards the bedroom to change again. "I saw that!" I call back, looking back to see Matt nudge Connor. The pair of them stare at me, guilt written across both of their faces.

Back at my wardrobe, I flip through the remainder of my clothes in frustration. In one regard, Matt is correct. It's been a long time since I've been on any kind of date. These days I'm so used to wearing jeans and t-shirt – not forgetting my leather jacket, of course – that I've almost forgotten what it's like to dress up. I pull out a tight sheath dress. I know I look good in it. The problem is that I still need something I can move around in if I'm going to meet O'Shea later and breach the army base. I hang it back up and sigh, telling myself I only care about what I'm going to wear because I need the press to believe I really am on a date. It's got nothing to do with caring what Michael thinks.

In the end, I pull on a little black dress, deciding not to subject Matt and Connor to my indecision any longer. It might be boring but it'll suit a date and it's short enough that when I need to spring into action-hero mode later, it won't hamper my movements. Not to mention that the colour will help with camouflage. I don't want to waste a single precious moment of darkness in doing something as mundane as getting changed when I get back from the 'date'. I'm tempted to put on a pair of flats but I'm fairly certain Michael is canny enough to make note of them and realise I'm up to something. The last thing I'll need tonight is either him or his Montserrat sidekicks following me to Brigstone. I'll simply go barefoot later when I need to – the addition of some heels at dinner will make me feel less like a midget.

When I stroll back out, Connor is nowhere to be seen. Kimchi has plonked himself on Matt's lap and is vigorously lapping at his face. At least my bloodguzzling buddy doesn't seem to mind.

"Connor told me," Matt says between licks, "that he's got vital work to do for your grandfather."

I half snort. "Anything to get out of a fashion parade."

Matt stretches his neck up and peers over Kimchi's head. "That one's really boring. Don't wear it."

"This from the man who was wearing a paisley shirt with a velvet suit a few nights ago."

"You asked me for advice, remember?"

I raised my eyebrows slightly. "Are you feeling alright, Matt?"

He seems surprised. "Yes, fine. Why do you ask?"

"Because," I smile, "that response was almost sarky."

There's a flicker of alarm. "I wasn't trying to be rude!"

"That's not what I meant," I reassure him. "Just that maybe the effects from the spell are starting to wear off."

His eyes grow wide. "I'm not sure I want them to."

"Why ever not?"

"I wasn't a nice person back then."

I look at him in sympathy. I'd like to disagree, but he's right.

Pre-enhancement spell Matt was a pain in the arse. "People change," I say softly.

He still seems miserable. "Try," he tells me. "Try to tell me to do something and I'll do what I can to resist."

I bite my lip. "Okay. Um, lick Kimchi back."

He scrunches up his face in a bid to avoid mindlessly following my instruction. It doesn't work. His tongue lolls out, and he licks a delighted Kimchi across his muzzle. "You could have asked me to do something nice," he bemoans.

"Sorry. It was kind of cute though."

Matt spits out a hair. "Yuck."

AFTER I LET him off the hook and Matt vanishes to leave me in peace, I stare firmly at Kimchi. "So," I say, wagging my finger, "this is how things are going to go. It's important you pay attention." Kimchi's tail thumps against the sofa. "When I give you the signal," I make a swiping motion with my right hand, you are going to whine loudly and lie down. I'll tell Michael you're obviously sick and that I need to take you home. Got that?"

He barks. I nod to myself. "Let's try it. Whine now." Kimchi barks once more and starts panting. "No. Whine. Like this." I give him what I think is a very good impression of an unhappy mutt. Kimchi leans his head to one side and looks at me as if I'm crazy. "Come on. Give it a shot."

He barks again. I shake my head. "No, like this." I whine again, combining the noise with my hand gesture.

Kimchi still looks confused but he does give me a tiny whine in response. "Well done!" I scratch his ears. "Now lie down and look sick."

Unfortunately at that point the door bell rings so, naturally, he completely ignores me in favour of rushing to the door and bouncing up and down next to it like some sort of demented yoyo.

"Kimchi," Michael commands from the other side. "Sit!"

My mouth drops open as he does exactly what he's told. "Traitor," I hiss, and gently nudge him out of the way to open the door.

Michael is looking damn good. He's also far more casually dressed than I am, in dark jeans and a leather jacket in Montserrat midnight blue. If I'd known I could get away with denim, I'd have bloody well done so.

The corner of his mouth crooks up. "A dress?"

I frown at him. "I wear dresses. They're just not practical when I'm working." I emphasise the point. When I skip out early, the last thing I want him to think is that I have a job to do. He wouldn't approve of breaking into an army base and, besides, this one is for me.

"You look beautiful." His eyes, filled with serious intent, meet mine. I'm just not sure what the intent is actually for.

"Thanks," I mumble. "Can I bring Kimchi along?"

He draws a thumb across the stubble along his jaw. "It's not the kind of place that normally allows animals." His smile deepens. "But you are the Red Angel. I'm not sure there are many people who will gainsay you at this particular moment in time."

"I really hate all that stuff," I whisper.

The amusement in his gaze vanishes. "I know. I know you don't want to go out with me either. You've been dealt a shitty hand, Bo, and I'm sorry."

I tug at my ponytail, suddenly feeling both awkward and vulnerable. "It's not that I don't want to go out with you, it's just that you and me would be so … complicated."

"Would we?"

"We're supposed to be friends, remember?"

"I think we agreed on friends with benefits." For a brief moment, his eyes spark again.

I just swallow. Sensing the banter is making me uncomfortable, he merely holds out his hand. I eye it warily for a moment, then take it, grabbing Kimchi's lead with my other hand and stepping outside to the hallway to join him.

"Wait." He snaps his fingers. "I almost forgot. It's a shame you're wearing black because it won't really show up against that colour." He hands me over a dark blue rose. "It's been genetically engineered to match our House colours."

"I'm not technically Montserrat…" I begin.

"No," he says, interrupting me softly. "But I am. By giving you this, it'll imply that you belong with me."

My eyebrows snap together. "I don't belong to anyone."

He watches me carefully. "I said belong with, not belong to. Bad choice of words either way though."

Looking at his expression, I'm not sure he really thinks that at all. I tell myself not to react and tuck the flower carefully into my hair. It scratches my scalp and feels unnatural but it makes sense to put it somewhere the press will notice it. That is what this is all about, after all.

SOMEONE, I'm guessing either my grandfather or Michael himself, has tipped off one of the big tabloids. Not only do the pair of us get snapped getting into the Montserrat limo outside my building but there's also a healthy bustle of paparazzi outside the restaurant. Kimchi seems to take umbrage at their presence, growling and snapping at several of them who get too close. I glance at the dog with newfound respect.

"Bo! Is this a business meeting?"

I smile prettily and wave, smoothing down my skirt to draw

attention to its lack of material. "Yes," I say firmly. "We are discussing important vampire business."

Michael looks down at me, a tender expression on his face. "Very important," he adds softly.

Several cameras flash in an excited explosion of light. Michael and I enter the restaurant without another word.

"Do you think that worked?" I ask him in an undertone.

"From the pound signs I saw in every damn photographer's eyes, I'd say so," he grunts. He actually sounds annoyed.

We're led to a prominently positioned table, right in front of the window. Every other patron in the place watches us take our seats. Kimchi, for once behaving, settles himself at my feet.

"Ms. Blackman?" A well dressed woman appears. "I'm Deborah, the manager of La Maison. I'm thrilled that you have decided to join us tonight." She glances down at Kimchi. It's clear what she wants to add but she's too nervous to actually say the words. "Lord Montserrat," she murmurs, "it is, of course, a pleasure to have you here again with us also. If there's anything I can do to make your night more enjoyable, do please let me know."

She melts away, leaving me raising my eyebrows in Michael's direction. "You come here often then? With dates?"

"A few times. I'm normally the one who's acknowledged first," he jokes. "Being around you will be good for my ego."

I frown. "Is that a good idea?" I ask tightly. "To come somewhere you've already been seen with other women?"

A tiny smile plays around his mouth. "You're not jealous, are you?"

"No," I snap. "This is make-believe, remember?"

"So what's your point?"

"If you want people to believe this ... relationship is special, then we should go somewhere new. Not where you take any old flame."

"Bo," he says with such conviction that I fall momentarily dumb, "this relationship is very special."

A heartbeat later there's another camera flash, making me blink and look away. "Good work," I mutter. "At least that photo will make it look like we were staring into each other's eyes."

His voice is low. "We were."

I'm rescued from having to add anything to that comment by a waiter appearing and smoothly offering us a bottle of wine – 'compliments from the manager'. I do what I can to graciously accept, sipping it once it's poured into my glass. It's hard not to wince at its tartness.

"You can send it back if you don't like it," Michael says, amused.

"I'm sure it's lovely. It's just not what I normally drink." I pat my mouth with my napkin to hide my expression of distaste.

"We have some very good vintages back at the mansion. There are some even better ones at my apartment. I'm sure I can find at least one that you'd enjoy."

I draw in a deep breath. "I'll look forward to it."

He raises his own glass and chinks it against mine.

A shadow falls across the table. "What are we drinking to?"

Both Michael and I look up at the unwelcome interruption. "What do you want, Medici?"

"Last time I checked, I was still Lord."

"Not mine," I spit.

Kimchi, sensing my antagonism, jumps to his feet, his hackles visibly raised across his spine. Several people at tables near us recoil away and there's a further flurry of camera flashes coming in our direction from outside.

"Now, now, Ms. Blackman, there's no need to be rude. Although perhaps that's what comes from the media's darling."

His cold eyes sneer at me. "It won't last, you know. The more they love you now, the more they'll hate you later when it all goes tits up. And it will go tits up. You're far too reckless to stay on the straight and narrow for long."

"You know nothing about me."

"I know enough." He pulls over an empty chair and sits himself down next to us.

"Lord Medici," Michael says, the venom in his voice belying his polite address, "this is a private dinner. If you wish to speak with either us, please make an appointment for a later date."

Medici, unfortunately, looks like he's enjoying himself far too much to even consider leaving. I grab Kimchi's collar and bring him round to the other side of the table so that he's further away from the vampire Lord. The last thing I need is for him to bite and snap in full view of all these people. Medici would start crowing about the Dangerous Dogs Act before I could do a single thing.

"Come, come," he drawls. "We're all friends now, aren't we? Especially now that New Order includes representatives from us all."

I forget to breathe. Is he admitting that he sent Dahlia to us?

"You've changed your tune," Michael interjects.

Medici reaches over to Michael's place setting and takes his napkin, carefully unfolding it and tucking it into his collar to form a bib. "I didn't have much choice. Damn female fledgling ran away to join you, didn't she? I should have known recruiting her was a bad idea."

"You didn't recruit her," I say through gritted teeth. "You forced her."

He looks up as if trying to remember. "Oh yes. I'd forgotten about that part." He shrugs and gives me what I suppose is meant to be a charming smile. "Oh well."

"Her defection reflects badly on you. Why haven't you tried to bring her back?"

Medici's gaze turns unpleasant again. "I will. I'm just waiting for the right moment."

My eyes narrow. Either he wants to force Dahlia back into the Medici fold at the point where it'll cause Arzo the most pain – or all this is a bluff to make us think she's not still working for him. A ball of frustrated ire rises up inside me. He knows every single button to push to achieve maximum effect in pissing me off. The only way I can win this is by making myself stay calm and playing him at his own game.

I gently kick Michael under the table to give him as much prior warning as I dare. His eyes snap to mine as if he's afraid about what I'll do. I decide that he really shouldn't worry quite so much.

I raise my hand to the waiter and indicate that he should set an extra place for Medici. He understands instantly and rushes over while I carefully extract the Montserrat engineered flower from my hair and pass it over.

"Here," I say. "Isn't it pretty? You should wear it in your lapel. It would look fantastic against that Medici red."

The only hint I have that he's affected by my actions is the faint tightening around his mouth. I try not to yell out a happy yippee.

"I couldn't possibly," he demurs. "It was so becoming in your hair."

"Oh, but I insist. After all," I smile, "we're all friends now."

Left with little choice, he takes the little bloom from me, pinching it in between his thumb and forefinger as if he's afraid it'll bite him. He shoves it into his pinhole and forces a smile. I cross my fingers, exulting again when another of the pavement paparazzi nabs a shot. That'll look good in the morning papers – Medici wearing Montserrat colours.

Unfortunately for me, Medici hasn't finished playing either. He leans across the table, taking my hands in his. For propriety's sake, I resist recoiling away although his touch makes me shudder. My mind flashes to the white pebble in my clutch on the table. I hold it in my mind's eye while Medici goes in for the kill, planting his own mouth firmly on mine. There are delighted shouts and a strobe light effect as yet more cameras go off.

I pull away, using every part of my body to resist slapping him round the face – or worse, breaking his slimy neck. Michael's body is rigid, his fists clenched. He starts to rise from the table and I know with a sinking certainty that he's about to punch Medici in the face. It would be a PR nightmare. I hastily stand up and interject myself between them.

"That wine has gone right to my head," I exclaim loudly. "I really don't feel very well at all. Michael, darling, take me home, will you?"

I can tell that my words are falling on deaf ears. I know what it's like to be filled with burning rage. The last time it almost overtook me, Michael brought me back from the brink. It's time for me to return the favour. I coil my arm round his neck and reach up on my tiptoes to kiss him deeply. He doesn't immediately respond. I don't give in, however. A few seconds later, I feel his body relax against mine. His hands move to my waist and he deepens the kiss. He tastes not only of the wine but something deeper and more masculine. I forget about Medici behind me until one of the paparazzi, who somehow had managed to sneak inside the restaurant itself while everyone was preoccupied, takes a photo from bare inches away. I pull away from Michael, telling myself that my rapid heartbeat is because of the tense situation with Medici, not the kiss.

"That was lovely, darling. It even got rid of the bad taste in my mouth. I still think I should go home though." I pat my stomach. "I just don't feel quite right."

Medici turns to the photographer and bares his fangs. I could swear he's actually about to bite the man. I almost hope he does. Vampires are above human law but no-one would be able to ignore such a blatant act of aggression. It's a shame he manages to restrain himself just in time and the hapless journalist escapes.

"She does look rather pale," he comments as if nothing at all untoward has just happened.

Michael takes my shoulder, gently pushing me to one side. My stomach drops when he steps up to Medici, going almost nose to nose. "Try that again and I will kill you."

Medici throws back his head and laughs. I silently plead with Michael to let it go. For a moment I think it's still touch and go, then he turns back to me, folding my arm under his and we stroll out of the restaurant.

MICHAEL DROPS me back off at home. He had been virtually silent the entire journey back, his expression a brooding maelstrom of emotions. I can't tell if he's angry at me for what happened with Medici but, when I get out of the car with Kimchi by my side, he comes out also and kisses me gently on the cheek.

"I'm sorry for tonight," he says. "I'll make it up to you."

"It wasn't your fault. We need to do something about Medici. He's sailing too close to the wind."

"I know," he answers grimly.

I wait until he drives away into the night before I spin on my heel and quickly open the main entrance door to the building, letting Kimchi inside. He starts immediately sniffing at Drechlin's door as if he's expecting some doggie treats to miraculously appear. I leave him to it and head back out and down the street rather than following the dog in myself. I'm back much earlier than I'd anticipated but I still don't want to waste a second of what's left of the night, even if it means taking a moment to change my shoes. I'm relieved to see O'Shea leaning against the wall, waiting for my arrival.

"Hey," I call out. "It's time." It may feel like I've already had an epic evening but the reality is that I'm only just getting started.

CHAPTER 6

TRACKING AND TRACING

We park the bike some distance away from the base, concealing it in a copse of trees. I double check the paths leading out, imprinting them firmly in my mind. If we need to make a fast exit, I'll need to know what our options are. I kick off my high heels and leave them there.

"You should wear shoes like that more often," O'Shea tells me.

"Because they make me look taller?" I ask distractedly, peering across the expanse of darkness for any sign of activity.

"No," he grins, "because it means I get to drive the bike." He flips back his hair. "I think it makes me look rather James Dean."

"You're certainly a rebel without a cause," I mutter.

O'Shea laughs and puts an arm round my shoulders. "Darling," he whispers, "you're my cause."

I snort and push him away. "You don't have to get involved in this, you know. There's no guarantee it'll even work or I'll find out anything about Renfrew. It *is* entirely freelance. You might not get paid..."

"I'm not completely mercenary, Bo. Does anyone else know what you're up to?"

"No."

"Not even Michael?"

I shake my head.

"Well, then, I need to stick around. If something happened to you while I knew you were up to no good, he'd have my head. I can protect you."

He starts walking off, stumbling over a tree root that's jutting out of the earth and going flying. I just manage to pull him back before he lands face first in the dirt. "You do that, O'Shea. I need a big strong man like you around to keep me safe."

He sticks his tongue out and I laugh. "Come on." I check my watch. "We've got five hours. Let's find a way inside then get that Trace thing going."

We jog down a small hill towards the base itself. From this elevated viewpoint, I suddenly see what O'Shea had meant. It's a sprawling complex. It would have taken me far too long to locate the time bubble orbs – not just because I can only operate during night hours unless I want to spontaneously combust, but also because the more time spent inside the base means the more chances I'll end up getting caught.

I wrinkle my nose at the high fence. It's looped with barbed wire at the top and I have no doubt that it extends far enough underground to negate digging our way in. "How did you get inside when you had your, um, assignation?" I ask.

"I had a visitor's pass, of course." He squints at me. "Do you mean you don't have a plan for how to get in through the gate?"

"Why do you think I came and asked you for help in the first place?"

O'Shea throws up his hands. "Do I have to think of everything?"

I glance down towards the road leading into the base. Two headlights on full beam are bearing down. "Actually, no. We need to run though."

We're in luck that the vehicle is some kind of large truck. It'll mean there's more room underneath the chassis. This is far from an ideal method of transportation but I'm counting on the fact that we won't be travelling far and it definitely won't be at high speed. The difficult part will be how to bring the damn Trace along with us.

I reach the slow moving vehicle long before O'Shea does. It's helpful that there are speed bumps all along this stretch although it will inevitably be more painful. I take care to keep to the truck's blind spot directly at the back, flinging myself underneath as it slows down before another bump. Then I use my fingers to cling to the undercarriage, pulling up my feet and gaining enough purchase with my toes to keep my entire body off the ground. The metal is searingly hot to the touch but I'm a vampire. I can stand a bit of pain. I rest the box containing the Trace spell on my stomach, doing what I can to keep my body level to avoid it falling off. That would be disastrous.

I'm starting to think that O'Shea won't make it before we hit the main gates to the base. Just when it's almost too late, however, he appears, squeezing himself up to join me. Just about the only part of him that's visible are his eyes. He doesn't look exactly happy.

"This is a really bad idea!" he hisses to me.

"I know it's hard to cling on but it won't be for long," I soothe. "You're a daemon. Your fingers are virtually made of asbestos anyway."

"That's not what I mean!"

"What then?"

The truck comes to a juddering halt and there's the sound of muffled voices. I hear a clank and my insides freeze as I realise someone is checking underneath with a small angled mirror.

"That. Drop!"

Both O'Shea and I fall to the ground. I hug the Trace box to me and roll away from the moving mirror. I can only pray that there's just one guard. If we have to deal with two checking both sides simultaneously we've no hope. It's the night shift though so we're in luck. At least they're probably looking for bombs – not a vampire and a daemon.

When the boot covered feet move round the back of the truck, O'Shea and I scoot forward and to our left. He keeps muttering something under his breath. I catch the words 'fucking stupid'. He's not wrong. It's not until the vehicle finally jerks forward that I think we might just be in the clear. I reach up and grab on again, ignoring the blisters forming on my fingers and toes. I count to twenty in my head as the truck begins to accelerate. I can't cling on for much longer and I daren't so much as turn my head to look at O'Shea and see how he's doing. The very moment I breathe out twenty, I let myself fall. My back bangs against the tarmac, sending a jolt of pain through me. A second later I hear a thump as O'Shea follows me. I stay flat on the road until the truck has driven far enough away and then crawl over to the side of the road. I lie on the cool dewy grass and pant.

"Thanks," O'Shea says sarcastically above me. "Thanks a lot."

I peek up at him. He has every right to be pissed off. "I'm sorry," I whisper, clambering slowly back to my feet. "I should have thought that through better."

He points to a dark stain on his shirt. "I'm covered in grease. You're paying for my dry cleaning bill, Blackman!"

There's another smear down his cheek, shaped oddly like a

black witch's tattoo. I stifle a giggle. It's not really funny but, for some reason, mild hysteria overtakes me.

Unimpressed, O'Shea lifts his fingers to his cheeks. When he sees the dark grease, he shudders delicately. It just makes me snigger even more.

"You're covered in oil too," he points out. "I'm just too much of a gentleman to make a thing of it."

I touch my own cheek, feeling the sticky substance clinging to my skin. I manage to get my giggles under control and sober up. "What does it look like?"

"Like you've been clinging to the underside of a freaking truck. What do you think it looks like?"

I reach over and adjust the smear on his face so it looks like a witch's tattoo again. "I have an idea," I say. "Can you make the oil look like a black witch's signet?"

His brow furrows. "Huh?"

"One of their tattoos? There are going to be cameras all over the place. It might depend how high tech they are but if we both look like we're witches and the cameras happen to pick us up..."

He nods in sudden understanding. "Gotcha." He steps over to me and peers down. "There's a lot of grease on both your cheeks. Without some soap I'm not sure I can clean enough off."

"No problem," I tell him. "Make me look like a hybrid." I hate those bastards. It'll appeal to my sense of self-right-eousness for one of them to get blamed for this ill-advised heist.

O'Shea does what he can while I twist my hair into a tight knot. My face might currently be one of the more recognisable ones on the planet but if I have a more boyish hairstyle and keep my chin down, I might just get away with this. Eventually, O'Shea steps back, vaguely satisfied. "It won't hold up to close inspection."

"If anyone gets close, we're already doomed," I say. I lift the lid off the Trace box and stare doubtfully down. "How do we make this work then?"

"Pick it up."

I start to do as I'm told, my fingers extending downwards. They barely brush against the cool glass of the orb, however, when I receive a shock of static and draw back, hissing through my teeth.

O'Shea juts his bottom lip out. "Aw. Did the big bad vampire get an electric shock?" I narrow my eyes at him. "Sorry. I meant little bad vampire."

I don't rise to the bait. Instead, I simply try again, this time managing to scoop the globe up and hold it in both hands. Almost immediately it tugs me forward. I blink.

"Cool, huh?" O'Shea grins.

"If it works."

"Bo, you're just no fun these days."

"We're not out on a jolly," I tell him. "This is a serious matter. If anyone catches us ... or even sees us ..."

He casts an airy hand around as I'm yanked forward yet again. "No-one's around. It's the middle of the night, after all. Just let yourself relax."

"We're slap bang in the centre of an army base surrounded by lots of soldiers and lots of guns. I'm not about to kick back and chill until we've got what we came for and we're safely away."

"No," he says, "I meant relax and the Trace will be able to do its job." He winks. "Trust me, Bo. I'm a daemon."

For some reason his words put me in mind of X and his ridiculous antics at the television studio. I have to force myself to concentrate on the matter in hand though, doing what I can to follow O'Shea's instructions. I loosen the tension in my muscles while the Trace continues to exert its pressure on me. It's one of those things that's considerably easier said than done but it's not too long before we're moving at a brisk pace while I keep the Trace out in front of me. I stumble several times as it leads us down the immaculately kept road fringed with a lawn that has such evenly cut grass I almost imagine some poor band of recruits out here every morning measuring each blade to ensure absolute conformity.

The Trace is just starting to pull me over to the left when the sound of voices from up ahead drifts over. O'Shea and I exchange quick glances and run to the nearest building, letting the heavy shadows around it conceal us as best as they can. I'm still nervous about cameras capturing our images so I keep my head down. A moment or two later, two soldiers appear. Both have identical crew cuts and straight-backed postures. The army certainly keeps its worker bees in line.

The pressure from the Trace is growing. I shift its weight in my sweaty palms, doing what I can to keep hold of it as it continues to try and force me to move. In an attempt to exert more control, I hug it to my chest but it that only gives it the unhelpful quality of jerking at my entire body. I grit my teeth and concentrate on remaining upright while the soldiers pass by.

They're about ten feet away in the opposite direction and heading out towards the main gates when the Trace apparently decides enough is enough. With a burst of uncontrollable energy it flings me forward. I can feel O'Shea grabbing at the back of my dress to keep me back but it's too late. My feet kick up the gravel that lines the building like a moat as I try to regain my balance. The only thing I can do is crouch down into a ball but even then I can feel the bloody thing still pulling me forward. I start to wonder what Isaac Newton would have made of a Trace when I realise the soldiers have stopped and are turning in our direction.

"Shit," O'Shea breathes, almost inaudibly.

My natural instinct is to run. But if we try that we'll be spotted for sure. My mind races as the soldier nearest us starts to walk over in our direction.

"Is anyone there?" he calls out, peering towards us.

Our only current saving grace is that we're enveloped in enough darkness to be invisible from the road. My mind races as I work through our options. We could rush him and escape that way but then we'll have no hope of getting anywhere near the orbs we actually need. I'm still wearing the dress. I could use O'Shea's story about the Lance Corporal and wander out to chat to them, making it seem like I have permission to be here. It would buy us probably about five seconds before they discover the truth. And what the hell do I do with the damned Trace? Right now I'm convinced that if I even try to stand up, it'll start yanking me again with such power that I'll either drop it and allow the soldiers to pinpoint our presence exactly or it'll fling me directly in their path. Bugger, bugger, bugger. This was such a stupid idea.

There's a crackle from the second soldier's radio. He unclips it from his belt and holds it up to his face. Whatever is said is inaudible to me but he nods briskly.

"We've got to go."

"But…"

"It's probably just a damn cat. You might want to get on Arbuckle's bad side but I'm not in the mood for another bawling out."

"That was Colonel Arbuckle?" Even in the darkness, I can see his face pale. "But…"

"We're wanted in the Sit. Room. Now."

The soldier's Adam's apple bob as he swallows nervously and turns away. My eyes track them as their heavy boots clump away. All the same, I remain where I am, hunched over the

Trace as it continues to try and tug me to move, until I'm absolutely certain they've gone.

O'Shea peels himself away from the wall. "That was too freaking close."

"Did you hear his radio? Do you know what was said?"

He shakes his head. "Just a word or two. I guess this Arbuckle fellow is kind of scary."

I gnaw on my lip. "Yeah," I say slowly, "I guess so." I imagine another identikit crewcut but with a thicker neck and harder eyes to go along with it.

"Can you stand up?"

I grimace. "I have the feeling that as soon as I do, I'll be flying through the air at a velocity that will defy the laws of physics. No sodding wonder these Traces aren't used very often."

"It's following your orders."

"To find the orbs."

"Yup."

"Well, in that case, let's find them and get the hell out of here. We don't need any more close encounters like that."

I carefully uncurl myself. As expected, the momentum has been building in the Trace so as soon as I'm halfway upright again, I feel myself being hurled forward like a cork popping out of a champagne bottle. My arms are outstretched and my feet almost drag along behind me as I'm shoved straight onto the road. If we'd not managed to hide ourselves in time, I'd probably have run smack bang into the soldiers.

"Can't you control that thing?"

"You're welcome to try," I throw behind to O'Shea as I continue to be rapidly propelled along the tarmac before I'm swung to my right and thrown flat against the wall of another building.

"No, thanks," he says, catching up.

I step back, only to be thrust involuntarily against the wall again. It's pebble dashed and sharp little stones dig uncomfortable against my skin. I turn my face to the side but I'm still being squashed thanks to the Trace's actions.

"Do you think it wants us to go inside?" I ask, my voice muffled against the stone.

"Pardon?" O'Shea leans towards me. I think he's enjoying this moment.

I drop the Trace, almost immediately feeling as if a great burden has been lifted from me. I fall back a few steps and stare at the damn thing. It looks pretty innocuous now I'm no longer touching it. I turn my head and look at the wall. There's a dark smudge where the grease on my cheek rubbed off. I shiver and shake myself.

"Bloody chunk of…"

O'Shea stops me. "Semi-sentient, remember? Perhaps you don't want to piss it off."

I roll my eyes. "Bloody thing. Come on. Let's find the damn door."

Rather than pick up the Trace again, I kick it gently along the ground, mindful of O'Shea's warning. Every time my foot connects, I feel another burst of static rippling through me. It doesn't particularly help when we reach the door and discover it's tightly locked with only a keypad for entry.

"We could try a window," O'Shea suggests.

I crane my neck upwards. There are small panes of glass set up against what must be the second story. I'm spry enough to be able to reach them but I'm betting they're alarmed.

"I have a better idea."

I turn round and jog over to the nearest patch of grass, digging my fingernails underneath to grab some soil. It's not rained for a week or two so it's dry enough to suit my purposes. I crumble the clumps into fine particles and return to the door and blow them gently onto the keypad. As I'd hoped, several stick to the buttons where traces of oil from human skin linger.

"One, two, three, seven, eight," O'Shea reads, flicking me a look. "Not necessarily in that order though. There are only fifty fine thousand and forty-nine possible permutations. That won't take us long." When I stare at him, he shrugs. "Maths and magic go hand in hand. At least for mixing potions like I do anyway."

"I don't suppose you have a potion for this?"

"Give me six months and I can come up with something."

"Helpful," I murmur, staring at the numbers. "Maybe it doesn't matter which order you press them in."

He snorts. "Yeah, right."

I shrug. "There's no harm in trying."

"Of course you can try. We'll only maybe set off an alarm that'll wake up the entire base if we get it wrong."

"I'm sure it'll give us a few attempts at least," I say, not feeling very sure at all. A troubling little thought nags at the back of my mind but I push it away.

O'Shea grins. "In for a penny, in for a pound." He pulls his sleeve over his finger to avoid leaving his prints and presses the numbers in quick succession. There's a whirr followed by an almost immediate click. Then the door opens.

"Huh," he says, "well, I wasn't expecting that."

He starts to move forward, but I grab his arm and shake my head. "No."

"What?"

I keep my voice low. "It's too easy. All this is too easy. They know we're here."

He scratches his nose. "Explain."

"Getting through the main gate like that was a stretch. But those soldiers veering off right at the last minute because they happened to get an order in the middle of the night? Now this? It's too pat."

O'Shea's eyes dart from side to side as if he's expecting a platoon to suddenly appear from every corner. "We need to get out of here."

"If I'm right, leaving now won't make any difference. They're not going to let us stroll off the base."

"We've not done anything illegal yet."

I raise my eyebrows. "Other than venture onto a military installation, you mean."

He looks uncomfortable. "Other than that."

"They probably don't know who we actually are. In fact, our little ploy with the grease might be working. They might still think we're witches."

"All they need to do is catch one glimpse of your face in the light and..."

I hold up my palms. "I know, I know."

"So what do we do?"

I outline my plan. O'Shea looks at me as if I'm crazy – which may well be the case.

"That'll never work," he says flatly. I don't say anything. He puts his hands in his pockets and sighs. "Alright then."

"Turn round."

"You know, as lovely as your legs are, they don't actually do anything for me."

"O'Shea..."

"Fine, fine," he grumbles, facing away from me.

I bend down and pick up the Trace again, making sure I'm away from the open door when I do so. I hike up my dress and shove the Trace underneath and against my belly, only just managing to keep my balance as I do. I still have to brace myself with one hand against the wall when I pull the hem back down again. The dress is tight enough that the Trace is snug against my skin.

"Okay."

O'Shea turns back round. "You realise you look like you're about five months' pregnant?"

I glance down. "I guess so. This baby has got a hell of a kick for five months though." The words have barely left my mouth when I'm flung against the wall once more. The only thing that stops me from being squashed against it again is the bulge of the Trace itself acting as a blocker between the pebble dash and my skin. I pray it doesn't break easily.

"Ready?" I ask grimly.

O'Shea bites his lip and nods. "I hope when they lock me up and throw away the key, I at least get some good looking soldiers to guard me." His light words bely the faint tremor in his voice. I shouldn't have dragged him into this. It's not even as if I'm investigating Tobias Renfrew for any good reason other than professional curiosity. We've come too far now though. I wish I had my little pebble with me. I could do with some reassuring solidity right about now. Instead I take a deep breath. "Okaydokey."

I side-step back to the door. The Trace reacts almost immediately, and I'm thrown through to the corridor on the other side. A split second later I'm being dragged down the hall as the Trace continues its inexorable pull towards the time orbs.

I'd have let it yank me the entire way there but I spot a bucket outside a small and unimpressive looking door and force myself to halt. Although it feels like I'm fighting against gravity itself, I lurch over and fling it open.

"Bo, what the hell are you doing?"

"Here," I say, reaching inside and grabbing a broom then tossing it in his direction.

He catches it and frowns. "I'm well aware that I'm your

sidekick, but that doesn't mean I'm going to act as general dogsbody too." I give him an exasperated look. "Wait, you're not going to..."

"We, O'Shea. We are going to."

He tuts to himself. "I'm never going to live this down."

"If it works," I promise, "no-one will ever know."

I relax slightly and let the Trace continue its magnetic pull. Now that it must be getting closer to its destination, it's easier to handle. I hope the theory that the further away it is from whatever it's seeking, the stronger it feels, is one that holds true once we start leaving the base too. It's the only way the escape plan is ever going to work.

We twist one way then another through the labrynthine corridors, passing all manner of laboratories and offices and classrooms. Things become slightly more awkward when the Trace yanks me down a set of stairs leading to what can only be the basement as it makes staying on my feet almost impossible. I think I've just about managed it when I only have a few steps to go. Unfortunately, however, my over-confidence is my downfall and I trip, tumbling headfirst and landing in an ungainly heap at the bottom.

"Bo! Are you okay?"

My ankle feels twisted and sore. If I'd still been human I'd probably be unable to walk – but then again when I was human, I'd never have attempted something as foolhardy, reckless or illegal as this. I let O'Shea help me up and try to stumble a few steps, gingerly testing out my weight. With each step, the pain dissipates.

O'Shea registers my look of surprise and grins. "Cool to be a vampire with those regenerative skills, huh?"

I smile back. "You know, it actually kind of is." Then something else hits me. "The Trace," I whisper. "It's not pulling me any more."

Both O'Shea and I immediately start looking around. There are several boxes piled neatly on the floor, each one with an official looking tag prominently displayed on the front. I crouch down and open the first one, then recoil.

"Fingers," I say, utterly disgusted.

"Eh?"

O'Shea peers inside. Rather than having a similar reaction to me though, his expression changes to one of awe. He reaches in and pulls one long-nailed specimen out while I recoil away.

"Do you know how rare these are?"

"Jesus, get rid of it! We don't have time for sightseeing anyway. You do remember that all those soldiers with big guns are onto us?"

"I certainly hope they have big guns," he mutters. He does at least return to finger to the box though.

I pull aside the next crate. Bafflingly, it's filled with what seems to be drug paraphernalia. The next one is a collection of empty glass vials. I throw open box after box. There are no damn time bubble orbs anywhere.

"Uh, Bo?"

"What?" I snap.

"Look." His voice is quiet.

I glance up, following his pointed finger. There, directly opposite us at the end of the room is a door marked 'Incinerator'. I briefly close my eyes. "You have got to be kidding me." No wonder we're surrounded by all manner of illicit materials. This is where they are sent to be destroyed.

"We're too late."

"This is ridiculous! Why would they destroy them? We could use them! They could use them! Bloody British nanny state bureaucracy!" I kick at the nearest box before realising I'm giving off a very good impression of a tantrum. "Sorry," I murmur. "I've dragged you into this and made you commit what could be construed as a terrorist act for absolutely nothing. I swear that this is the first and the last time I'm ever going to try breaking the law."

"Don't be so hard on yourself," O'Shea chides. "I've broken the law lots of times. Sometimes it pans out and sometimes it doesn't. Much like life."

"O'Shea," I sigh, "as much as I love you to pieces, you're not exactly my role model. At least when I screwed up with Bergman I had an excuse. This time there's no-one to blame but me."

"You remember what you were saying about the men with big guns?"

I meet his eyes. "You're right," I say quietly. "We need to get out of here." What's left unspoken is whether we can.

I know from my own experience of being a good guy that the easiest way to catch a thieving bad guy and have an airtight case against them is to wait until they're leaving the premises with the stolen property in their possession. Our only wiggle room if we do get caught is that we don't actually have anything belonging to the military on us. Apart from the broom anyway. I don't imagine my fabulously overblown reputation as the Red Angel will endure a stint in jail however – not to mention what might happen to O'Shea with his already colourful record. Still, at least I can be certain that we're safe until we exit the building. When O'Shea and I finally make it back to the keypad door, we both stop and listen.

He points to his ear and shakes his head, indicating he can't hear a thing. If these army guys are any good they'll be as quiet as the damn grave though. I give him a shrug and take the broom from him, turning so my back is to the door. Then I straddle it carefully. O'Shea sidles up behind me, his arms going round my waist.

"You'd better hang on damn tight," I whisper.

"We're going to look like idiots when this doesn't work," he says.

"It'll work. It has to." I squeeze my eyes shut. I want to find the moon, I think to myself. I want to find the moon. I envisage it in my mind, round, full and complete with craters. I want to find the moon.

The Trace, still stuffed under my dress tugs. "Start backing out, Devlin," I say. "Slowly and carefully."

He does as he's told. We shuffle out, neither of us looking to see what's there. I'm gripping the shaft of the broom with both hands and O'Shea's hold around my waist tightens.

"Stop right there," a deep voice yells, followed immediately by the sound of a dozen guns cocking. "Hands up."

"Oh no," O'Shea whispers.

The Trace pulls at me. I mouth the words. I want to find the moon. Then the force almost takes my breath away. The Trace flies upwards, taking both O'Shea and I with it. He screams aloud as we rise into the air. The soldiers below seem to panic.

"I said stop!" followed by "They're fucking flying!"

The material of the dress is starting to give. We're not high enough yet – neither are we close enough to the fence.

"Lean left!" I yell to O'Shea.

Our combined weight is just enough, although a gust of wind helps. There's a loud rip. "Any seco..." My voice falls away from me as the material finally gives and both O'Shea and I start tumbling. I catch a glimpse of the Trace as it's freed, hanging against the night sky for a fleeting instant and no longer in the shape of an orb but now as a tiny moon. A moment later it's gone. Trees and buildings blur as I do what I can to turn my body so I can land in a roll and avoid any real injury.

The thump when I do hit the ground is extraordinary. It's as if all my internal organs have mushed together. I lie there for a moment, groaning. It bloody hurts.

"I am never ever doing anything with you again, Bo Blackman," O'Shea moans. "You are dead to me."

"As long as you're not dead," I tell him, slowly getting up to my feet.

There are already shouts from within the base. It won't take the soldiers long to find us. We really have to hurry. I pull O'Shea up. He winces dramatically and there's a nasty cut on his cheek but, as far as I can tell, he's going to make it.

"Can you run?"

"You bet your arse I can."

We take off. We'd landed further from the fence than I'd even been hoping for but reaching the top of the hill where the bike is hidden is hard. My side is burning and there's still a pain in my ankle – and O'Shea is doing far worse. Halfway up, I stop and beckon him onto my shoulders. We complete the rest of the ascent piggyback then I run as hard as I'm physically able to until we're weaving through the trees and reach the bike.

"Thank fuck."

"You still need to drive, O'Shea. I can't do it barefoot."

He flashes me a quick grin and gets on. I leap behind him. "Go!"

Before he turns on the engine, there's a rustle. At least twenty camouflaged soldiers appear out of nowhere and they all have guns. Big ones.

CHAPTER 7

THE CAMERA NEVER LIES

O'Shea and I are dragged off to separate rooms. I'm trussed up like a chicken and left able to do little more than blink. Colonel Arbuckle, who it turns out has long hair tied back tightly in a bun instead of a crewcut, is even more stern and scary looking than her soldiers had suggested. It's less because of her stature, which is actually fairly diminutive, even next to me, and more because of the freakishly hard lines around her face. If it weren't for her lack of tattoo, I'd have said she was a black witch. It doesn't help that there's something remarkably peculiar about her eyes. The colour in her irises doesn't seem quite right. I squint and realise it's because she's wearing tinted contact lenses. Is Arbuckle trying to pass herself off as human when in fact she's something else? Daemons are generally welcome in the armed forces these days so I can't imagine why it would particularly be a big deal. Unless being a daemon in the army as well as a woman just makes life too complicated.

"You know Trace spells are notoriously ineffective," she says, leaning against the wall with her arms folded. "I'd love to know where you got that one from."

I look at her. "Considering my position, I'd say the one I had was pretty ineffective too," I say, trying to keep my tone mild.

"What were you looking for?"

"A broom. I had the sudden urge to clean and mine was broken."

Arbuckle's strange eyes narrow. "This is not the place to be flippant, Ms. Blackman. Even if you happened to think that disguising yourself as a witch and flying away on a broomstick was a good idea."

It wasn't as it turns out. "I made an error of judgment. It was all my doing. I forced Devlin O'Shea to come along with me. He has nothing to do with this."

"It's not very heroic," she continues, as if I hadn't said a word, "breaking the law to sneak into a military zone and steal a time bubble orb." I must have looked surprised because she laughs sharply. "You might think army intelligence is an oxymoron, Ms. Blackman, but I can assure you, I'm not stupid. What I don't know is what exactly you were planning to do with it once you got it."

I mull over my options. I could fabricate some sort of story but I'll be tangling myself in a further web of lies. At least the truth is vaguely honourable and might display my good intentions. I'm going to need something to extricate O'Shea from this mess.

I tilt up my chin. "I want to find Tobias Renfrew."

Arbuckle's eyebrows shoot up. "Well," she says, "I wasn't expecting that. He's been missing, presumed dead, in fact, for over fifty years. What makes you think that you would be able to discover the truth? And why would you even care?"

"If you've been paying any attention to the news lately," I tell her drily, "you'll know."

"The fake ear that purportedly belonged to him?" she scoffs.

"That's why you're engaging in activities that could see you locked up for the rest of your natural life?"

"There's more to this than a severed ear. I had friends who almost died because of it." My voice is quiet but there's a hint of challenge to it which I know she can hear. My implication is obvious. Threaten me or mine and face the consequences.

"It probably had nothing to do with Renfrew," she dismisses. "It was just some scam between a bunch of lowlife criminals."

"All the same," I shrug. "I'm going to find them and I'm going to find Renfrew. Whether he's dead or alive."

Arbuckle taps her mouth thoughtfully. "You thought a time bubble would help you." It's not a question. "You were going to use it as some sort HG Wells inspired time machine and travel back to the night of his disappearance to find out what really happened." I smile. Arbuckle, however, rolls her eyes. "The reports of your sleuthing skills are greatly exaggerated."

The disdain in her voice makes me stiffen. "What do you mean?"

"You don't think others have tried? That the police haven't attempted to make use of time bubbles to solve crimes?" She blows air out in an expression of disgust. "There would be no criminals loose on the streets if that were the case."

I frown. "But..."

"Time bubbles were evolved in laboratories during the nineteen seventies in order to keep dangerous chemicals safe. They are meant to exist in order to provide a form of stasis, not tourism. That's why all those companies use them as the latest type of cryogenics. But being inside a bubble is entirely different to being on the outside. You can't just plug it in and see who was on the grassy knoll. You can't go back and kill Hitler. They're bubbles. You're trapped inside. Your movements are limited. What do you think would happen if you engaged a time bubble here and now? If you set it to go back, say, a year and there's already someone inside this room in that time?"

I simply stare at her. She sighs in exasperation. "The past is set in stone. It's already happened and you can't change it. A bubble will not establish itself where living beings already are. It would displace them from their own time and time will not allow that. You can only use a time bubble to go back to places which are empty of people. If you think you can transport yourself to Renfrew's mansion on the night of his party and see what really happened, you're kidding yourself. Those serial killers you murdered..."

"I didn't murder them!" I splutter.

She dismisses my interruption with a wave of her hand. "Those serial killers knew what they were doing. They knew history. They probably experimented somewhat as well in order to take themselves out of our time and into another. But they didn't interact with the past. They merely existed inside it for a short period. In fact they probably saw nothing other than a few buildings or trees."

I remain stubborn. "It doesn't mean it wouldn't prove useful."

Arbuckle shakes her head. "As useful as looking at a photo or a painting."

"Renfrew might be using a time bubble," I point out. "It makes sense. No-one has seen him since that night in 1963. If he used a bubble, he could..."

"Didn't you hear me tell you they were developed in the seventies?"

"He still could have..."

"No," she says flatly. "He couldn't."

"How can you be so sure?"

For a long moment she doesn't answer. Instead she just

regards me with a steady expression before finally nodding to herself. "Wait here." She stands up and walks out.

I can't move a bloody inch. I can't do anything else but 'wait here'. I go through the motions of straining against my bonds but it's a pointless effort. They're not even vampire-proofed like Magix's damn handcuffs – it's simply that the army clearly have considerable experience in dealing with tribers who have advanced physical attributes. What makes it worse is that right now I have an uncontrollable itch on my face, probably from the oil that's congealed there on my skin. No matter how I attempt to contort myself, I can't reach it. At least it gives me something else to focus on now that Arbuckle's revelation that utilising a time bubble to investigate Renfrew would effectively be a waste. Not only was breaking into Brigstone the worst idea I've ever had, it was also for absolutely nothing. Even if we'd succeeded, we'd have failed. I can already picture the look on my grandfather's face. Assuming he doesn't immediately disown me first, of course.

Arbuckle strolls back in. She places a heavy file on the table in front of me. A fountain pen is clipped over the front page and at the top, in the corner, I can see the words 'Renfrew, Tobias'. A squirm of excitement shoots through my belly. She's really going to let me see the army's own records?

"I have spoken to my superiors and I can't show you all of this," she says. "In fact, even what I am going to let you read is already classified."

"So why are you doing this?" I ask, virtually salivating at the thought.

"Because we need to do something to make you desist from your current course," she answers briskly, turning over the cardboard cover to the first page. A photo of Renfrew himself stares out at me. His head is turned slightly towards the camera so the famous ruby in his ear is prominently displayed. His mouth is curved into the semblance of a smile but there's hard look in his orange daemon eyes that even the camera hasn't failed to capture. I glance down. He's perched over a desk with a pen in hand. It's apparent that he takes – or rather took - his own health seriously. His body is lean and the faint shadows around his arms where his suit is bunched up make it clear that there's also muscle and strength there.

"I've never seen this shot," I say.

Arbuckle snorts. "We're not the Daily News. Like I said, this is all classified."

She flips over several pages at once. I try to take in as much information as I can but Arbuckle does a good job of keeping the important parts concealed. As far as I can tell, they all related to Renfrew's own military career. When she stops at the next report, however, I can feel my heart in my mouth. The date at the top is January 17th, 1963. That's the night of the party. The last time anyone ever saw him alive.

AT 22-30 HOURS, the guests assembled at the front courtyard. Extensive interviews have stated that the numbers exceeded eight hundred, including staff. The subject took to the stage at 22-38, wearing a mauve smoking jacket rather than the tuxedo he had initially worn earlier on. Neither the tuxedo nor the jacket were ever located.

"HE CHANGED HIS CLOTHES," I breathe. That little fact had never been released.

"Well," Arbuckle says, rather pragmatically, "there had been a considerable amount of blood." She turns the page to the crime scene photos. These I have seen before, although the scale of the brutality displayed never ceases to turn my stomach. There's evidence of five separate corpses, all hacked to pieces.

"At least you can say he was an equal rights killer," she continues, pointing to the different limbs in turn. "Witch. Human. Daemon." A tiny smile lifts the corner of her mouth. "Vampire."

"You think he did it then? He killed all of them?"

"I don't think, Ms. Blackman. I know."

"Where's the evidence then?"

"His fingerprints are everywhere."

I lift my eyes from the file. "It was his house. Of course they were."

"His prints were on the bodies too. What was left of them anyway."

"There's no motive."

Her expression doesn't change. "Isn't being psychotic enough of one?" She doesn't wait for an answer, merely reaches and starts turning more pages. I try to crane my neck round to catch more glimpses of what's contained within the file but this time her body blocks my sight entirely. She takes out one large photo and stands back as she studies it. Then she looks at me. "Searching for Tobias Renfrew is a waste of time."

I suddenly have a good idea about what exactly she's holding in her hands. A kind of nausea fills my stomach, although whether it's due to disappointment, rubber-necking excitement or the thought of seeing yet another body, I can't say. I wait until, with a flourish, Arbuckle turns it over to let me see. I'm right. It's a photo of another corpse, in lurid technicolour. The bright red ruby glitters in his earlobe, the colour mirroring the pool of blood around his head. His face is obscured partly because of the position of the body and partly because of the fact that half of it seems to be blown off. His right hand is outstretched next to him, one finger curled round the trigger.

"He killed himself."

Arbuckle nods. "As you see."

"But why?"

"Who's to say? Guilt perhaps after the bloodbath at his house," she suggests. "Or he knew the net was closing in and it was only a matter of time before he got caught. Either way," she says as she taps the corner of the photo, "by 1965, Tobias Renfrew was dead."

I shake my head in disbelief. "If you know this, when why don't you tell people? Release the damn photo?"

"I have already told you that we are not the Daily News, Ms. Blackman."

"The amount of money that's going into looking for him though! The people who've searched! His family members! All that wealth…"

"Indeed," Arbuckle comments, "all that wealth. If Renfrew is declared legally dead, who gets the money?"

"His descendants, surely."

Her eyes flicker. "They're all thugs. A billion pounds in the hands of that lot? No-one wants to see that happen."

"I know they don't exist any more but if you knew he was dead you could have done something back then. You could have let the charity take the money…"

"That charity is defunct because they couldn't manage their own finances. They'd have frittered away the Renfrew millions in a heartbeat."

"If you can prove he really killed those people, then the Agathos Court can confiscate his wealth. Surely the army approves of them?"

"There are some who believe the Court already has too

much power." At my look, she shrugs. "Not just humans. There are high ranking daemons who think the same."

"People should still know!" I argue.

Arbuckle's defence is simple. "Why? It doesn't serve any purpose. Well," she amends, "not any purpose that serves the army anyway."

"It's not your decision to make," I protest.

"And neither is it yours." She holds the photo up. "Classified. You can't tell anyone."

"But..."

"Even if you do, the army will deny it."

I stare at Renfrew's corpse. This is ridiculous. I open my mouth to argue further then I see something and change my mind. "Do you know where his body is now?"

"An unmarked grave. I personally don't know where. There are deliberately no records of the location and few people still living who know its whereabouts either."

I lick my lips. They're cracked and dry. I could really do with some damned O neg right about now. "What about the gun?"

"It was buried with him." She pulls the photo away and replaces it back in the file.

"That makes sense if you want to hide all the evidence," I say slowly.

"It does." Arbuckle straightens up. "I realise it looks like a cover up to you but almost no-one benefits from knowing the truth. Revealing his death will only cause more problems. No-one will win."

I bite my lip and nod. "So what happens now?" I ask. "To me, I mean. And O'Shea."

"I've spoken to high command. If you can keep your mouths shut, then we are willing to let you go. Assuming that is, you don't ever try and return." She smiles humourlessly. "We do have some extensive video footage of your little romp that we'll happily refer to if this ever comes to court."

"I think I've learnt my lesson," I whisper.

She fixes me with a cold-eyed glance. "I'm glad to hear it." As I watch she walks to the door and beckons a fresh-faced soldier inside. He moves round towards my back and begins undoing the knots keeping me in place. He's obviously terrified. I can hear his rapid breathing in my ear. I have the distinct certainty that it's Arbuckle who scares him rather than me though.

When I'm eventually freed, I stand up and rub my wrists. All my joints are sore. Arbuckle begins leading me out, down a strip-lighted corridor and into the freedom of the night. Both my bike and O'Shea are standing there waiting.

"I didn't tell them a thing, Bo!" he exclaims loudly as soon as he sees me.

"That's alright, Devlin," I say softly, throwing him a warning look. "They already know."

"I sincerely hope our paths will not cross again, Ms. Black-man," Arbuckle interjects as she throws me the keys. "You should probably use your time more wisely. Such as investing in a new wardrobe."

I look down at the gaping rent down the black dress. It's wide open, revealing my underwear. Thankfully, I manage not to blush. "Just out of interest," I say, "when did you know we were here? In the base, I mean?"

"The second you left that thing," she nods towards the bike, "in the trees."

I look down. So much for all our ducking and diving then. What Arbuckle doesn't realise, however, is that now I know this little 'adventure' has been far from a waste of time after all.

O'Shea climbs on the bike. I get on behind him. He turns on the engine and looks in Arbuckle's direction. "Colonel," he says, with a sloppy salute that will achieve no results other than pissing her off.

I jab him in the ribs. "Enough."

He nods dutifully and takes off.

WE'RE FOLLOWED all the way back to the outskirts of London. O'Shea sticks to the speed limit and we make no effort to lose them but, all the same, I'm relieved when the military vehicles finally peel away and leave us in peace. I can feel the prickle across my shoulder blades indicating that the new day isn't far away. I'm not particularly worried, however. I have far bigger things occupying my mind.

When we pull up back outside New Order, O'Shea turns to me with a low whistle. "That was some evening."

"It was." I consider the revelations of the night. "Did you know that even if we'd gotten hold of a time bubble, it would have been next to useless?"

He shakes his head. "I'd rather hoped I'd be able to use it to go back in time and re-live my greatest moments. Once," he adds hastily, "we'd finished with all this Renfrew business, of course. I guess that's all done with now though. There are still other avenues we can go down to find who's behind those pricks who tried to kill the kid."

I look up at the last few remaining stars. "I'm not done with Renfrew. Not by a long shot."

O'Shea's eyes widen in alarm. "I don't think the army would take too kindly to us continuing to investigate him."

"She showed me a photo," I tell him. "Of Renfrew's corpse."

He sucks in a breath. "He's dead?"

"Apparently since 1965. He committed suicide."

"No way." He watches my face. "You don't believe it?"

"Not for a second. There was another photo of Renfrew holding a pen. In his left hand."

O'Shea nods. "He was left-handed. Lots of important famous bigwigs are. In fact," he adds with a confident air, "So am I."

"You're sure about this?"

"Yeah. I can show you by trying to write with my right hand. It's virtually illegible."

I tut in exasperation. "I mean about Renfrew."

"I'm sure. I was the only leftie in my class at school. I made a point about researching other people who were too so I didn't feel so left out." There's an odd note in his voice, revealing a hint of vulnerability that I rarely see from him. It makes me reach out for a moment and squeeze his hand. "Why does it matter?" he asks.

"Because in the photo Colonel Arbuckle so proudly showed me, the gun he'd used to blow his brains out was in his right hand."

A slow smile spreads across O'Shea's face. "The army killed him?"

"Either that or," I pause, "it wasn't even Renfrew in the photo because he's still actually alive and they don't want us to know it."

Our eyes meet. "I guess," he says with a little grin, "that our investigation is only just getting under way then."

"You bet it is," I agree. Up until now, Tobias Renfrew had been a means to an end – discovering the motives behind the bastards that attacked the Agathos Court and Rogu3 so that I could find them and make damn sure they never tried anything again. Now I'm suddenly far more invested in discovering the truth about the billionaire daemon as well. There's nothing like a few blatant lies from highly placed officials for stirring up my interest even further.

CHAPTER 8
DODGING THE TRUTH

The stifling weight on my chest is making it difficult to breathe. For a moment, I'm completely disorientated. When I receive a long lick down the side of my neck and hear a tiny whine though, my muscles relax.

"Bloody dog," I grunt, gently pushing Kimchi off my body. He seems determined not to leave the bed until I get up. His large soulful eyes hover over mine. "You still need to lose some weight," I tell him. I'm gifted with another lick.

Dragging myself to my feet, I pull on some clothes and pad into the small living room cum kitchen. I leap back half a metre in ridiculous fright when I see I'm no longer alone.

"Vampires have enhanced senses, Bo," my grandfather says, lifting a bushy eyebrow in my direction. "You should have known I was here."

I scowl at him, making a show of it. Then I tilt up my chin and walk to the fridge, taking out a bottle of blood and glugging it noisily down. I can't live off blood unless it's fresh from the vein but it's always handy to have some decanted for when I really need it. And I know the action will piss him off. I'm only really annoyed at myself of course though. He's right – I should have known he was here. I tell myself it was because I was focused on Kimchi that I missed hearing him enter. Although, speaking of Kimchi, he should have noticed too.

"This is my flat," I say, wiping my mouth with the back of my hand. "You can't just barge in."

"Technically, it belongs to New Order. Not you."

I'm tempted to point out that I was part of our little investigative firm before he was but I have a sneaking suspicion he wants me to do just that so he can then accuse me of being petty and childish. "It's my home."

"We're family. Share and share alike."

I hold up the now almost empty bottle and offer it to him. "Well, in that case…"

His lip curls. "I'm not even going to deign that with an answer."

"Suit yourself," I shrug. "Why are you here?"

"Did you sleep well?"

"Yeah, I guess."

He tuts. "Yes."

I give him a confused look. "Yes what?"

"It's not yeah. It's yes. Yes, I slept well. Thank you for asking."

"Any time."

He rolls his eyes and holds up a mauled piece of black fabric. "Would you like to explain this?"

I stare at the tattered remains of my dress. Bugger it. I peeled it off and dropped it next to the sofa the instant I returned home. I should have planned on having an unwelcome guest. I should always plan for that these days. I turn to look at Kimchi. "Did you do this?" I demand. "Bad dog!"

He gives off a very good impression of guilt, hanging his head and looking shame-faced. Kimchi missed a career in acting apparently. As bad as I feel for laying the blame on him, it's a calculated move on the dog's part. He knows I'll make it up to him. I'm pretty sure I still have some of his favourite doggy treats lurking in the back of one of the cupboards. So much for the diet though.

My grandfather is unimpressed. "That dog is a liability."

I stroke his ears. Actually, he's very handy to have around whenever I need to avoid the truth. "He's better than your cat," I say. "And you still haven't told me why you've barged in."

He takes a newspaper from his side and tosses it disdainfully onto the coffee table. My curiosity is piqued enough to pick it up and unfold it so I can read what's written there. When I see what the lead article is, however, I wish I'd not bothered.

"Oh," I mumble. I put it back down. "That's not really my fault." It's not my better side either. My nose looks squashed against Medici's and there's a wide-eyed expression on my face which seems to suggest I'm turned on by his kiss instead of simply surprised.

My grandfather sighs heavily. "You were supposed to very publicly display your affections for Michael. Not him."

"Michael was there. It's not my fault Medici showed up out of the blue. In fact, I actually did a very good job of defusing a fight between the pair of them. You should be impressed."

His expression is stony. "Where did you go?"

"Some swanky French place called La Maison." I sniff. "Apparent Lord Montserrat takes all of his dates there."

"After that."

Uh oh. "Back here," I squeak. Has Colonel Arbuckle already dobbed me in?

"Then why was Kimchi out in the hallway and tearing strips off the wallpaper when Arzo arrived?"

I blink. Arzo got to work before I got home? He normally takes the day shift unless... "He was here early for Dahlia?" She's like me – too young to venture out during the daytime.

"I told you he was keeping tabs on her work."

I half snort. "I'm sure that's all he's keeping tabs on."

"Stop evading the question, Bo. Where did you go?"

I breathe a silent sigh of relief that he doesn't seem to already know the answer. As much as I trust him, he did used to be the head of MI7. If he was aware that I'd effectively broken into an army base, he'd flip his lid. We are supposed to respect other national peacekeepers (or warmongers, depending on your point of view). Somehow I don't think my little jaunt with O'Shea would fall under that remit.

"Is it Medici? Did you go to confront him about this?" he asks, pointing back at the paper.

"No."

"Then what?"

I look away. "Um ... Tobias Renfrew," I hedge. I don't have to mention Brigstone specifically.

My grandfather's nose wrinkles. "Really, Bo?"

"Rogu3 almost died because of him."

"Alistair Jones," he says sternly, refusing to use Rogu3's hacker alias, "almost died because of his association with *you*. Besides, Renfrew is dead."

I meet his eyes, tingles of dread threading their way across my veins. Was he part of the army's cover-up too? Were MI7 working with them to fake that photograph? "How do you know?" I ask, my voice sounding overly casual, even to my own ears.

"Someone would have found him by now if he were alive," he says as I start to relax again. "Countless people have tried. The only thing he can be is dead." He fixes me with a steely stare. "Don't tell me that because you could enter his mansion without an invitation, you think that's proof of life?"

Actually, visiting the scene of the crime is next on my list. The sudden knowledge that I'll be able to go inside is particularly welcome. As is my grandfather's assumption that Renfrew's house is where I'd begin. "Erm..." I prevaricate.

"Honestly, Bo. I thought your investigating skills were better than that. What did they teach you at Dire Straits? It's been open to the public for decades. It's the only way they could find the money for its upkeep." He tsks. "All that money locked away in bank accounts and no-one's allowed to touch it, not even to preserve such a national treasure."

I'm confused. "You think Renfrew's house is a national treasure?"

"Not because of the daemon, I assure you. But the gardens were designed by Capability Brown. The building itself is a sixteenth century masterpiece. That's without even mentioning the contents."

He was a showy billionaire. I can probably imagine. "Look," I say honestly, "investigating Renfrew is not going to prevent me from showing up to these dates with Michael. If you're going to allow me to complete assignments for New Order, then I'll stop because they will always take precedence. But I can't just sit around and twiddle my thumbs. Have you ever tried to watch late night television?" I shake my head. "I can't take it."

He looks exasperated. "You could begin a new hobby. Learn something."

"Like what?"

"Flower arranging is very satisfying."

I splutter. "Flower arranging? You have to be kidding me!"

"The Japanese have turned it into quite an artform. Ikebana is not for the faint-hearted."

"Grandfather..."

He cast his eyes heavenwards. "You're going to look into Renfrew no matter what I say. I just don't want you to be disappointed when there's nothing to find. What happened with the ear that Devlin found could have been because of anything."

"Then why go to such trouble to get rid of anyone who knew about it?"

"I don't know. But there's no way that Tobias Renfrew is still living and breathing. No way at all."

HIS WORDS ARE STILL RINGING in my head when I finally make my escape. It was a real daemon ear. And it was made to look as if it belonged to Renfrew, even if the DNA testing proved otherwise. It has to be related to the real billionaire somehow. The idea that these are two completely separate crimes is plausible but I reckon if I can solve one, then I'll solve the other too.

With Kimchi in tow, I decide to forego the motorbike. There are other ways to move around the city and I want to make a stop first anyway that's within walking distance. Kimchi, delighted to be out and about, does a little doggy dance of delight then jerks me over to the nearest lamp-post. While I pause with him, I feel an uncomfortable prickle behind my neck. I half turn and see a pair of middle-aged women nudging each other and looking in my direction. They both grin when they see I've noticed them. I sigh inwardly and smile back.

"Bo! Wait up!"

Squeezing herself hurriedly out of the door, Dahlia waves. She jogs over to me, ignoring the women, and beams. "I thought we could walk Kimchi together," she says brightly.

"I'm actually pretty busy," I tell her. "I don't have time for chit chat."

Her face falls just as I catch a flicker of movement on the pavement opposite. I glance over just in time to see a man with a remarkably short haircut duck into a nearby doorway. I frown and scan further down. Sure enough, sitting in a car not too far away, is another one. Well, well, well. It appears that Colonel Arbuckle – or indeed her superiors – don't quite trust me.

"Sorry, Dahlia," I amend, "I didn't mean to be rude. It would be lovely to have you along."

Her surprise is obvious. Rather than wait to hear her simper some reply, I turn and continue walking down the street. Kimchi takes his time sniffing at every car, post and wall. I don't look behind again. I don't need to – those army types will no doubt be on my tail either way.

Dahlia trots by my side. "He's a cute dog."

He's a slathering rotund beast. "Yes."

"He doesn't seem to like me very much."

Of course, he does still have very good instincts. And bags of intelligence. "Mmm."

"You don't like me very much either." It's not a question.

"I hardly know you, Dahlia."

"It's okay," she says softly. "I understand. You want to protect Arzo. I'm not going to hurt him though."

"You already did," I tell her simply, tugging at Kimchi's leash so we can cross the road.

"I know what I did was wrong."

I pause in midstep. "What did you do, Dahlia? Spell out for me just what you did." I want to see if she realises the extent of her past actions.

She drops her eyes. "I betrayed him. I know I did."

"You ran off with his best friend," I grind out. "Not only that but you made him think you'd been recruited so he would turn vamp and be out of your hair forever. You destroyed his life."

"I fell in love. I couldn't help that."

"You didn't need to send Arzo to the Montserrat Family though, did you? You could just have sent him a Dear John letter." It's hard not to keep the anger I feel on Arzo's behalf out of my voice.

"Yes, I could have. I was young and not thinking straight. Arzo was … obsessive. He'd never have left me alone. It seemed like the best thing to do at the time."

"He could have died. Do you know the statistics for newbie vampires?" I shake my head in disgust. "You could have killed him."

She looks up at me, an odd note of desperation in her expression. "Haven't you ever made a mistake, Bo? Done something you will spend the rest of your life wishing you could take back?"

I don't answer her. Instead, I carry on walking, holding myself stiffly upright.

"I'm paying for it now, aren't I?" she calls out, before catching up with me. "I didn't ask to be made into a vampire either. My husband didn't ask to be blown up."

I try not to snort. "He shouldn't have messed with the Triads then."

"I'm going to make it up to Arzo, you know. And to New Order for taking me in. I'll spend the rest of my life paying for my mistakes if that's what it takes."

"And how," I ask calmly, "are we supposed to know whether you're telling the truth? How are we supposed to know whether Lord Medici hasn't just sent you here to spy on us?"

She's silent for a moment before answering. "I can see why you'd think that. He didn't though. I hate him." The venom in her tone makes me almost believe her. "I'm going to get you trust me, Bo. Everyone respects you. Not just because of this Red Angel thing. I respect you too. One day you'll see that along with the fact that I'm not your enemy. We could be friends."

"I don't need your respect. And I have enough friends."

Dahlia's head droops slightly. I quash down the tiny flicker of sympathy I can't seem to help feeling. "I tell you what," I say, against my better judgment, "you can start out by doing me a favour."

Her chin jerks up. 'What?"

"There are two guys following me, one in a car and one on foot. I need you to distract them so I can get some peace and quiet."

Her eyes go round. "Why are they following you?"

"Does it matter?"

She shakes her head rapidly. "No, no. What do they look like?"

"Crewcuts. Muscles. They walk like they have rods jammed up their arses."

"Soldiers?"

When I glance at her she blushes slightly. "I know the type."

"Why am I not surprised?" I mutter. "Just delay them for a few minutes so I can get away."

She bobs her head vigorously. "Yes. I can do that." She touches my arm. "Thank you, Bo."

I flinch slightly and she drops her hand. Without giving her another glance, I speed up and leave her to worry about them although right now I don't particularly care whether she's successful or not. The army can't clap me in irons for doing nothing more than visiting a friend.

I FIND Foxworthy in Stallworthy's, an old fashioned pub typically frequented by members of the police force. When I make my entrance, the reaction of the punters is almost comical. The conversations mute and every head turns in my direction. I wouldn't be surprised if the balls on the pool table also came to a stunned frozen halt.

Foxworthy raises his pint in my direction. "Bo Blackman!

Why are you darkening my door?" His light tone encourages the others to relax although I still receive several long wary glances as if they're afraid I'm about to start biting several jugulars just because I can. It helps that Kimchi bounds up enthusiastically towards the gruff policeman and starts slobbering over his feet. Dog lovers, even dog lovers who are vampires, can't be all bad, right?

I join him at his table, pulling over a stool. His companion mutters something about getting another drink and quickly scoots off in the direction of the bar.

"So," he says, leaning his head to one side, "I see you've been a busy girl."

I guess he's referring to my well-publicised exploits at La Maison. I shrug. "It wasn't quite how it looks."

"It never is," he responds cheerfully. "Why are you here?"

I don't waste his time with a long preamble. "The ear," I say. "The one that isn't Tobias Renfrew's. What do you know about it?"

He takes a sip of his drink. "I know it isn't Tobias Renfrew's."

"The man who had it initially...?"

"The one your little daemon mate stole it from, you mean?"

"He didn't exactly steal it," I say, doing what I can to defend O'Shea's dubious honour, "he just, um, found it."

"And took it without permission."

"Wouldn't you?"

Foxworthy purses his lips. "Perhaps. Either way, by the time we knew of him, there was no trace. Whoever he was, he disappeared," he clicks his fingers, "into the night."

"Did you find out anything about him at all?"

He looks at me over the rim of his glass. "Believe me Bo, no stone was left unturned with that investigation. We are talking about terrorists who attacked the Agathos Court and a damn school disco. Nothing was found. Of course there's the three who went to Venezuela and the government is still negotiating for their extradition. We all know it's merely lip service, however. They're not coming back unless it's in body bags."

"So the guy who initially had the ear vanished just like Renfrew," I muse.

"Bo, Tobias Renfrew is dead."

"How do you know?" I ask softly.

Foxworthy gestures at me in frustration. "He has to be."

"Everyone seems to think that."

"Because it's the only thing that makes any sense. He had his fingers in lots of pies. He pissed off the wrong person and ended up at the bottom of the bloody ocean or in some deep grave. If you're looking into him then you're chasing after ghosts and wasting your time."

"What about the ear? It has to have something to do with him. You can't tell me that trying to find out what happened with that is a waste of time. We have no way of knowing whether there's more to it than those bastards in Venezuela. What if they try something again?"

Kimchi whines at the rising note in my voice. I reach down to pat his head in reassurance, my free hand searching inside my pocket for the white pebble. I roll it across my fingers and remind myself to breathe.

"Then we'll stop them just like we did last time," Foxworthy says. His expression is calm but he seems concerned about me. "You're not the only person looking into this, Bo. And it's not your responsibility to find the mastermind behind the attacks. You can't take the weight of the world on your shoulders, as much as you might want to."

I laugh slightly, although there's not the faintest trace of humour to it. "Is that how you feel about your cases, Inspector?

That they're not solely your responsibility and if you don't solve them it doesn't matter because someone else will?"

A ghost of smile lights his face. "Just because I understand the sentiment doesn't mean I think it's healthy. I know very well how chasing after dead ends can take over your life."

"That's where you're wrong," I tell him. "There are no dead ends. Just lots and lots of questions. And I'm going to find out the answers."

He looks at me with a mixture of sympathy and dismay. "Don't let the questions destroy you, Bo. Because if you let them, they will."

CHAPTER 9

BREAKING AND ENTERING

O'Shea pitches up in a battered Volkswagen Beetle. I give it the once over. Despite its cratered bodywork and myriad of scratches, it seems remarkably sound. I pat its bonnet in approval while O'Shea pops his head out of the window.

"Are you bringing that thing along?" he asks, frowning dubiously at Kimchi. "I don't want my upholstery ruined."

I peer inside the dusty windows. The back seat is littered with rubbish and I'm sure I spot a familiar brand of Tampax from peeping out from underneath a crisp packet. "*Your* upholstery?"

"I'm not quite sure what you're trying to imply, Bo," he says, with an affronted expression on his face. "I bought Barry fair and square from a woman I know in Soho. I've just not had time to clear out all her stuff yet."

"Barry?"

"Barry to you," he says with a flick of his fingers. "When you become better acquainted, you might get to call him Baz."

Kimchi sniffs at Barry's wheel, then glances back at me with an expression on his face that suggests he'd rather gnaw off on his own tail than get in. "Were you followed?" I ask O'Shea. Surprisingly, I've not seen any sign of my square-headed followers since I left Dahlia to deal with them. It doesn't mean there aren't others, however.

"Oh, yes," he responds cheerfully. "There were two of them waiting outside my flat."

"And?"

He grins. "And a rather large friend of mine who enjoys dressing up as Tallulah at the weekends helped distract them for me. I'm clean."

I nod at Kimchi. "Sorry, buster. We're climbing on board." He cocks his leg in response, urinating on the rear tyre.

O'Shea leans further out. "What's that dog doing?"

"Nothing." I open the backseat door and Kimchi jumps in, immediately setting about sniffing at all the litter in case there are any stray crumbs to be found. Then I go round to the passenger side and get in next to O'Shea. Unfortunately it's a bucket seat that seems to have seen better days. The second I sit down it groans loudly and there's a rush of air. My bottom sinks until I'm only just able to see over the dashboard.

"I have a great recipe for a growth spell," O'Shea tells me.

I stick my tongue out. "Just drive."

RENFREW'S MANSION sits at the far end of a leafy suburb on the very outskirts of the city. It's remarkably well signposted, adding weight to my grandfather's information that it's become a tourist hotspot. There's something macabre to me about wandering around the scene of a mass murder on a jolly family day out. That thought is only solidified when I spy the gift shop at the front. O'Shea cups his hands against the glass and squints inside.

"Books, keychains, mugs…" he announces. "Nothing useful here."

"Did you think there would be?"

"I was hoping for a Cornetto. I'm rather peckish."

Kimchi barks. I wag my finger in his direction. "There's no way you're getting an ice-cream," I tell him sternly. A trail of drool drops down from the corner of his mouth.

"Don't mention F. O. O. D. when the dog's around, O'Shea."

He rubs his fingers across his mouth and eyes Kimchi thoughtfully. "There's quite a lot of meat on him, isn't there? He'd keep me going for a while. Is that why you're fattening him up?"

"You're hilarious."

"And I'm here all week, ladies and gentlemen."

From the far corner of the house, a beam of a light from a torch appears. I tap O'Shea on the shoulder. "Torch," I grunt. "Must be a security guard doing the rounds."

O'Shea points to Kimchi. "He was the one making all the noise."

I roll my eyes. "Come on. Let's head round the back before they get here."

The three of us jog away in the opposite direction, past a row of large darkened windows encased in sandstone. It's hard to believe that this entire building was all for one triber alone. I can't imagine what on earth he did with all the space.

It's an odd experience when we make it to the far side. Even with the absence of lights, it's such a familiar vista that the creeping sensation of déjà vu momentarily overcomes me. I've seen this same spot in so many old photographs that it's definitely very weird being here. Clearly, I'm not alone in this sentiment. O'Shea squeaks and dashes forward.

"This is the spot, Bo," he calls out in a low, reverent tone. "There's even a plaque."

I join him and look down. He's right. A small blue tile marks the very place where Renfrew had been standing when he vanished all those years ago. "He was on a platform though," I say, attempting to be pragmatic even if I still can't avoid the slight shiver that runs down my spine. I gaze out across the shadowed garden, trying to picture what it would have been like to be here on that night. All the people and the noise and the music ... it must have been a sight to behold.

"It's a damn shame," O'Shea murmurs, "that we can't create a time bubble here."

I fervently agree. There aren't many places in the world where there's such a strong sense of history.

"Shall we?" I say eventually, jabbing my thumb in the direction of the house.

O'Shea's eyes gleam in the darkness. "Let's."

I turn my back on the plaque and the gardens, heading for the nearest window. It actually helps that the building has been preserved for posterity in the same condition that Renfrew left it in. It means that the old-fashioned sash window is ridiculously easy to jimmy open. O'Shea and I pause nervously, in case an alarm starts to shriek and alert the security guards to our presence. When all remains quiet, however, we squeeze our way inside, one after the other.

We find ourselves in a large sitting room. There's a grand fireplace at one end and a collection of matching furniture. O'Shea bends down to examine a chair.

"Chippendale," he declares. "Only the best for elusive billionaires."

"Not that it did him much good in the end," I point out, dragging Kimchi away before he can start gnawing on a priceless chair leg. "We need to head upstairs."

"To the scene of the crime?"

"Indeed."

I carefully open the door, wincing slightly as it creaks. I needn't have worried though. It's so silent and still inside that it's quickly apparent the guards only patrol the exterior of the mansion. We pad softly down the corridor until we reach a staircase. I motion to O'Shea and we ascend.

As tempting as it is to spend time exploring the whole house, there's really only one room I want to examine – the bathroom where the dismembered corpses were discovered. It's not that I'm expecting to come across any clues. After all, every inch of the room has probably been minutely studied and pored over. I want to get a feel for it, however. Old photographs are no substitute for the real thing.

Despite the mansion's size, the room is easy enough to locate thanks to the many signposts no doubt placed to help the eager tourists find their way to the very same place. 'Only fifty feet to go!' one proclaims with some photo-shopped blood spatter for effect. I flatten my mouth in disapproval. It seems to me that there's a considerable lack of respect as far as the five victims go. They died horribly – and most probably at Renfrew's own hand. It appears that the public just can't get enough of celebrities and death though. The only slight sign of deference to the crime that occurred here is that when we finally do reach the bathroom itself, it's roped off to prevent people from traipsing around inside.

Kimchi sits down by my feet, his tongue lolling out and his nose twitching. I can't help wondering whether he can smell the traces of decades old blood. Even my vampire nose can't pick anything up although it's hardly surprising considering how long it's been and how vigorously the room was probably cleaned afterwards. Little yellow markers are laid out, lurid against the white marble and pointing to where the different body parts were discovered. Other than that, it looks like nothing more than a typically opulent bathroom.

O'Shea licks his lips and glances at me wide-eyed. "Do we go in?" he whispers.

As uncomfortable as it makes me feel, I nod and duck underneath the barrier before I change my mind. I step gingerly into the middle of the room, taking care not to knock over any of the markers and look around.

There's a shaft of dull moonlight coming in from a small window set high into the far wall which bounces off the white tiles on the floor. A large claw footed bathtub sits against one side. I edge over and peer inside. It smells faintly of bleach. I crouch down to see if there's anything noteworthy underneath but before I can get right down, I hear a whine and a muffled protest from O'Shea. Kimchi's paws scrabble across the floor, knocking several of the markers over. Alarmed, I spring up, just in time to see the dog sail over me, landing inside the bath itself.

"Goddamnit!" I hiss. "Kimchi, get out of there!"

He wags his tail in delight as if this is some kind of game. His claws scrape loudly against the ceramic as I grab his collar and heave him out, the sound echoing across the room and making me wince. I only just catch sight of O'Shea rolling his eyes as I yank Kimchi back outside, remonstrating with him all the while. Then I tie his lead round the leg of a side table and go back in to assess the damage.

The carefully laid out markers are all over the place. I sigh inwardly and begin doing what I can to stand them back upright again, hoping I'm getting them back in at least vaguely the right position. O'Shea stands over the bathtub, frowning down.

"You could help, you know," I tell him in an irritated undertone.

"Look at this, Bo," he says, ignoring me.

I prop up the last marker and join him. My stomach drops

when I see what he's staring at. Kimchi's claws have managed to scratch the bath in several places. Even in this dim light, the marks are painfully obvious. So much for being discreet, then.

O'Shea reaches into his back pocket and pulls out a coin. Then he pivots round towards the large sink and bends down, drawing it across the ceramic.

"What the hell are you doing?"

He gestures towards it. "It's scratched here too now."

"You've damaged it? Shit in a hell basket, O'Shea, at least Kimchi doesn't know any better! We're not trying to advertise ourselves. This is supposed to be an undercover operation!"

"Do you think it's the same suite that was here when the murders happened?" he muses, not even noticing my admonishments.

I shake my head in confusion. "Why wouldn't it be?"

"It's so easily damaged."

I shrug. "So what? It's not like the sort of durable plastic you get nowadays." Then I falter. "Oh."

O'Shea stands back up. "Because of the amount of blood, it was always assumed the murders took place here."

I nod slowly. "I've never heard it suggested otherwise."

"But how can you kill five people, four of whom are in fact tribers, and not leave a single mark, blood and guts aside, when in less than five minutes we've managed to scratch the surfaces without even really trying?"

"You think they weren't actually killed here at all? They were murdered somewhere else and then transported here?"

His eyes meet mine. "If someone wanted to frame Tobias Renfrew, it would make sense. It was the Sixties, after all. Forensics weren't as good as they are now."

"It might just be a replica suite. We could get in touch with the National Trust and ask them."

O'Shea smiles. "Or we could check out the gift shop at the front."

"Eh?"

"There were a lot of books inside. I bet some of them are about this place in particular."

"Good idea."

O'Shea beams. "See? I'm not just a devilishly handsome face. I've got smarts too."

I smile back. "How about putting those smarts into action a bit more and working out how we can hide all these scratches?"

He rubs his chin. "Um, Tippex?"

IN THE END, we have no choice but to leave them as they are. The mark O'Shea made on the sink is concealed enough, but Kimchi's scrapes inside the bath are horribly obvious. I can only hope that the next batch of visitors assume they aren't fresh. I take snapshots of everything with my phone so we can compare them with the original photos later on, then head out to retrieve Kimchi.

He's lying next to the side table, his head on his paws. He cocks his head up at me and his tail gives me a tiny wag as if he's trying to ask whether he's forgiven or not yet. I tut at him and untie his lead from the table leg. When I stand back up again, I catch the corner of my forehead on the table's edge and wince in pain. An expensive looking vase sitting on top wobbles rather dramatically but I manage to catch it just in time before it falls. I set it carefully upright again, underneath a pretty land-scape painting of a farm. A tiny figure sits underneath a tree in the far corner, while golden fields stretch out in front, leading down to a quaint looking farmhouse. I decide that Tobias Renfrew had good taste in art. Then I spot the scrawled signature in the bottom and start. 'T.Renfrew'. I gaze back at the painting with renewed interest. The fact that the ex-military daemon also dabbled in painting is a new one on me. Out of nothing more than vague interest, I also take a photo of it. Maybe it's a place that had some significance for him. You never know.

I meet O'Shea back at the stairs. Kimchi nudges his hand with his nose and I see a slight smile cross his face. I raise my eyebrows at him. When he catches me looking, he abruptly changes his smile to a scowl. "Damn dog," he growls.

Kimchi wags his tail again and I grin. "You love him really."

We exit the same way we entered, carefully closing the window shut again behind us. The guard from earlier seems to have helpfully disappeared so it's an easy jaunt back to the front and the gift shop. I pull out my trusty lockpick and let us in. Unfortunately there's a bell above the door which jangles jarringly when we enter. I hiss through my teeth and all three of us freeze. When no-one comes running, I force myself to relax.

"What is this?" O'Shea asks, cheerfully, "the third place in two nights that you've broken into?"

"Second."

"Brigstone, the mansion and now here," he says, ticking off his fingers.

"I'm counting this and the mansion as the same."

He snorts. "If you say so. I'll make a hardened criminal of you yet."

I stick out my tongue in response and make a beeline for the bookshelves. There's a vast array of titles, all pertaining to Tobias Renfrew. I take one of each, balancing them in a pile. Then I dig out my wallet and leave enough cash on the side to cover them all.

"Bo, is that really necessary?"

"We're not thieves." I give him a look. "Okay," I amend. "*I'm* not a thief."

"They're hardly going to notice them," he says. "Look at this one. It's covered in dust. It's probably not even been picked up in years."

I glance at the small book on the top. He has a point. Even the cover is twee and old-fashioned with a hand-drawn picture of Renfrew standing in a pile of bloody bodies. "It might be useful," I say.

"Mm." He sounds doubtful. "How about this instead?" O'Shea holds up a keyring of a miniature Tobias Renfrew. He shakes it and the tiny plastic ruby in its ear lights up while the theme tune from the Twilight Zone plays.

"Put that away," I hiss.

"It's kind of cute. I'm going to keep it."

"Then pay for it."

"Bo, you really do suck the fun out of life sometimes."

I open my mouth to answer him when Kimchi suddenly growls. I glance down and realise all his hackles across his spine are raised.

"Either he also doesn't think you should take the damn keyring," I whisper, "or we're about to be interrupted."

O'Shea nods. "Hide."

A beam of torch light reappears and we duck. Kimchi growls again so I pull him down onto the floor too and hush him. He does as he's told but I can still feel his body vibrating with anxiety from through his thick fur. I try to crane my head upwards to check whether the guard is heading for us just as there's a sudden popping noise and the glass in the shop window splinters, spraying out shards in every direction.

"He's shooting at us!" O'Shea screeches.

There's the sound of running feet on gravel and distant shouts. There's only one door out of the damn shop and, thanks to me, it's lying wide open. Keeping my head down, I scoot over and slam it closed with one hand. My fingers fumble with the lock, twisting it closed just as a pale face suddenly appears, pressed against the glass. A set of orange eyes, wide with fear, blink down at me. Then there's another shot and the daemon, whoever he is, slumps forward before crashing down to the ground.

I throw myself backwards towards Kimchi and O'Shea, keeping as low as I can.

"Bo, that sodding door is made of glass! They'll come through in a second!"

"Quiet!"

"But..."

"I don't think we're the targets," I tell him in an urgent undertone.

He stills. I place a protective arm around Kimchi as the voices get louder.

"Did you get him?" a man asks. He sounds as if he's right outside.

There's a thud. "Yeah, he's gone."

"Good riddance," he spits. There's a pause. "Your aim is off. Now we need to fix the shitty window too."

"No need. They'll just blame it on kids. Get his ear."

"I got it last time. You take it."

I debate with myself about what to do. Whoever these two are, they're clearly currently preoccupied with the daemon they just executed. I can't tell what manner of bad guys they actually are – whether they're tribers or humans – and I reckon I could probably take both of them out. They are, however, obviously armed and there may be more of them in the vicinity. It might be more prudent to see what they do next instead.

I keep my body frozen, not daring to move an inch. There's a heavy sigh and one of the men bends down in front of the door, grabbing the dead daemon's head. I see a flicker of steel before I'm forced to dampen down my nausea as he starts sawing away at the soft flesh.

"I hate this part," he grunts. There's a plopping sound as the cartilage rips away then he stands back up again. "Call the clean up crew. We need to dispose of this mess."

I reach into my back pocket and carefully slide out my phone as the men start walking away. Kimchi whines and I hush him, quickly typing out a message to Foxworthy. I glance in O'Shea's direction and he gives me a nod of agreement.

"What are we going to do?" he asks in a low voice.

"Follow those two, of course," I answer.

He groans. "I had a horrible feeling that's what you were going to say. They just murdered a daemon right in front of us, Bo."

"And sliced off his ear. There's no way I'm letting them get away."

Off in the distance there's the sound of an engine revving. "We'd better get a move on, then."

"I hope Barry can keep up," I mutter.

"Somehow I think my car is going to be the least of our worries."

Keeping low, we edge out of the gift shop, stepping over the daemon's body. I hug the pile of pilfered books to my chest. "Watch out for the blood," I warn. "We don't want to compromise the scene."

"Give me your phone," O'Shea says, dipping his head in agreement.

I toss it over to him, turning away as he bends down and takes a quick snap of the dead daemon's face. There's a screech of tyres as our two culprits start to speed off.

"We need to go now, O'Shea."

He stands up, a faint green tinge to his skin. He absently

touches both his own ears as if to check they're still there. "Let's go."

I flick a quick look back at the corpse. "I should have done something," I mutter. "I should have at least tried to save him."

O'Shea's fingers brush against my arm. "There was no time." His tone is soft. "There's nothing we could have done."

"Tell that to him," I say sadly. Then I start running to the car.

CHAPTER 10
CHASING SHADOWS

The two killers, whoever the hell they are, already have a good lead on us. I'm painfully aware of how easily the men who murdered Bergman Stuart slipped away so, at risk of offending O'Shea, I slip into the driver's seat.

"Buckle up," I tell him, my tone brusque and business-like. I don't wait for him to follow orders, however, I simply start the engine and head off.

Kimchi appears to have caught the urgency of the situation. Rather than remain in the back seat with the litter from Barry's previous owner, he squeezes his way forward and perches on O'Shea's lap, eagerly gazing out of the windshield and the dark road ahead of us. When we reach the end of the long drive, there's a choice – left or right. I curse inwardly and pause.

"A sodding Trace would be pretty handy right about now," I mutter.

"They don't work on people," O'Shea answers. "Go right."

"Why?"

"Because if it's left, we've already lost them. There are too many crossroads in the other direction."

I nod. He's right. My knowledge of London geography is

considerably less strong out here in the suburbs but I caught enough of the roads and the signs on the way in to the mansion to appreciate his words. With my heart in my mouth, I swerve to my right. I speed up although with Barry's headlights off as they are to avoid detection I'm forced to pay close attention to what's going on up ahead. I only just manage to avoid a rabbit that bounds out in front. I grit my teeth and change gears, accelerating even more.

We whizz round the next curved corner. In the distance a set of brake lights flickers on and I make myself slow down. This might not be them but it's the middle of the night and there's no-one else to be seen. I'll just have to keep my fingers crossed.

My phone beeps. O'Shea snatches it up from the dashboard and examines the text. "It's from that copper. He wants to know where we are."

"Just tell him to get to Renfrew's mansion," I say as the traffic lights turn green and the car ahead begins moving again. It glides forward onto a more well lit street where it will be harder for us to follow unobtrusively. I hang back, hoping we're far enough back to avoid raising suspicion.

The phone beeps again. "He says you're not qualified to chase down suspects," O'Shea tells.

"So I'll make a goddamn citizen's arrest. Besides, I still have my PI license. That'll grant me some leeway."

"Not if you're ignoring a police request."

"If they call out a bloody panda car, those guys will get spooked and we'll lose them in a heartbeat."

"Or," O'Shea comments, "they'll get arrested for murder."

I shake my head. "No. That won't help us. They're just like the Venezuelan crew. These bastards are following orders. We need to find out who's giving them."

I breathe again when the car turns down away from the

main road and the danger of the street lamps. Wherever they're going, they're smart enough to avoid taking a direct route. Unless they've spotted us, they can only be trying to keep away from the CCTV cameras and traffic hot spots. Either way it means they're professionals. I drop back further just in case.

A car approaches on the other side of the road. I catch a glimpse of a bleary eyed driver frowning in my direction. He flicks his high beams off and on and beeps his horn no doubt to alert me to own lack of headlights.

"Shit."

"Do you think they noticed?" O'Shea asks.

"Can't tell," I mutter. I turn Barry's lights on just in case, keeping a close eye on the killers' car to judge for myself if there's any reaction. They slow down fractionally. I bite my lip and make a decision, indicating left.

"What are you doing, Bo?" O'Shea cranes his neck round Kimchi's body, holding onto him so he doesn't fall over.

"Taking a gamble." This is a residential area. I'm betting I can find my way out further up ahead and will only lose a small distance between us and the other car. Just in case, I speed up again. The only thing to be thankful for is that all the people who live here are tucked up safe and sound in their beds. At least none of them will be getting in my way.

I twist left, spinning the wheel. Kimchi lets out a small yip while Barry crashes unfortunately over a speed bump.

"Bo!"

"Sorry."

"I've only had Baz for five minutes," he complains. "You can't kill his suspension just yet."

"Baz can take it." I narrowly avoid driving down a cul-de-sac and turn left, hoping I can find a way back out to the same street as before. I'm still forced to make several quick turns but we eventually make it. "Can you see them?" I ask anxiously.

"I can't see anything," O'Shea grumbles, "apart from the back of your damn dog's fat head."

"He's not fat," I say primly. "He's big boned."

As if understanding, Kimchi turns and licks my left hand as it tightly grips the steering wheel. My knuckles are white and taut with tension but I relax ever so slightly when I spot the car again up ahead.

"Stop," O'Shea hisses.

I slam on the brakes and all three of us jolt forward, saved only by the seatbelts and O'Shea's hold round Kimchi's body. "What?"

"Dead end," he answers, pointing to a sign only a few metres away. "Do you know what's up ahead?"

I shake my head. "Not a clue."

"I thought you were the Queen of the Streets."

"Not here unfortunately." I release myself from the seatbelt and leap out. "Leave Kimchi here," I call to O'Shea as I start sprinting.

I stick to the far side where it's more shadowed. All the same, if either of those goons look back, they'll still probably notice me – especially if they're tribers of the vampiric or daemon persuasion. Their enhanced vision makes it much easier to see in the dark. Despite my own bloodguzzling nature, I can't see what's up ahead unfortunately. I strain my eyes as I run, past row upon row of terraced houses that put me in mind of the Truman Show. It's not until I'm almost at the end of the street, however, that I finally spot the car again.

It's parked at an angle, in a haphazard fashion that no self-respecting driver should allow. I take it, peering inside the windows. The seats are empty. In fact, there's not even the slightest trace of a chewing gum wrapper or piece of ID. I pull back and note the scratch on the exterior, just underneath the passenger window. I grimace to myself. No doubt they stole the damn thing.

O'Shea catches up, bending over double and panting. "Do you have to run so fast?" he gasps.

"We can't let them get away." I search ahead, noting a high fence leading onto a railway line. "Come on. They must have gone that way."

I jump up, hauling myself over. Where once, when I'd been human, I'd have found it impossible to avoid ripping my clothes on the rings of sharp barbed wire at the top, I now find it easy to vault over them by flipping up in the air. O'Shea obviously is struggling. I can hear the metal links rattle behind me, along with several colourful curses. It doesn't matter now though. As soon as I cross the rail tracks, I can see where the men are. Their two shadows running across wasteland and into some kind of abandoned warehouse less than fifty metres away. I turn back and help O'Shea clamber over.

"This is a designer suit," he complains, fingering a rip in the fabric.

I pat him on the shoulder. "Don't worry. We've almost caught them."

We edge forward towards the building, keeping low. Towards the far end, a light flickers on and I smile in satisfaction. They don't realise we're onto them.

"Do you think this is their hide-out?" O'Shea asks. "I always wanted one of my own."

"Tell you what," I say, stepping past a collection of gorse bushes, "once we catch these pricks, it's all yours." I pause. "Unless it belongs to someone else."

"You're all heart, Bo," O'Shea mutters as we reach the building itself.

There's a single steel door leading inside. I reach over and give the doorknob an experimental tug. It doesn't budge. There's no visible lock to pick either.

"I got this," O'Shea whispers.

I step to the side to allow him his moment of machismo. He cricks his neck and leans back, ready to launch forward and kick it open. Then I spot the tiny wire hanging out of the frame and stop him just in time. I place my fingers to my lips and point upwards. His eyes follow, narrowing when they see it too.

"Bend down," I tell him.

He does what I ask. I hook my legs round his neck and pat him on the head. He stands back up, wavering slightly. "Have you put on weight lately, Bo?"

"Shh. Move a bit closer."

He shuffles forward. I lean over and inspect the wire, nodding in thoughtful irritation. "It's alarmed," I whisper. "Do you still have my phone with you?"

O'Shea passes it up. Using it as a makeshift torch, I peer closer, gingerly touching it with the tip of my finger. The smell is unmistakable. "Well, we know one thing now," I say. "Whoever they are, they're human." The alarm system includes an anti-triber coagulant. As far as I can tell, it's a damn expensive one too, meaning that even if I were confident enough to bypass the alarm, our presence would be immediately advertised anyway.

"We could try the roof," O'Shea suggests.

I glance upwards. "Too risky," I decide. "It might be alarmed too. Let's skirt right and see if we can get a better look inside from over there."

We jog down the side of the building, traversing its length until we reach the far end where the light is still shining out from the windows. They're high up but I manage to reach the sill with my fingertips and pull myself up just enough to peek inside. Unfortunately all I'm able to see are some shadows moving around.

"They're still there," I inform O'Shea when I drop back down again.

"So what do we do?" he asks in a low undertone. "Screw the alarm and storm the place? We know they're armed."

I run a hand through my hair, my fingers snagging on a tangle. I work it out as I think aloud. "Probably a bad idea. We don't know what else is inside and we'll already be scuppering our chances when we lose the element of surprise."

"We can wait them out."

"We can. Although that only works until dawn for me," I remind him. I check the time. "Three hours, give or take, before I'll need to find shelter."

He shrugs. "It's better than nothing."

I nod. "I'll stay at this end. You watch the far door."

O'Shea snaps off a salute and walks back. I watch as he takes up position behind another clump of bushes then clamber up the muddy slope towards the front side of the warehouse. Whoever owns this land isn't much into landscape gardening. There's nothing to hide behind at this end – not unless I want to head back across the railway line anyway. I hunker down on my belly and use my hands to push together a small wall of mud. As long as I stay flat it should be enough to hide me if the two men decide to venture back out again. It's unfortunate, however, that the mud is particularly slimy and smelly. I can already feel my skin starting to itch.

There's another beep on my phone. I wince at the sound and change it to vibrate. It's another text from Foxworthy.

Nothing at mansion. Only a sleepy security guard. What's going on and where are you?

I stare at the message. That can't be right. We left less than thirty minutes ago. I frown and jab out a reply.

Check gift shop.

A minute later, I get a response.

We did. Broken window. Nothing else.

Damn. These guys – or whoever they work for anyway – are bloody efficient. I gnaw on the inside of my cheek.

Get some luminol. There must be blood traces. And the smashed window is from a bullet. You might find it inside.

Tell me where you are.

I wrinkle my nose. I'm going to have to let him know sooner or later. With time running out on me, it probably makes sense to tell him sooner. Part of me still doesn't want to ask for his help. I want to get these bastards on my own. I yield to the inevitable, however, and send him my location, along with a caveat to stay stealthy. I don't want my targets spooked.

I shift my position. From this high point, I can still make out the flicker of moving shadows from within the warehouse. Whatever they're up to, they're certainly being bloody busy. My stomach grumbles noisily, reminding me that I really need to drink some fresh blood. I lift up my head to check how it's doing and I'm rewarded with a faint sensation of dizziness. I blow air out through my teeth in annoyance. Super speed and super strength are all very well but when you need to recharge every twelve hours, it's easy to realise your own limitations.

My phone vibrates, indicating a call coming in. Assuming it's Foxworthy, I don't bother to check the screen, simply answering in a hushed voice.

"Hey."

"Where the fuck are you?" Michael asks. He sounds remarkably pissed off. My belly still does a little flipflop of traitorous delight though.

"This really isn't a good time," I say evenly.

"It never is with you."

I blink. I'm well aware that things were awkward between

us after Medici's intervention during our first 'date' but the level of enmity in Michael's voice takes me aback.

"Are you with him right now?" he snarls.

"With who?"

"You know damn well who."

"What happened the other night with Medici wasn't my fault, Michael. You know that, right?"

"I'm not talking about Medici."

I'm puzzled. "Then who?"

"The lawyer."

My brow furrows. I'm prevented from responding further, however, by the sound of distant sirens. They sound stomach-droppingly as if they're heading this way. "Goddamnit," I hiss. "I've got to go."

"Bo, wait..."

I hang up. From the far end, O'Shea half stands, his hands flapping in my direction. I gesture towards him to get down. I shouldn't really have bothered though. Less than ten seconds later, no less than five bloody police cars screech round from the other side of the building. Several black dressed people pile out and race to take up positions around the warehouse. I can't see Foxworthy amongst them but I'm still cursing him viciously under my breath.

I hear a shout. One of the officers is grabbing O'Shea by his elbow, forcing him up to his feet. I scramble to my knees, receiving a bright light in my eyes and a muttered command to put my hands up for my trouble. Then I'm being hauled up also, squinting to try to make out who exactly has decided that I'm suddenly the enemy.

"Don't move," a voice tells me, their tone brooking zero argument.

I open my mouth anyway but I'm forestalled from saying anything but the sudden crash of the door to the warehouse being blown open. The alarm immediately peals out, ear-splittingly loud. I can only watch as the warehouse is entered. There are shouts from within, but at least no shots are fired.

My hands are dragged down and someone fixes a pair of handcuffs round my wrists. "Sorry, Ms. Blackman," they mutter. "Protocol."

I don't bother telling them that they're using normal cuffs which I could probably break out of in about three seconds flat. Instead, I just watch helplessly as the two killers from the mansion are dragged out and bundled into one of the waiting vehicles. For all their bluster back at the mansion, they didn't put up much a fight. Annoyingly, with the stupid light still shining in my eyes, I still can't get a good look at their faces.

At last I hear a familiar voice. "What's going on here?" Foxworthy shouts.

I ignore my captor and stumble up to my feet. "I told you to be quiet and stealthy! We needed to find out what they were doing to try and discover who they're really working for! Now they'll lawyer up and we might not get anywhere!" My frustration is palpable.

"This wasn't me," he says, his tone sounding surprised. "I don't travel around with Special Forces in tow. I don't even know why they're here."

The man holding the light in my face drops it to the ground, allowing me to finally make out a balaclava-covered head. Only a set of slightly puzzled eyes are visible. "We got a call," he says.

"Not from me, you didn't."

He shakes his head. "Anonymous tip about an armed gang."

"There are only two of them," I scoff. "Not much of a gang."

"They're not armed either," he says.

My eyes narrow. "But..."

He shrugs, not noticing my reaction. "Just two guys playing cards inside an old empty building. Looks like they've been here all night. We'll release them to you for questioning anyway, Inspector."

Foxworthy glances at me. "What's going on, Bo?" he asks softly.

I wipe my cheek, clearing it of the claggy mud that's somehow attached itself in chunks to my skin. "They killed someone," I answer. "Back at the mansion. They killed him and took his ear."

The Special Forces guy looks doubtful. "Are you sure?"

"I..." my voice trails away. "I thought I was."

He grunts and shrugs. "Everyone makes mistakes." He steps back and gives me the once over. "You know, I kind of thought you'd be taller. Could I have your autograph?"

CHAPTER 11

CARS, CARDS, BARS AND KISSES

The nearest police station is situated in a new building. Inside it's all sleek lines and chrome finishes, as if the government has decided that what London's coppers need is to look like they work out of a bizarre cross between a diner and Blade Runner. I give my statement to a blushing young constable who can barely look me in the eye then head out to the front to meet O'Shea and get the hell home before the sun comes up.

It's a surprise to see Connor's smiling freckled face in the waiting area. He waves at me and grins. "Hi Bo!"

"What are you doing here?" I ask.

"Inspector Foxworthy thought you looked hungry. He gave me a ring and sent a car to pick me up and bring me here."

I raise an eyebrow. The good Inspector is growing even more amenable to vampires than I'd have thought possible. "I am hungry," I admit. "I really appreciate you coming out all this way."

There's a flicker of relief in his eyes. "I wasn't sure if you'd want me to. You know, because you're drinking from other people nowadays." He still seems oddly uncomfortable with the idea, as if he preferred it when I only used him alone. The trouble was that 'used' was the key word. It wasn't fair on him. In fact, it's not fair on him right now to have been dragged out at this ungodly hour to satiate my blood lust. It's unfortunate that beggars can't be choosers.

"If you don't want to…"

"I do! I do!" He stretches out his neck, displaying his jugular in what is obviously an open invitation.

I catch the wide-eyed stare of the desk sergeant. "Maybe we should go outside for this," I suggest.

We're just finishing up when O'Shea trips down the steps to meet us. "I'm not used to being on the right side of the law," he drawls. He catches sight of Connor. "But it's good that I am!" he suddenly declares. "Devlin O'Shea is a new man who enjoys helping out the police in all matters." He scratches his neck and looks away. I watch him, fascinated.

"Hi Devlin," Connor beams.

"Oh hi," O'Shea mumbles. "I didn't see you there. It's Connor, isn't it?"

"We've met a few times."

"Yeah, yeah. So we have." He casts around as if searching for something to say. "Where's Kimchi?" he finally asks.

"In the car. I took him for a short walk while you guys were inside," Connor answers. "He really is a great dog."

"He's the best," O'Shea agrees, before lapsing into an uncomfortable silence.

"Thank you, Connor. You didn't have to do that," I say. "I won't have time to walk him properly now myself."

He grins in agreement. "You're right. We should head back while it's still dark. If we leave now, we should make it in time. Unless you want to hang around here? Maybe the police have a safe room you can stay in?"

It's a nice idea. I don't really want to stray too far from my two suspects. I'm not quite sure, however, that even with my apparent status as hero I'd fully trust the police to keep me safe while I slept. One stray shaft of sunlight and it would be adios muchachos. Home makes more sense. I glance through the revolving glass and spot Foxworthy. He notices me and comes out.

"What's happening?" I ask.

He grimaces. "They're not saying a word until their counsel gets here."

"Did you find the ear?"

"No." He seems troubled. "No ear and no guns. It is possible these aren't the guys, Bo."

I bite my lip. It is. It seems unlikely though. "Do you have people at Renfrew's mansion?"

"It's still too dark. As soon as first light hits, forensics will be out in force. Speaking of first light…"

I nod. "We're just going. You'll keep me updated though?"

"This isn't my jurisdiction but the chief constable is an old mate. As soon as anything happens, he'll tell me. And, yes, I'll tell you."

I blow air out through my cheeks. "Great." We shake hands and he heads back in. I watch him go. He's already warned me about getting too personally involved – but this isn't his case and it's still barely five o'clock in the morning. I'm not the only one with obsessive workaholic tendencies.

"I'll bring the car round," Connor interjects, clearly still eager to help out. "It's kind of messy though, Bo. I'm not sure why you bought it. Maybe you should stick to the bike. I can clean the car out once we get home."

I glance at O'Shea. Unbelievably, he appears to be going red. He coughs. Deciding to rescue the daemon, I just smile encouragingly at Connor and he bounds off.

"What's with you?" I ask curiously.

O'Shea sounds defensive. "What do you mean?"

"With Connor. It's like you have a schoolboy crush or something."

He doesn't reply.

"Devlin," I say, "he's really young."

"He's not a child, Bo. You think of him as young but he's actually much more mature than you know."

Perhaps he's right. "This isn't like you though. You're normally more … confident with your conquests."

O'Shea shuffles his feet. "So?"

Understanding dawns on me. "You really like him, don't you? I mean, *really* like him."

He shrugs. "He's a nice guy. Is he…?" his voice trails off.

"Gay?" I try to think. I've never seen Connor with any girls. But I've never seen him with any guys either. "I don't know," I say truthfully. "He's a bit of an innocent though, O'Shea. It wouldn't be fair of you to corrupt him."

"Please! I wouldn't corrupt him." A tiny smirk appears as the real O'Shea makes a return. "Not much, anyway."

I give him an assessing look. "I can find out his preferences," I offer. "But if he's not interested then you have to promise to back off completely."

"No, don't do that," he begs. "Let me keep my fantasies just a little longer. I'll speak to him when I'm ready."

"If you're sure."

He dips his head as Connor drives up and sticks his neck out of the window. "For all the mess, this car does kind of have character," he says. "We should give it a name."

I smile. "How about Barry?"

Connor grins back. "I like it! We could call it Baz for short!"

I firmly button my lips and open the back door, pushing the clutter to one side so Kimchi and I can get in. O'Shea can ride shotgun this time.

I'm woken up much earlier than I should have been thanks to the incessant ringing of my phone. It's particularly irritating because I'd been enjoying a rather racy dream involving myself, Michael (with a scowl which still confounds me as to its reason) and a can of UHT cream. I fumble across the bedside table to grab it, disturbing Kimchi's snoring slumber in the process. He leaps up to his feet in the mistaken belief that it means it's feeding time.

"Bo Blackman," I mumble.

"I'm sorry for waking you up," Foxworthy says, "but I thought you'd want to know straight away."

I bolt upright. "Know what?"

"Your two have just walked."

"They've what?" I screech.

"There was nothing to hold them on. You couldn't positively identify them from the scene. There wasn't a single thing to suggest they'd been doing anything illegal whatsoever."

"Were they even properly questioned?"

"Bo, that's not fair."

I rub my eyes. "I'm sure it was them. It has to have been them."

"There's no body. There are no traces of blood. All we have is a broken window and a single bullet embedded in the wall of the gift shop. We can't hold them on that without evidence."

"No blood?" Disbelief overtakes me. Just how good is their damn clean up crew? "What about their car?" I ask desperately. "There must be some traces inside."

"We couldn't examine it."

"Why the hell not?"

"Their barrister got involved. We didn't have a leg to stand on. He's a canny bastard. And," Foxworthy pauses, "I believe he's somewhat of a friend of yours."

My eyes narrow. He had to be kidding me. "Harry D'Argneau."

"That's him."

Sodding hell. I'll string him up when I find him. "Do you at least have an address for them?" If the police are going to cut them loose, then I'll have to deal with them myself.

"I can't give it to you, Bo."

"Foxworthy, come on. I'm not going to hurt them. I won't even talk to them. But they need to be watched. They murdered someone in cold blood!"

"Maybe. They maybe murdered someone."

I shake my head in despair. "Please."

"I really can't. But don't worry. I've put a team onto them. Every move they make will be catalogued. If they are your killers then sooner or later we'll know about it."

The trouble was that it might end up far too bloody late. They could very well kill again. Angry frustration gnaws at me. "At least you believe me," I say finally, squeezing my eyes shut. "I appreciate that much."

"Of course I believe you," he answers quietly.

"Can you tell me their names?" I plead in a last ditch effort.

"Sorry, Bo."

I get up, stalking to the bathroom and glaring at myself in the mirror. Then I let out an inarticulate scream and punch the wall. Plaster flies off and my fist leaves behind a rather unsightly dent, with several hairline cracks leading away from it. Kimchi comes up and nudges my hand, whining softly.

"Sorry," I tell him. "I didn't mean to scare you." I look down at the phone in my hand, debating whether to call D'Argneau or not. I'm still too worked up though. I can feel the hot anger coursing through my veins. If I can't speak to him like a calm intelligent adult, then I'll never get anywhere. Besides, I want to look the slimy lawyer in his goddamn eyes.

I TAKE Kimchi with me to D'Argneau's offices. I'm certain that dogs aren't allowed inside but I don't care. Let them try and stop me. It helps, of course, that I make absolutely no effort to conceal myself. I use public transport and keep my head and face uncovered. By the time I reach the gleaming façade, I've garnered myself a considerable following. I don't bother questioning any of the people behind me as to why they don't have better things to do than wander around after me. Neither do I let the incessant questions from the few journalists who've decided to tag along bother me. From time to time I reach into my pocket and touch my white pebble then simply smile prettily for all the cameras and allow the seething churn of emotions inside to solidify into something very cold and very hard.

"You can't bring him in here," the doorman states firmly.

"What if I told you he was a guide dog?"

"He's not."

"How do you know?"

He gazes at me helplessly. "Ms. Blackman, you're not blind. And I've seen the dog on television. He's not trained. Not for anything."

Sometimes this fame business works for me and sometimes it works against me. I glance down at Kimchi who's enjoying all the attention. "I guess you're as famous as I am." He just wags his tail. "Why can't I bring him in? He's only a dog. He won't hurt anyone."

"I'm sorry. It's the rules. I don't make them."

I run my tongue over my teeth and consider the matter. I

don't want him to lose his job by bending the pointless rules just for me. I'm not leaving my dog behind though. "Kimchi," I say with the sweetest tone of voice I can muster up, "attack."

The guard's eyes widen and he backs away. Kimchi requires no further encouragement. He bounds towards the man and immediately leaps up, placing both his paws on his chest. Then he starts to furiously lick at the buttons on his shirt. I stroll in.

When I reach the bank of lifts, and one dings open, I call Kimchi back to me. He runs over to me, his ears flapping in the air. "You see?" I say, raising my voice just loud enough for the doorman to hear. "He is, in fact, very well trained."

The pair of us walk into the lift, leaving the poor man now covered in drool staring after us.

My presence in the building is clearly pre-advertised. By the time the lift arrives as D'Argneau's floor, he's already there and waiting. A woman wearing an incredibly short skirt skitters over with a tray and a crystal cut glass containing blood. I raise my eyebrows at the lawyer.

"Service around here has definitely improved."

He gives me a professional smile. "We have many triber clients now, Bo. Including several vampires. I told you about the Stuart Family, didn't I? I've had to expand. We've taken on over twenty new people lately."

"Good for you," I sniff. "But it's not the vampires on your client list that currently interest me."

"Why don't we go to my office? Your..." he flicks a distasteful look at Kimchi, "animal can wait out here."

"The dog stays with me. And I don't need to go to your office. I just want to know why you took on those two new clients last night."

"I don't know who you mean," he replies smoothly.

I take a step towards him. The woman stiffens and backs

away but D'Argneau doesn't so much as flinch. "Oh," I purr, "I think you do."

"Andrew Wyatt and Steven Creed, you mean?"

I file away their names. That was even easier than I'd thought it would be. "Why?" I demand. "Why take them on? They're not tribers. Did they call you?"

"Everyone deserves legal representation, Bo."

"Yes, but you're a triber hungry megalomaniac. You wouldn't sign them up unless there was something in it for you. I want to know what."

"My office?" His face takes on a faintly strained quality. "Please? You can bring the, er, dog."

I mull it over, then acquiesce as gracefully as I can manage. I'd rather been enjoying having it out with him in front of all his employees. If it means he gives me more information, however, I can make the switch to privacy.

D'Argneau smiles in relief then gestures at me to follow him. We pass by row upon row of cubicles and glass fronted rooms. From every single one, I'm watched. I relax my shoulders and wave at them all, like I'm the goddamn Queen.

Once we're inside D'Argneau's own sanctuary, he offers me a seat. I politely decline.

"I'm not sure exactly why you're here, Bo," he says, perching on the edge of his desk. "Client privilege..."

"I'm not asking for any state secrets, D'Argneau," I spit. "I just want to know how you got hired and why you took the case."

He sighs over-dramatically and runs a hand through his tawny hair in a good impression of someone under pressure. "If it was anyone else, Bo, then I would ask you to leave."

"Give it up. You're not fooling me for a second."

His eyes meet mine. Then he grins and shrugs. "Fair enough." He walks round to the back of his desk and opens a drawer, pulling out a single white card, about A5 size. "Here." He throws it in my direction. "This was couriered to me at around one o'clock in the morning."

I stiffen. By my reckoning, that was before O'Shea and I had even entered the gift shop. I read the carefully inked words.

Two humans may well be arrested tonight in the vicinity of the Renfrew mansion. Ensure their swift release and you will be rewarded.

"That's it?"

"It was a simple matter to scan the police frequencies and find out what had occurred." He gives me a pointed look. "I knew you were involved, of course."

I shake my head in confusion. "Why would you even care?" I wave the card around. "This doesn't mean anything at all."

D'Argneau's expression is one of infinite patience. "Dear Bo. Do you really mean to tell me that if you received a mysterious message in the middle of the night that you would ignore it? Such a missive would appeal to anyone." His eyes light up. "The mystery and drama of it all!"

"It could have just been a practical joke!"

He tuts. "The Renfrew mansion? After all that business with the ear? Even if it were a joke, do you think I'd just go to sleep and forget about it? No go, Bo." He smirks at his own little rhyme. "If this Tobias Renfrew investigation is continuing, I want some of the action. Besides, my time was well spent."

I stare at him suspiciously. 'What do you mean?"

He grins, reaching down for a briefcase and laying it on top of the desk. He opens it up with a flourish. "My retainer."

Three shiny gold bars are nestled inside. D'Argneau picks

one up. "You can hold it if you want to. It's not as heavy as you'd think. I can assure you, however, that it's definitely the real thing."

"These came with the note?"

"No. They arrived upon my return. Once I'd secured Wyatt and Creed's release." He winks at me. "Someone was paying close attention and it wasn't just you."

"The courier...?"

"He was questioned, naturally. He knew nothing. It was an anonymous drop off set up online." D'Argneau leans towards me, dropping his voice to a conspiratorial whisper. "I don't know about you, but I'm excited."

I roll my eyes, even though there's a considerable part of me that unwillingly agrees with that sentiment. "Why you?" I demand.

He looks offended. "Why not me? I'm a good lawyer."

"No. There's another reason." I chew my lip and think it over. I'm betting it had something to do with me and my association with him. I don't need to tell him that though. "Why does Michael Montserrat seem to think there's something going on between us?" I inquire, still wondering what had been going on with his pissed off phone call from last night.

"Lord Montserrat believes we're having a fling?" A look of pleasure drops over D'Argneau's face. "Interesting. It could work, you know. After all, we almost did have a night of tumultuous steamy passion. The Red Angel and the lawyer. It has a nice ring to it."

"We did not almost have a night of passion. It was almost a night of seedy stupidity. And," I enunciate, "the key word is almost." I look over at Kimchi, who's sniffing at the gold bars with obvious interest. "Come on. We're leaving."

He barks in response. I straighten my back and point at

D'Argneau. "If you get any more of these cards, you let me know."

"I don't work for you, Bo. Unless you want to revisit the passion aspect..."

I snort loudly and turn round, stalking out.

I'M STILL THRUMMING with irritation when I walk back outside again although I take the time to smile politely at the doorman who keeps himself well away from Kimchi.

"If anyone gives you any trouble because of him," I say, "give me a ring." I throw him a generic business card for New Order.

"Uh, thanks," he stammers. "Your car is waiting at the side of the road."

I frown at him. "Car?" I look over and see a sleek limousine in midnight blue sitting less than twenty metres away. I bite my lip. This could be interesting.

I tug at Kimchi's lead to avoid him from attempting to lick the man again and stroll over. My heart rate is picking up but that's definitely only because I'm still angry at D'Argneau for getting in my way. Definitely.

I rap on the passenger window. It winds smoothly down and Michael's dark, impassive face glances out at me.

"Hey!" I say brightly. "Are you still in a mood?"

His eyebrows fly up. "A mood? I'm not a teenager, Bo."

"Then what you call the way you acted on the phone last night?"

He hisses. "So you're allowed to blow hot and cold all the time but the moment I get annoyed, I'm immature?"

I blink. "That's not what I said." Not exactly anyway.

"Why are you here anyway? What does that lawyer have?"

I purse my lips. "A white card and three gold bars."

Michael's brow creases but, before he can ask what I mean, there's a shout from the other side of the street. "Ms. Blackman! I want to talk to you!"

I realise with a sinking sensation that it's Arbuckle. It's obviously taken her all of two minutes to realise I'm not dropping anything to do with Tobias Renfrew. Crawling around the Renfrew mansion and getting half of London's police force to meet you there will do that to you.

"Actually," I say to Michael, making a quick decision, "if you give me a lift, I'll explain everything."

"Someone you're trying to avoid?" he inquires, less irritated now.

"You could say that."

His eyes scan my face. I wish I knew what he's thinking. "Fine," he answers slowly, "but you need to kiss me first."

I blink. "Eh?"

"There are quite a few cameras around, Bo, if you hadn't noticed. Half the world still thinks you have a thing with Medici. We need to abuse them of that notion."

I look over at Arbuckle. She's weaving her way across the road. Damn it. "Make it quick," I mutter, bending my head down.

Even though I'm expecting it, the kiss still takes me by surprise. Michael's hand snakes round my neck and his mouth is hard and possessive. There's a smattering of flashes from behind as the mob of followers and journalists snap away in glee. I barely notice them however. I can taste an odd mixture of salty blood and heady masculinity from Michael's tongue and there's a flutter deep in the pit of my stomach. Alright, less my stomach and more my loins. I reach in, one hand grazing the stubble on his cheek. Why does this have to feel so damn good?

"Ms. Blackman!" Colonel Arbuckle says, from no more than a few feet away.

I growl, a strange rumbling sound deep in my throat. Michael pulls away and the car door opens. I hastily get in.

"Ms. Blackman!"

The door closes behind me. Michael watches me with an unfathomable expression on his face. Arbuckle raps loudly on the window but both of us ignore her as the car moves off.

Michael's fingers twitch, an inch away from mine. "Who was that?"

I swallow, trying to get my pulse back under control. "Army."

"Let me guess," he says drily, "Tobias Renfrew."

I blink. "How did you know?"

He laughs. "It would hardly take a genius, Bo. I knew you'd go after him sooner or later. He has to be mixed up in this ear business somehow. He was originally a military man too. Unless you've decided to sign up, I can't think of any other reason why the army would be bothering themselves with you."

"You don't think I'm worth bothering with?" I hate the fact that my voice still sounds breathy.

He gives me a small crooked smile. "Oh, I didn't say that." He raises his hand and brushes away a loose strand of hair from my face. "Now, tell me what the fuck is going on with D'Argneau."

The abrupt change in tone takes me aback. Still unsure as to why he's so pissed off about the lawyer, I explain what happened last night. His eyes spark. "You keep forgetting that you're still a fledgling vampire. You need to take more care. If you're caught outside when the sun rises..."

I hold up my hand. "I know, I know."

He leans forward. "Anyway, that story still doesn't explain why you were out with him the other night."

"What do you mean?"

He sighs, reaching into a folder and sliding out a glossy magazine. I'm not quite sure why he took the time to keep it in the folder. The pages look twisted and ripped, as if Kimchi himself had gotten hold of it and chewed it up. He flicks through to the centre pages and points. "There," he says flatly.

I glance down. There's a full page photo of myself and D'Argneau. His hand rests on my shoulder and he's licking his lips suggestively. I groan inwardly. It's one of the selfies from the bar. The only way the magazine could have gotten hold of it is because D'Argneau himself gave it to them. Prick. I wish I'd known that half an hour ago when I confronted him.

"It's nothing," I say. "I met him in a pub to see if he could help me get hold of a time bubble. He couldn't."

Michael's eyes scan my face. Eventually he nods. "While we continue our relationship," he begins.

"Such as it is."

"Such as it is," he nods, although I can see a faint tightening around his mouth, "I'd prefer it if you didn't see him. It will only muddy the waters. Things are bad enough after Medici's little display."

I don't particularly want to see D'Argneau at all. I might be forced to, however. "Nothing's going on between us. It's just business. I can't promise I won't meet him again. Whoever is pulling the strings of those bastards from last night has involved him."

He's silent for a moment. Then he lifts up his chin. "Fine. But at least do me the favour of not meeting him alone. Take O'Shea or Connor with you."

I want to tell him he has no right to be jealous – and certainly not of bloody D'Argneau. I'm reminded, however, of how I felt at the restaurant when I was confronted with the knowledge that Michael had taken other dates there. I had no right to be jealous then either. "Okay," I say softly. "That much I can do."

"Thank you."

We look at each other. The silence grows, stretching out between us. Light prickles dance across my skin. I drop my gaze. "Are we going on another date now?" I finally ask.

"Would you like to?"

I actually really would. I bite my lip and nod. Unfortunately the car comes to a halt and the driver, a Montserrat vampire I vaguely recognise from my time with the Family, opens the divide with an apologetic look.

"I'm sorry, Lord Montserrat. There's a call coming in."

"Tell them I'm busy."

"It's Ursus. He says it's urgent."

Michael mutters a curse and takes the phone. I try to give him some privacy by turning away and looking out of the window but, as he talks, he reaches out for my hand and squeezes it.

When he hangs up, he sighs. "I'm sorry. We're going to need to take a rain check."

I push away the illogical flicker of disappointment I feel. "Anything I can help with?"

"No, it's better if I deal with this alone. Medici has turned up on Gully's doorstep and is demanding all the Family Heads meet for a vote on contacting the Kakos daemons to see if they'd like to work with us."

My mind flies to X and I gulp. "Kakos daemons don't work with anyone else."

"Not to mention they're bloodthirsty monsters who slaughter everyone they come across." He flashes me a quick grin. "Present company excluded of course."

I try to smile. I don't do a very good job.

"No," Michael continues, "Medici is just trying to cause

more problems. There are rumours that Lord Stuart used to have a business agreement with a Kakos daemon. It's all nonsense but he'll use it drive a wedge between us."

"He probably doesn't like that the four other Families are working together more closely than you ever have before," I murmur, wondering whether the information about Stuart's 'agreement' is actually true.

"Probably," he agrees. "Shall I drop you back at New Order?"

"Yeah, I guess." No doubt my grandfather will have already heard all about last night's antics and will be there waiting to scold me for them. Frankly, it's a miracle he didn't barge into my flat again to do just that. I likely only escaped because I was woken up so early. As long as he doesn't find out about my little escapade into Brigstone, I'll probably survive.

CHAPTER 12

PIZZA, SALAD AND BEER

"What in the world were you thinking of, Bo?" my grandfather bawls. "Storming an army base? It's … it's …"

I'm not quite sure I've ever seen him lost for words. "Preposterous?" I ask, squirming where I stand.

"Exactly!"

The Stuart, Gully and Bancroft representatives make a hasty departure. Even Arzo seems to have vanished. The only other people who remain in the office are Connor, Matt and, irritatingly, Dahlia.

"Did O'Shea grass me up?"

"That poor excuse for a daemon? No, he did not."

I frown. "Then who?"

My grandfather marches to his office door and pushes it open. Sitting primly inside, with the damn cat on her lap, is Colonel Arbuckle. My stomach sinks.

"Oh."

"That's all you have to say? Oh?"

I sigh and meet Arbuckle's eyes. "I thought you didn't want our paths to cross again."

"And I thought you were going to leave this Tobias Renfrew business alone," she answers.

"You're chasing after ghosts," my grandfather thunders. "The man is dead."

Considering he'd already been well aware of my investigation into the daemon billionaire, his obvious anger is just that. Too obvious. The canny bastard is playing up for Arbuckle's benefit. He's clearly not happy that I breached Brigstone but the old man is more on my side than hers. The knowledge is remarkably satisfying. "I'm not so sure," I say calmly, raising my eyebrows at the Colonel.

"How much proof do you require, Ms. Blackman?"

I tilt up my chin. "Your stupid secret photo was staged."

She seems taken aback. "Don't be ridiculous."

I watch her carefully. Arbuckle is far too young to have been involved in Renfrew's disappearance. She's probably as much in the dark as the rest of us are. "He was left handed," I tell her.

"So?" she sneers.

I simply wait. It takes a second or two for her face to drop. "There you go." I fold my arms.

My grandfather looks from her to me. "Would you like to explain this?"

I shrug. "I can't. It's classified."

Arbuckle hisses in annoyance. "We have a file," she says. "And a photo of Renfrew's corpse." Dahlia gasps audibly.

"Supposed photo," I remark, enjoying the fact that everyone in the room just sat up that much straighter.

She stands up, ignoring the fact that my grandfather's cat takes extreme umbrage at being dumped unceremoniously back onto the floor and swipes at her leg. "I will look into this further," she says stiffly, then stalks out.

My grandfather's expression remains impassive until it's clear she's not coming back. Then he gives me a glance filled with approval. "Well, well, well. You may just have uncovered a decades old conspiracy. There's never been anything about a photograph of Renfrew's corpse in MI7's files."

"I don't get it," Connor says slowly. "If I understand what just happened correctly, then the army have a fake photo of Tobias Renfrew's death. But if they faked it, then why didn't they release it for the world to see?"

"I have no idea," I answer. "It might have been Renfrew's body in the picture. I couldn't tell for sure either way. If it is him, then I believe the army killed him. If it isn't him, then goodness only knows what they were hoping to achieve."

"It's not exactly New Order's remit to investigate daemons," my grandfather says, "but I think in this case it's time we made an exception."

I can't keep the beaming smile off my face. "Brilliant."

He jabs a finger at me. "If I hear you've been sneaking into any more army properties, however, I'll lock you up myself and throw away the key."

"It was a one time thing," I say absently.

"What can we do?" The eagerness on everyone's faces is clear.

I consider it. "I want to check up on the two daemon killers from last night. They might have something to do with all of this and they might not but, either way, I'm not about to let them get off scot free. It might be helpful to bring Connor along as a fresh set of eyes."

Matt looks crestfallen. "Not me?"

I look from him to Dahlia. "I have some books I'd like the two of you to look at."

"Books? But that's so boring!" he complains.

"It's necessary," I say briskly.

"What's the daemon going to be doing?" my grandfather asks.

"O'Shea?" I sneak a glance at Connor. He simply smiles. "I'll call him. He can come along to Creed and Wyatt's with us. Matt, come upstairs and help me grab the books, please."

He mutters under his breath. I grin at him. I'm still convinced that the enhancement spell that's warped his mind is starting to lose its effect even though his feet are already leading him out of the room. I quickly follow.

Once we're in my flat upstairs – and the door is safely closed - I grab the pile of Renfrew related books from the gift shop and hand them over to him. "This is important," I say in an undertone. "Dahlia was in that room too so I can't escape her involvement, much as I'd wish otherwise. I trust you and I don't trust her. You need to cross reference all the material in these books to see if there's anything new we can learn about Renfrew. You also need to cross reference what she's doing."

"Why can't you trust Dahlia?" he asks, confused. "I like her."

"She might be working for Medici," I say, pointing out the astoundingly obvious.

He mulls it over. "So I'll be like a super spy, will I?"

"Exactly. That's why I need you here instead of out in the field."

"Okay, Bo. I can do this."

I pat him on the shoulder. "You're the best, Matt."

There's a knock on the door. Leaving Matt to balance the books, I open it half an inch. For some reason it's Drechlin.

"I have your dog," he tells me, with a curl to his lips.

I open the door further. Kimchi leaps forward, bowling me over. I receive several slobbering licks to the face.

"Thanks," I say, doing what I can to keep my face away from Kimchi's lolling tongue. I am pretty certain I'm fighting a losing battle.

"You should take better care of him," Drechlin sniffs. "This came for you too. Some lazy courier who was too lazy to climb a set of stairs."

I freeze. Kimchi's blocking my sight but I have a sudden feeling I know exactly what Drechlin is holding. I gently push the dog out of the way. In his hands there's a single white card. There's not even an envelope.

"When?" I demand. "When did it arrive?"

He shrugs. "About half an hour ago."

I grind my teeth. Damn it. I'd really have liked to talk to that courier. I eye the card as if it's a snake. Why now, I wonder?

I wait for Drechlin to hand it over, but he doesn't seem particularly keen. "There are too many of you bloodguzzlers now," he says. "It's a fire hazard."

I'm not quite sure what his beef is. I know for a fact that since the crowd of journalists elected to leave the street outside, Drechlin's little dentistry has been teeming with customers. From the way I've been accosted several times on the stairs, it's more because they seem to be hoping they'll catch a glimpse of the Red Angel while getting their fillings than for any other reason.

"I'm sure we meet all the regulations." At least I'm sure Arzo and my grandfather have covered that aspect of our tenancy anyway.

"I could complain, you know."

I give him an exasperated look. He's complained about us often enough in the past. I'm not sure what's stopping him this time. "That's your prerogative, Dr Drechlin."

He seems to be waiting for something. I have no idea what. When he realises I'm not going to say anything else, he exhales. "I could be persuaded to stay quiet."

My nose wrinkles. Does he want a bribe?

He shuffles forward. "It must be difficult keeping your, uh, fangs clean. A vampire's teeth are vital."

"You are suggesting I come in for a check up," I say in sudden epiphany. "Perhaps have my photo taken while I'm there."

"Perhaps."

"You're usually closed by the time I'm up and about."

He smiles, revealing his own blindingly white teeth. "I can make an exception. In the interests of being neighbourly."

I only just manage not to roll my eyes. "How about next week then? Monday? Around eight?"

"I suppose I can do that."

I lean forward and take the card from him. "I'll see you then," I say firmly, waving him back outside. Wonders will never cease.

"I thought he didn't like vampires," Matt says. "I tried to get him to clean my teeth a few weeks ago and he refused."

"He wants to jump on the fame bandwagon." My fingers tighten around the card. With my heart in my mouth, I flip it over to read what it says. The handwriting is exactly the same as it was on D'Argneau's little missive. Even the colour of the pen is the same.

Leave Creed and Wyatt alone. *They're a dead end.*

Well, well, well. I reckon I'm on the right track with those two after all.

"I've got to run, Matt," I tell him. "Make sure you keep that eye on Dahlia."

I virtually leap out the door, Kimchi at my heels. Speeding into the office downstairs, I find my grandfather in his chair. I fling the card down in front of him. "Look!" I say, almost shivering with excitement.

He quirks up an eyebrow and reads the card. "Real ink," he murmurs. "You don't see that often these days."

"Real ink?" I splutter. "That's all you can say?"

"It's certainly interesting," he says.

Dahlia walks in, placing a cup of tea in a delicate flowered china saucer in front of him. Her eyes flick down to the card. "Who's that from?" she asks.

"The tooth fairy," I answer shortly. Her mouth tightens at my gruff tone. Keep your enemies close, Bo, I remind myself. "By the way," I add, "I meant to thank you for keeping those soldiers from tracking me. You did a good job."

A grateful smile spreads across her face. "Thank you!"

"You're welcome." I try not to soften towards her. She can't be trusted, no matter how nice she acts in person. "Connor and I are leaving now."

"Remember the police are watching them too, Bo," my grandfather warns. "Don't do anything foolhardy."

I scoff. "As if."

"I HAVE A LOCATION FOR CREED," Connor informs me, "but I've not been able to find much on Wyatt. His last known address was Manchester."

"Good work!" I grin. "Where are we heading?"

"Kensington."

I'm slightly taken aback. It's a pricey area more suited to the well-heeled London contingent of large bank accounts and four wheel drives. "You're sure?"

He nods. "It's an unusual enough name. I'm certain that's our guy."

I wonder how Creed's neighbours are taking to having a police presence in their leafy street. It'd be nice to hope that whoever's assigned to the stake-out is being discreet. My alleged killers will already be on edge after their arrest and subsequent release. I need them relaxed and unworried – they'll be more likely to screw up in that scenario.

"Can you let O'Shea know?" I ask.

"Already have," he says cheerily.

I flick him a look. There's nothing in his tone whatsoever to suggest he thinks any more of the daemon than a potential work colleague. I'm tempted to ask him about his personal inclinations but I'm mindful of O'Shea's request to the opposite.

I settle for bland niceties instead. "O'Shea seems to be turning over a new leaf. He's been helping us out a lot and he's even got himself a gig as a mystery shopper."

"I hope he's not working too hard," Connor says. "He needs to give himself time to go to the gym and keep that hard daemon body all buff and muscular." My mouth drops slightly. Connor winks at me. "I'm not stupid, Bo. I know what he wants from me."

"And," I ask slowly, "does it offend you?"

"Not in the slightest. I have eclectic tastes." The corner of his mouth lifts up in a mischievous smile. "Humans. Vampires. Daemons."

"Men?"

"And women. Devlin though..." he pauses, "there's something special about him."

This is a brand new Connor that I'm seeing. There's a dancing glimmer in his eyes. If O'Shea is acting uncharacteristically shy around the red-haired human, then Connor is doing the complete opposite.

"You seem very self-assured," I tell him. "Unusually so."

"I don't understand why people get so nervous about relationships. There are some things in this world that it makes sense to be scared of. Your grandfather, for one. His cat for another. Hybrid witches. Kakos daemons." He sneaks a quick glance. "You."

"Me? I'm not scary!"

"You're the Red Angel, Bo. You're bloody terrifying." He puts his hands in his pockets. "But being frightened of those things is logical. Being frightened of love? That's just daft."

I shake my head fervently. "Love is the scariest thing there is. You're more likely to be hurt when you love someone. There are complications and problems and arguments about toilet seats." I think about Michael. "Unnecessary jealousy."

Connor gives me a half smile. "You're not scared of falling in love. You're scared of being hurt." His eyes grow serious and intense. "But, Bo, believe me, it's much scarier to walk away from love than it is to experience it."

"You're not in love with O'Shea, are you?" I ask suspiciously.

He laughs. "No. Not yet anyway. Maybe I never will be. I meant love in the sense of the possibility of the word, and all its meanings. I'd been hoping that Devlin was going to see that too but I think perhaps I need to give him a nudge first. He's quite a lot like you. That's probably why you two get on so well."

"We don't get on," I protest. "He's just useful. We argue all the time."

He pats me on the shoulder. "Lord Montserrat and you argue all the time as well."

"I don't really get on with him either," I mumble.

"Yeah, right." Connor's eyes twinkle. "Bo, I'm not telling you that relationships like that are easy. I'm telling you that they're worth it."

I stand staring at him for a moment. "When did you get to be so wise?"

He smirks. "I'm not just a pretty face. Now, come on. We've got some murderers to catch."

WE MEET up with O'Shea at the far end of Creed's street. Connor gives him an easy smile and touches his arm – and the answering look of delight from the daemon makes my heart squeeze. He coughs and looks at me.

"There are two coppers," he says. "They're parked several doors down."

"Are they obvious?"

He purses his lips. "Actually, they're doing well. Foxworthy must have come through and made sure that they're experienced. I knew they were there and it still took me a while to spot them."

A glow spreads through me. It's nice to be trusted – especially by the gruff policeman. "All the same," I say, "they're probably not going to hang around forever. Not with a complete absence of evidence."

"Then we do what any self-respecting private dick would do," he declares.

"I'm the only official PI around here," I remind him. "And I hope you're not thinking what I think you're thinking."

"I think I'm thinking exactly what you think I'm thinking."

I roll my eyes.

"Er, what?" Connor asks.

O'Shea turns to him, his old self starting to shine back through. "We go through their rubbish, of course."

I wrinkle my nose. "Wonderful."

"Won't the police stop us if we try to rummage through their bins?"

O'Shea beams, clearly proud to display his knowledge off to the younger man. "That they will. But if you look behind you, you will see the number fifty nine night bus."

Both of us twist our heads. "Perfect timing," I say as the bus trundles towards us. "All the same though, you should probably grab the bin bags, Connor. Both the police and the killers know who we are. If they see you, however, there's less chance they'll be suspicious."

O'Shea frowns. "He's human. We shouldn't put him in any danger."

Connor flashes him a smile. "Don't worry, Devlin. I've got this." He dashes to the other side of the road and waits for the bus to reach him. As soon as it does, he begins to jog down towards Creed's place. The bus should be just enough of a barrier to block the view of the watching police officers. It's unlikely that Creed will happen to look out of the window and spot him at the same time but it is still possible. Connor's going to have to be quick to minimise his chances of detection.

"That's amazing," O'Shea breathes, as we watch Connor make his way down.

"As long as he doesn't draw too much attention to himself," I add.

"No." He shakes his head. "That's not what I meant. He called me Devlin. It's amazing. The sound of my name on his lips…"

"Ask him out," I say suddenly. "When he gets back."

"What?" His eyes widen. "No, no, no. We're on a job right now. We need to stay focused. I'll do it, um, tomorrow. Maybe."

"Devlin," I say quietly, "just ask him."

Connor draws level with Creed's house. I hold my breath. He flips open the lid of the wheelie bin and snatches up a large green bag from inside before the bus passes by him completely. In less than three seconds he's already sprinting off, his waves of ginger hair flapping in the wind.

"Good boy," I say satisfied.

O'Shea smiles. "He's no boy."

It takes Connor at least ten minutes to circle back round the long way and meet up with us again. We find a quiet spot in the corner of a nearby park and sit down crosslegged.

"Well, at least they're environmentally friendly daemon killers," O'Shea says, reaching out for the biodegradable bag and untying it.

The reek of rotting food reaches all our nostrils. I recoil away.

"That's rank," Connor groans, wafting his hand in front of his face.

I delve inside my leather jacket and yank out a pair of gloves. "Tools of the trade," I tell the other two.

"Well, as you're the only one with those tools, you can be the one to do the rummaging," O'Shea says.

I walked into that one. I sigh and pull the gloves on then start picking my way through. There are several hardened – although not yet mouldy or stale - pizza crusts with traces of tomato sauce and basil clinging to the edges, screwed up utilities bills that I smooth out and put to one side, and numerous crushed beer cans.

"I guess they're not that environmentally friendly after all," I mutter, shaking off the drips of stale beer from my fingers. "They're certainly not recycling anyway."

I extricate several old batteries, crusted acid leaking from each one. I'm starting to get the impression that Creed is not particularly house proud. There's a carton of milk, dated to almost eight weeks ago, a half-eaten salad still in a throw-away plastic container, a ripped charity donation envelope which I place next to the bills and the contents of what appears to be several ashtrays, along with the source of the bad smell – some kind of slimy meat that should probably have been thrown out days ago. And there's pretty much nothing else.

I rock back on my heels and stare at the rubbish now strewn

across the grass in front of me. "So, boys, what does this tell us?"

"They like pizza and beer," Connor says solemnly. "If we knew where they ordered it from, we could find out when they've been at home with an obvious alibi."

"There's no pizza box. And we're trying to prove that they are the killers we're after. I'm not looking for an alibi."

"It's strange," O'Shea comments, "that they like pizza *and* salad."

I pick up the salad tub and frown at the contents. It's nothing exciting – just some leaves, shaved radishes, and squashed cherry tomatoes. "I guess Creed likes pizza and Wyatt likes salad," I shrug. "Or vice-versa. Both the leftovers are certainly a lot fresher than the milk and that meat anyway."

I peel open the salad lid and peer inside.

"Bo," O'Shea says drily, "I'm not sure that investigating lettuce is going to help us."

I'm about to tell him that the key to a good rubbish retrieval is considering each item in depth and linking it to the others to get a rounded picture of your target, when I suddenly pause. "That's not lettuce," I say slowly.

"Rocket, spinach, raddichio ... who cares?"

Connor shoots him an overly admiring glance. "You know your greens."

O'Shea blushes. "I like to eat healthily."

"So do I."

"Maybe ... maybe we could eat healthily together?" He coughs awkwardly. "There's a good restaurant not far from New Order that I go to sometimes."

In terms of charming date requests, this is hardly going to top the charts. For once, however, I'm really not interested. I reach in and pick out one of the darker leaves and hold it up to the moonlight. It looks more like a herb than something more substantial such as lettuce. I keep my eyes on it as if it's about to attack and sniff. Then I drop it and run.

"Bo!" O'Shea shouts. "What are you doing?"

I don't slow down. I sprint down Creed's street, ignoring the watching police officers. With my vampiric speed, I reach his front door and have it kicked open before they can even get out of their car. I burst inside, the fact that my entrance is unimpeded confirming my fears.

They're both in the kitchen, lying flat on their backs and staring up at the ceiling with unseeing eyes. One of them – for some reason I decide it's Wyatt – has vomit trickling down from his mouth. The other is clutching his stomach.

The plain-clothed police arrive about ten seconds later. "What are you doing?"

I stand up and turn away. They've been dead for at least a couple of hours. There's no point even attempting resuscitation.

"Creed and Wyatt are a dead end," I murmur, thinking of the strange white card that Drechlin handed me. "Ha. Ha."

The first policeman mutters something into his radio while the second looks at me in pure confusion. "How did you know?" she asks. "You're the Red Angel and I know you've got powers but how did you know they're dead?"

"Hemlock," I said simply. "They ate hemlock." The pizza sauce wasn't laced with basil and the salad leaves weren't bloody spinach. Creed and Wyatt had been poisoned and whoever had sent me the card was responsible.

CHAPTER 13

JUSTICE WILL BE SERVED

I'm forced to endure yet another round of questioning and statement giving. Forget the Red Angel. I should be re-named Key Witness Number One. Unfortunately at this rate, it doesn't seem likely that I'll ever get to give evidence in a courtroom. Not when there aren't any suspects to hand.

"I had to pull a few strings to get that stake-out set up," Foxworthy tells me when he finally appears. "Suddenly I'm being inundated with orders to investigate all this more thoroughly."

"You should send a team back to that warehouse. They had to have done something with the ear and the gun before they were arrested."

"It's already in motion." He gives me a shrewd glance. "Does it feel good to be right?"

I rub my forehead. "Not particularly. Even with the stake-out, they still died. The food could have come from anywhere. Maybe it was planted in Creed's own damn fridge."

"If we'd kept them locked up," Foxworthy says, "they'd still be alive."

I look away. "Yeah," I admit. "I guess they would have been.

Now all we're left with is some leftover food and two useless corpses who won't be able to tell us a bloody thing."

He lays his hand on my shoulder and squeezes, leaving without saying anything else. I'm not quite sure what else there is to say right now.

"I spend more time inside police stations now that I'm a super sleuth," O'Shea complains when I meet both him and Connor back outside again, "than I did when I was a criminal." He throws Connor a panicked look and hastily backtracks. "Not that I was an evil criminal or anything…"

I sigh. "Another lead down the damn drain. Let's get out of here."

"Actually," O'Shea whispers, "that's not true."

"What do you mean?"

He pulls out a crumpled piece of paper. I recognise it as the charity envelope from Creed's rubbish. O'Shea checks over his shoulder then waves it at me. "I took this," he says in a conspiratorial undertone, "before the police came and bagged everything up."

I'm confused. 'So?"

He tuts. "I must be the only super sleuth around here. What's the charity?"

I read it. "Checkers Children's Charity." I'm none the wiser.

"Bo, Bo, Bo." He shakes his head in dismay.

Connor thumps his arm. "He didn't get it either, actually. It was me who pointed it out."

"Pointed what out?"

"That charity. It's been out of business for decades. And…"

"Oh God," I breathe. "It's the one that was named in Tobias Renfrew's will."

"Should we tell the police?"

I think about it. Even with Foxworthy on my side and my reputation as heroine of the hour glaring all of us in the face, the police still let Creed and Wyatt go – and look what happened to them. I reckon we can probably manage this better on our own.

WE RACE back to New Order. It's time that only old-fashioned research can take over. We need to find out what Matt and Dahlia came up with as far as the pile of stolen books goes and it's imperative that we search out for as much information as we can possibly get on the charity. Rather than being holed up inside and poring over information, however, Matt is outside on the street throwing a ball to Kimchi.

He waves enthusiastically at the three of us. Kimchi isn't interested. The colourful ball clearly holds far more allure. I'd be offended if I didn't already know that it's one of those doggy contraptions that contains a hidden snack.

"Why aren't you inside?" I think about Dahlia and wonder just what in the hell is going on.

Matt shrugs. "They told me to take a walk."

My eyes narrow. They?

I swivel round and open the main door, then walk upstairs. I keep my footsteps light. More than half the staff are vampires so they'll all have preternatural hearing. It doesn't I mean I want to be obvious though.

When I reach New Order's door, my hand hovers over the doorknob for a moment. Then I push it open with a sudden heft. Arzo and Dahlia spring apart, him wheeling his chair back with such force that it clunks heavily against a desk. Sodding hell.

I give Arzo a look filled with dismay. It's not that his romantic return to Dahlia is unexpected, but I'm still so very disappointed. At least he has the grace to appear embarrassed.

"Bo," Dahlia begins, "it's not what you think."

I completely ignore her. "How could you?" I ask Arzo. "After everything she did to you? And you know she's probably still working for Medici."

"She's not, Bo."

"You don't know that!"

"He forced me to become a vampire against my will. I hate him," Dahlia interjects.

"You mean kind of like you forced Arzo to become a vampire?"

"I'm Sanguine," he says calmly.

"Only through a quirk of fate!" I shoot back. "We can't trust her."

Dahlia steps forward. "I understand why you feel like that, Bo..."

"Do you?" I snarl. "Really? Do you? I was there when your beloved husband was blown to smithereens. I know what he was like as a person and I know what you're like as a person. You're a user. A bitch who..."

"That's enough, Bo." Arzo's voice is quiet but it's filled with menace. His fists are clenched and there's raw anger written across his face.

"You're making a mistake," I ground out.

He meets my eyes. "It's my life," he says simply. "It's my mistake to make."

I falter. How can I argue with that? My shoulders droop and I reach inside my pocket, pulling out my white pebble. I stare at it sitting benignly in the palm of my hand, then curl my fingers round it and squeeze. "We need to work," I tell them both coldly. "You want to shag each other silly then get a damn room."

"It's really not like that."

I hold up my palm. "I don't care."

We all stand there for a moment, the uncomfortable silence growing and growing. Eventually, Arzo speaks up. "We will leave you to it then." He wheels himself out. Dahlia, white-faced, shoots me a nervous look and follows him. I sink down in the nearest chair and press the base of my palms into my eyes.

"Bo?" It's Matt.

I drop my hands and look up at him, smiling weakly at his worried expression. "It's alright," I tell him. "Everything's alright."

"They deserve a chance to be happy."

"She can't be trusted." I shake my head. "I don't know why he can't see that."

"Redemption should always be possible. For everyone."

I bite my bottom lip so hard I draw blood. "Maybe you're right. It is the premise behind all the Families' recruitment policies, isn't it?" I sigh heavily. "Maybe I'm the bitch."

He takes my hand and gives it a reassuring squeeze. "You're just worried about your friend. He'll be fine though. Arzo can look after himself. Besides, Dahlia came up with the goods with that stuff you wanted."

I swallow down the salty tang. "The books?"

Matt nods. "The bathroom suite in the murder room is the original one. That's not what's interesting though." He beams at me. "You'll like this."

He pulls over a chair and sits next to me. Connor and O'Shea tiptoe into the room. I can't help noticing that they're standing very close to each other. I try to smile at them both and beckon them over.

Opening three of the books to bookmarked pages, Matt points to the first highlighted area. "Here."

"'Although Tobias Renfrew never married, he was in a relationship at the time of his disappearance,'" I read aloud. "I'd never heard that before. Who was she?"

Matt grins. "Look here."

I glance over. It's a black and white photo from a restaurant. Renfrew is sitting across from a well dressed human woman, holding her fingers across the table. The caption simply reads 'Tobias Renfrew and companion'. It's dated three days before his disappearance.

"And this one," Matt says.

It's a forensic list from the murder scene. My eyes follow his finger where I read the highlighted area. "One of the victims had a birth mark on their arm."

"Check the photo again."

I flick back. Whoever the mysterious woman is, the short sleeved dress is displaying enough skin to reveal the splodge of a long thin mark. "He killed his own girlfriend?"

"Or someone killed her for him."

We all look at each other. "Why would someone do that?" Connor asks.

"That's easy," O'Shea shrugs. "Money."

I agree. "If he was seriously involved with someone else, then the beneficiaries of his will would be the most likely to be pissed off."

"Because a serious relationship might mean he'd change the terms of the will in her favour."

Connor's eyes are wide. "And the original beneficiaries were..."

"Checkers Children's Charity," I finish.

Every one of us absorbs the information quietly.

"We need to find who used to work for them and where they are now," I finally say.

There are nods all round. "Let's do it."

Kimchi appears in the doorway, the now somewhat mangled ball in his mouth. He lets it drop to the floor and lets out a bark, wagging his tail. In that moment, I think we all feel the same frisson of excitement. We might actually be getting somewhere.

In less than an hour we have seven names. Five triber daemons and two humans who were Trustees of the charity. Three of them are already dead – old age, cancer and a car accident respectively. Of the remaining four, one emigrated to Australia. The others, helpfully, still live in London. We're just about to start confirming their addresses when Lars, the Gully representative, lopes in.

"What are you guys up to?"

We exchange glances. In theory we're all part of the same team. He works for New Order now just like us. But the investigation into Tobias Renfrew and the severed ears isn't really a vampire matter. Somehow, by dint of silent agreement, we all decide to play dumb. It's not a matter of trust – Lars isn't Dahlia. I guess it's more because we are all finding it hard to believe that we have some actual leads and we don't want to share them. Or maybe it's because we're a tight-knit little group that traditional bloodguzzlers like Lars can never quite be a part of. Either way, there's considerable humming and hawing from everyone. Fortunately, Lars is more than keen to talk about his night tracking down the bastards who killed Bergman Stuart to notice.

"So I've spent every night checking all their known acquaintances," he says, "and either no-one knows or no-one's talking."

I feel a jolt of guilt for not doing more, even though it's at my grandfather's behest. "They obviously spent a lot of time at that nightclub," I say to him, doing what I can to be helpful. "Maybe you need to check out other similar clubs."

"That'll be like finding a needle in a haystack," he complains. "Do you know how many clubs there are in this damn city?"

"Good investigating involves a lot of legwork." I hope I don't sound too patronising. After my confrontation with Arzo and Dahlia, I don't want to piss off anyone else. I'm still smarting from the implication that I was trying to tell Arzo how to live his life. "X never marks the spot. You need to go searching."

He grumbles slightly but he doesn't appear particularly offended. "By the way," he tells me, "I think those journalists are back again."

I frown. "Really? I thought they'd gotten tired of hanging around out here."

Lars shrugs. "There is a mysterious looking car outside. When I passed it, a guy got out and asked me about you."

I sigh inwardly. Being followed around isn't really what I need right now. If I'm going to visit the high and mighty of Checkers Children's Charity tomorrow to find out whether they're responsible for the brutal murder of at least five people, it's going to be difficult to get them to talk with half the city's press in tow behind me. I can disguise myself enough to move around the streets but if I have to sneak out in the first place, I'm just asking for trouble. It'll be easier if they're not hanging around and waiting for me. Rolling my eyes, I mutter to everyone that I'm going to deal with them and head out.

I spot the car almost immediately. It's black and unshowy but it seems remarkably expensive looking for a journalist. I squint my eyes, trying to work out whether there's anyone inside or not, when a dark figure steps from the shadows.

"You know, Bo, sometimes X does mark the spot."

I glare at the Kakos daemon. He's wearing his smoothly

handsome human glamour. I know what lurks underneath his skin though. "What do you want?"

"Oh," he drawls, "come, come. Surely you can be more welcoming than that? After all, I've been a good friend to you. More than a friend, in fact. I'm like the Max Clifford of your little world."

"I didn't ask you to involve yourself," I hiss.

X smiles. "How many times have you come to me for help in the past? I should think you'd be more grateful."

"Leave me alone." I turn on my heel, ready to walk back inside.

"You still owe me a favour," he says. His voice is casual but I still stiffen.

I slowly turn. "You're coming to collect?"

He lifts up a shoulder. "In a manner of speaking."

"I'm kind of busy right now. Can it wait a few days?"

"You mean your ridiculous Renfrew crusade? Who cares? It's all ancient history now." There's a gleam in his eyes that suggests he thinks entirely the opposite to what he's saying. I feel my gut tighten. X's mind-reading skills mean that he knows far more than he ought to. I'm not going to ask him for help again though. I've damned myself enough as it is by getting involved with him at all. "Come with me, Bo," he says smoothly, gesturing towards the car. "We have much to discuss. Renfrew's waited this long. A few more hours won't hurt."

Every atom in my body is screaming at me to say no. I should walk – no, run – away. But as much as I'd like to forget, I do owe X. In return for not slaughtering Rogu3 or Connor or anyone else smart enough to realise that I turned Rogu3 into a vampire and back again, X made me promise to fulfil one favour. I'm a woman of my word. And if I tried to make a dash for it, he'd probably rip out my heart.

"Good girl," he says, obviously reading my mind.

I get into the passenger seat. The moment X also gets in and closes the door, the tinted windows concealing him from the rest of the world, he lets out a tiny moan and cricks his neck. His glamour vanishes, revealing the twisting tattoos and ever-present aura of danger of the daemon below.

"That feels so good!" he exclaims. "It's so good to be free, you know? To live your life the way you want to live it."

My eyes narrow. Had he been listening in to what happened with Arzo and Dahlia too?

"No," he tells me. "As surprising as it may seem to you, I don't spend my life running around after you and eavesdropping." I almost snort. He could have fooled me. "But," he continues, "it's screaming out from your conscience. You, Bo Blackman, feel bad about it."

I shift in my seat. I really don't need the inner workings of my mind to be revealed to me. "Should I trust Dahlia?"

X laughs. "How should I know? I've not met the woman."

"You know of her though. Her husband worked for you."

He puts the car into gear and drives off. "Water under the bridge now. If you'd like, I can go after her and…"

"No." My voice is flat. "It's fine."

He laughs again. "As you wish."

I fold my arms and stare resolutely ahead. "Where are we going?"

"Not far."

"Because the others back at New Order will wonder where I've gone. And it'll be daylight soon."

"Don't worry, little Bo. I'll have you back and tucked safely up in bed before the sun rises." There's such amusement in his tone that I look away and button up my lips. I'm not going head to head with X, not even with banter. Unfortunately, my refusal to engage him any further only seems to amuse him even more.

At least he was right when he said we weren't going far. We

pull up outside a remarkably familiar building. Wary, I stay where I am. I've done enough breaking and entering as it is lately.

X gets out and walks round to my side, opening the door and giving me a little bow. "I had no idea you were such a lady," he comments. "It's just as well I chose this location for our ... rendezvous."

"I am not breaking into Harrod's in the middle of the goddamn night."

His mouth crooks up. "Don't worry," he says in a confidential tone, "I've got the keys. Follow me."

Against all my better judgment I step heavily out of the car. He's already at the door. "Aren't you worried about CCTV?" I ask. "You're still you."

X chuckles. "I'm touched that you're so concerned about me." He opens the door with a flourish and bows again. "Ladies first."

I shake my head. "I'm not going in there."

"It's fine." His eyes glitter. "I've cleared it with the owner." When I don't move a muscle, he raises up his eyebrows. "If you don't come inside, then you won't get your present."

Oh God. Nausea squirms in my belly. This could be really bad.

"You'll like it, Bo." He grins broadly. "I promise."

I close my eyes briefly, dreading to imagine what's waiting for me. Up until the events at the television studio, I'd come to feel an odd amity with the daemon despite my natural terror of him. Now my initial instinct to run away screaming is all I can think about. With a deep sense of foreboding, I enter the famous store. X closes the door behind us and points ahead, before overtaking to show me the way.

He leads me to the food hall. He is obviously well aware of my fear because he seems to be taking perverse pleasure in goading me as much as possible. "I put your present here," he says, "because I wanted to keep them fresh."

Them? I swallow and stop in my tracks. "Listen, X," I say, painfully aware of the tremor in my voice, "I know I owe you. Believe me, I'm not about to forget. But you promised the favour wouldn't involve anything illegal. I appreciate that you thought killing Marcus Lanscombe was a good thing to do but there were avenues that could have been explored before that. The police…"

"The police are impotent. As you very well know." X shrugs, a languid motion that makes his opinion all the more obvious. "Besides, isn't legality a pointless argument? Vampires are above the law."

"It's not as simple as that," I answer stiffly. "We don't answer to human law but we have very strict laws of our own. And murder, kidnapping, whatever… they're dealt with far more severely than the humans ever care to consider."

"When it suits the Families' purposes." He traces his fingernail down a nearby display of caviar, tapping against various tins as if attempting to ascertain their quality. "They'd never have bothered themselves with Lanscome, would they?"

"Because no-one knew about him!"

"No-one cared to find out." He cocks his head and eyes me. "Favour or no favour, Bo – I won't make you do anything you don't want to."

I'm not quite sure what new trick this is. "X…"

"It's not a trick." He winks. "Trust me."

Like that's about to happen. I stare at the darkened shelves. I can't smell any blood. Not yet, anyway. "Fine."

X smiles as if my answer is what he'd expected all along. I take a deep breath and step forward.

"Towards the back. Keep going straight ahead. When you reach the Stilton, you'll know you've gone too far."

I do what I'm told. For some reason, X hangs back. I wonder how far his mind reading extends to. I'm guessing at least the length of the hall. I reach behind my neck and massage my shoulders. There's a stiff knot of tension. I knead it carefully, trying to work it out. It's a pointless effort. The deeper I go into the food hall, the more tense I become. I scan the darkness. Nothing's moving. Nothing's there. Perhaps it's just a practical joke. Any minute now I'll slip on a banana skin, X will laugh uproariously and we can all go home.

That's when I hear the moan. It's faint and muffled but it's definitely a moan. I wince and gingerly turn in its direction, past one shelf, then another. There's a scraping sound and an odd judder. Shit. I feel like I'm trapped in a horror film. I pause at an intersection, chocolate on one side and coffee on another. Then I peer round. Three seated shapes greet me. I blink and jerk back. Then I peer round again. My fangs elongate. It's not a conscious action, however. It must be a result of the stress. I still can't see who the people are. If X is setting me up again, I'm going to kill him. Or at the very least have strict words with him.

I shuffle forward. The flashing red of a nearby security camera is throwing shadows across the three people's faces. Who the sodding hell are they? The one on the left moans again. His nearest partner flinches and swings his head round as if to shush him. The contours of his face are momentarily displayed. I recognise him. It's the guy O'Shea shagged – the one who had the ear that started all this in the first place.

Leaping over, I grab his chin and tilt it up, just to be sure. "You," I hiss, "I know you."

His mouth is taped shut but the snarl in his eyes is enough of an answer. I stare at the other two. I know them too. They're the bastards who went to Rogu3's school. The ones who tried to kill him. They tried to gun down a kid for next to reason. I can't help myself. I throw a punch, smashing the first one in the face. His head snaps backwards. He's obviously tied to the chair. He can't fight back.

My breath is coming in short bursts. I do what I can to control and walk three steps back, keeping my eyes trained on them. I fumble for the white pebble. The instant I touch it, I feel better. It doesn't stop me from wanting to hurt these pricks very badly. But it helps me to remember that's not the way things should be done.

"You should have stayed in Venezuela, boys," I spit.

The one on the right has a muscle near his eye that's twitching furiously. Making a quick decision, I reach over and rip off the tape.

He bares his teeth. "Don't you think we wanted to?"

X. I spin round but the Kakos daemon is still nowhere to be seen. I wonder if this means that I owe him yet another favour now. It doesn't seem possible that this particular scenario helps him. I push away my worries about whatever game he might be playing and turn back.

"Why? Why did you do it? Why attack the Agathos Court? Why try to kill so many people?"

The man coughs, a dribble of spittle escaping his mouth. "Can I have some water first?"

I think about it. "No," I say finally, "tell me first."

I can see him mulling it over. "If I tell you, then I'm dead."

I tilt up my chin. "You're dead anyway."

"Nah, you're just a little girl. You won't hurt me."

I bare my fangs, leaning close into his pulsating jugular. "Guess again." The answering flicker of fear in his eyes is enough for now. I lick my lips, making a show of it. "You probably don't taste very nice," I muse. I lift up a shoulder. "I don't need to hurt you though. Back there, lurking in the darkness is the Kakos daemon who brought you here. He can read your mind. And he can hurt you a lot more than I can."

Shadows flit across his face. He knows I'm telling the truth. "We were given a lot of money," he says. "A lot of money to kill one little daemon, take his ear and deliver it to a specified address."

I hold my breath. "Who? Who gave you the money?"

He meets my eyes. "I have no idea." Damn it. He's telling the truth.

"How could not know?" I hiss.

"We were contacted anonymously through a broker. After that, all our communications happened through a series of dead drops."

"The broker? Where's he now?"

He smiles coldly. "The broker is broken. Chopped up into little pieces."

"You did that?"

"No."

One thing he is lying about is the broker. His eyes give him away. He and his damn buddies probably gutted him, hoping that torture would reveal who their employer was. I circle round him, clenching and unclenching my fists. He retains a stiff, almost military straight posture and there's defiance still flickering in his eyes. "Once you lost the ear, why go to so much trouble to get it back? Why try and kill so many?"

He sighs as if it's a stupid question. "Who cares?"

I harden my voice. "I care."

"There were going to be others. Three others. We couldn't advertise what we were doing because we couldn't allow them to be spooked and run off before we could kill them too. If we deviated from protocol, we knew our lives would also be forfeit."

"Which others? Who were they?" I demand.

He tries to shrug but his bonds prevent him from completing the movement. "I don't know. We were only going to be given each name separately. Once one contract had been fulfilled we were going to do the next one." His expression turns wistful. "We only managed the one."

I really want to hurt him very, very badly. Instead, I keep my tone even and my arms by my sides. "Whose ear was it?"

"Some woman. Madeline Gregory."

"And what was the address? The one you were supposed to deliver her ear to?"

He rolls his eyes. "So many questions. Does it really matter?" I don't deign to give him an answer. I simply stand in front of him and put my hands on my hips. He sighs again. "12 Forest Avenue."

I file it away. Now we're getting somewhere.

"Are we done now?" he asks.

I start to nod, then change my mind. "The money," I say slowly, "how much was it?"

He smirks. "It wasn't a wad of unmarked notes, if that's what you're thinking. It was gold. Three shiny gold bars. One for each of us."

It's all connected. I knew it. When these idiots disappeared from the scene, the mastermind behind all this simply hired more – Creed and Wyatt. When they messed up, they were summarily dispatched. Whoever is doing all this is desperate to keep their identity a secret. Is it a simple case of revenge or is there more to it?

"Tell me about Checkers."

He gives me a confused look. "Who?"

I look into his eyes, ascertaining the truth. "Never mind," I mutter.

All three of the captive daemons abruptly stiffen as their

eyes fall on something behind me. There's no mistaking their sudden fear.

"Are you done now?" X asks smoothly.

"I guess. I don't know." I turn and look at him. "Why? Why did you do this?"

He smiles. "I thought you'd appreciate the opportunity to take your revenge."

I hold the image of my pebble in my mind's eye. "It's not revenge, I want," I tell him. "It's justice."

X laughs softly. "One and the same, Bo."

"Was he telling the truth?"

He inclines his head. "He was. For the most part anyway. Poor Madeline. He was the one to take her ear, you know. Post-mortem." He points to the man in the middle. "He put the ruby in." He moves his hand to the last one. "And he let your little daemon friend steal it away before it could be delivered. Don't you think they deserve to be hurt?"

I stare at the three of them. They're bound and helpless but the malevolence and spite in their eyes remains.

"Think of Rogu3," X whispers. "What they tried to do to him. He's just a child."

"You brought them here."

His black eyes gleam and his tattoos twist under the dim light, writhing like inky snakes. "I have ... power abroad."

"Why have you done this?" I ask, shaking my head in confusion.

He answers me with another question. "Don't they deserve to die? Shouldn't they suffer for what they did? They're terrorists, Bo. Evil."

I turn away. "Call the police."

"You must possess unshakeable faith in the justice system."

"It's the right thing to do."

X steps up close, leaning in. "Is it?"

I swallow hard, reaching into my pocket and taking out my little white stone. I stare at it lying there in my palm, small and innocuous.

"You're not ready yet," X says. There's no disappointment in his voice. He says it as if he's merely stating a fact. "You will be."

I curl my fingers round the stone and meet his steady gaze. "Why?" I ask again. "Why have you done this?"

"I want a superhero. A dark avenging angel to sweep the streets of crime." He twinkles with entirely misplaced humour.

"You can do that all on your own. You don't need me."

"I'm a Kakos daemon." For the first time there's a trace of real emotion in his face. It hints at deep-seated bitterness. "No matter how hard I try or what I'll do, I'll always be the boogeyman."

"That's kind of what happens when you murder people live on television!"

"Oh," he tuts, "poor maligned Marcus Lanscombe." He glances down at me. "That girl wasn't the only one, you know." I repress a shudder and look away. X laughs softly.

"I still don't understand. Are you offering me a job in executions?"

"No. I'm offering you the opportunity to rid the world of evil. The public are already behind you. You'll become the power in London. The army, the police, the secret service all combined into one. Except you'll do more good than all of them put together."

"That's why you did that at the television studio?"

"You were already a hero. I simply made you a star along with it."

I press my fingers against my temples. My head is pounding. "Why do you want the streets cleared of criminals?"

"The entertainment value alone would be worth it."

I give him a narrow-eyed look. "Bullshit."

"We're not the bad guys you all think we are. You know the Families are responsible for pinning a vast amount of murders on us. You know I've been working to help the Agathos Court. I've even encouraged Streets of Fire to develop their charity work."

"You're all heart."

"They get in my way," he says in an undertone. "The petty criminals. The self-serving humans and the squabbling tribers. I want to concentrate on my own interests. I could rip the hearts out of every idiot I come across but that will only create an atmosphere of fear. That's not going to help me. A superhero working for the powers of good, however, will unite the country."

I glance back at the trussed up trio. "We're not in a comic book, X. Vigilantism isn't heroic. It's reckless and stupid."

"As I said, you're not ready yet."

"I will never be ready. The law is there for a reason."

He laughs again. "And Bo Blackman never ever breaks the law."

I ignore his jibe. "What are you going to do with them?"

"If you're not going to get involved, then it's got nothing to do with you."

"X..."

He grins. "I'll do as you ask, of course. I'll let the police handle them." He raises his eyebrows mockingly. "Justice will be served."

CHAPTER 14

MOMENTOUS DECISIONS

I pace around my flat. Kimchi watches me from the sofa, his head on his paws and his eyes large and expressive. I stop occasionally to stroke his ears but even his furry friendliness doesn't ease my frustration. Dawn is approaching so there's nothing I can do. I'm too amped up to sleep. I keep thinking of the cold, hard look in all three of the daemons' eyes. My heart is telling me that I should have just killed them and been done with it. My head reminds me that I did the right thing by walking away. X doesn't need a hero to clean up the streets for him; he needs a sodding conscience.

I force him out of my head and focus on what I know. Four potential victims. The Harrods three are responsible for one. Creed and Wyatt, based on their actions and conversation at the Renfrew mansion, at least two. That means there might be one person left. One person who might end up ear-less and in a bodybag. I need to find out who that is. I have my suspicions but I want to confirm them first. I can't do anything, however, until night falls again.

I press my lips together. Actually, that's not true - there is one thing I can do. I pick up the phone and slowly dial.

It doesn't take Michael long to arrive. When he knocks on my door, my stomach lurches. I still manage to smile when I beckon him in, however. He steps inside, motioning to Kimchi to stay put, he gives me a long measured look.

"What's wrong, Bo?" he asks finally.

I think of O'Shea. "I like it when you say that."

Michael's brow furrows. "Say what?"

I stare at my feet. "My name."

"Bo." He steps over to me, his fingers reaching under my chin and tilting it up so I'm forced to meet his eyes. "What's happened?"

I shrug awkwardly. "Everything. Nothing." I shake my head. "I don't know."

He watches me for a moment, then reaches out and draws me into a tight hug. I press my face against his chest and inhale deeply. His scent is heavy and masculine. Standing here, with Michael wrapped around me, I feel safe and secure.

"All the criminals you take in," I mumble, my voice muffled, "the ones you recruit into the Family and rehabilitate, aren't they bad people who deserve punishment?"

He releases me slowly, pulling back enough to gaze down at me. "We've been through this. They've already served their time. They deserve a second chance."

"But what about their victims? And their families? Wouldn't they want revenge?"

"There's no such thing," he tells me, shaking his head. "Revenge implies satisfaction and closure. Getting your own back doesn't actually make you feel any better. It just makes you feel even more empty. Forgiveness is a lot harder to stomach but it will heal your soul."

"Arzo has forgiven Dahlia. She ruined his life."

The corner of his mouth crooks up. "He's still in love with

her," he says simply. 'And love will beat out hate any day of the week."

I'm not convinced. "Even when that hate is deserved?"

Michael pulls out his phone. "Look. There were seven murders across the city yesterday. And you know what news is trending?"

"What?" I ask, scanning the screen.

"Us," he tells me. "Our kiss. The world wants love and happiness and peace. Not hatred and murder."

I stare at the photo of myself bent down, my lips firmly planted on his. "That's not even real though. We were faking it for the cameras."

"Were we?" His voice is quiet. He's holding himself back from me but there's still a silent plea in his eyes.

I bite my lip. "That was all arranged thanks to my grandfather." I half snort. "He's not much of a pimp."

"It was my idea."

My mouth goes dry. "Was it? Because you're so worried about your image?"

He laughs slightly. "Do you really think I would be? The Families have been in a bad place, sure, but it's happened before. People will come around. They always do."

"So why did you want us to play pretend?"

He takes my hands and squeezes them. "You know why."

I don't immediately answer. When I do, there's a hard lump in my throat. "What if what we feel is only because you turned me? You said there would be an attraction between us because of that. You said…"

He places his index finger across my lips. "I wanted you before that." I start and he grins at me. "Who wouldn't want a bolshy little dwarf who thought she had the power to take on a vampire Lord in an enclosed space?"

He's referring to the first time we met, in Arzo's hospital

room. "I wasn't trying to take you on," I tell him, " I was trying to bloody escape." I frown. "And I'm not a dwarf."

Michael reaches out and takes a tendril of my hair, running it through his fingers. "You're an Amazon."

I draw back, folding my arms. There's a flash of hurt in his expression. I'm not quite sure what I'm trying to protect myself from but I still feel afraid. "If you knew that there was a human, a rich human, who was doing something illegal, then would you do something to stop him?"

"It might depend on the issue at hand. If we're talking not paying his TV license…"

I interrupt. "Marcus Lanscome."

Michael stills. "The girl in his dressing room."

"There was more than one."

He nods. "So I've heard."

"If you knew," I repeat, "would you have done something? Or would you have invited him into the Family fold so he could seek redemption?"

"You know recruitment doesn't work like that."

"Please, Michael." My voice is strained. "What would you have done?"

"I like it when you say my name too," he says quietly. He sighs and rakes a hand through his hair. "If I'd known, honestly, I'd have wanted to rip his throat out. But that's not what I'd have done. He's a human so I'd have called the human police."

"Honestly?"

He nods. "Bo, I don't know what's going with you. If you don't want to tell me, then that's alright. Things have been hard for you. You didn't want to be a vampire. The PTSD, the blood aversion…"

"I'm past all that," I interrupt.

"I'm glad. But know that I will wait. I will wait until you're ready for me." He gestures between us. "Ready for this. You keep searching for reasons to stay away from me, whether it's because of your recruitment and how I turned you, or because you saw some stupid old photo of me and jumped to conclusions, or because of a conflict with new Order. They're just excuses and that's okay. Because I will wait until you change your mind. I know it will be worth it. If you want to stop the public dates, then that's fine. But, Bo," he says, placing a faint emphasis on my name, "I'm not going anywhere. No matter what you do or what you say."

I know in that instant what I need to do. It's been there all along and I've shied away from it. I take a shaky breath and shake my head. "No. Don't wait."

"Bo…"

"Shh. I don't want you to wait. I don't want to wait. I'm afraid, Michael. But I don't have any more excuses and I don't want to waste any more time."

He doesn't move a muscle. His body is still and frozen like a statue and eyes are fixed on mine. "Are you sure about this?"

I don't answer him. Instead I take one little step forward. I stand up on my tiptoes and press my lips against his. For a moment he doesn't react, then he groans and grabs my waist. He deepens the kiss. I coil my arms round his neck and sink against him. His fingers dance up my body, his movements light and wary, as if he's afraid I'll suddenly change my mind. I pull back, breathing hard. Michael stares at me. I smile and reach out to his pristine white shirt, undoing first one button then another. I run my fingers up his bared chest and he sucks in a breath. He shrugs out of his jacket while I unbuckle his belt.

"I want you to be mine," I whisper.

His eyes glitter. "Always."

WE LIE TOGETHER ENTWINED in damp sheets. His leg is hooked over mine and he's playing with my hair. I gaze up at the ceiling and, for the first time in a long time, feel genuinely at peace and content. Kimchi whines faintly from the other room.

Michael grins. It's a fully self-satisfied expression. "We should let him in."

"He'll only attack you," I murmur.

"Why would he do that?"

"Because you look just like the cat that got the cream."

His thumb traces a lazy circle round my nipple. "You were the one who was purring."

I reach down, my fingers trailing from his flat stomach to his groin. A deep grumble sounds from his chest and I laugh. "Who's purring now then?"

"Minx." He leans over and kisses me, snatching away my breath yet again. "Tell me," he murmurs, "what's changed your mind? You were so desperate to keep yourself away from me before."

I consider. "O'Shea and Connor, I suppose."

His face takes on an incredulous expression. "Devlin O'Shea?"

I giggle. "More Connor, really. He made me see the light."

"Well," Michael growled, "from now on, I only want you to see me."

"I already know you're the jealous type," I tease.

"Moi? I should think, Bo Blackman, that you're the jealous one around here."

I splutter. "I am not!"

He smiles wickedly. "Why were you so annoyed that I took you to La Maison then?"

The phone rings. I stick my tongue out at him. "Saved by the bell."

He punches me lightly on the arm. "I'll get it." He reaches

across me and picks it up. "Hello," he drawls, his eyes on me, "you've reached Bo Blackman."

His action and words are deliberate. He's staking his claim and, oddly, I don't mind. When his face shutters, however, I realise with a sinking sensation who is on the other line.

"D'Argneau."

Michael's jaw tenses. "Do you want to talk to him?"

I already know what the lawyer is going to tell me. I want to hear it from his own lips, however. I nod and take the phone, doing what I can to avoid the suddenly furious expression glittering in Michael's dark eyes.

"This is Bo."

"Well, well, well! This is a turn up for the books," D'Argneau says, evidently enjoying himself. "No wonder you didn't want to take up with me where we left off."

"Get to the point, Harry."

"There's no need to be snippy. I'm doing you a favour. I didn't have to call you."

"Tell me."

"I'm only doing this because you were so annoyed last time..."

Michael stands up, extricating himself from the bedsheet and pulling on his boxers.

I hiss in annoyance. "D'Argneau, spit it out."

"I have three new clients."

I close my eyes briefly. Unfortunately I'd been right. "Let me guess. They've got Venezuelan stamps in their passports."

I watch as Michael walks out of the bedroom to a suddenly delighted Kimchi. Harry D'Argneau sounds pretty delighted too. "You already know! Yes, I now represent all three of them and, between the two of us," he says in a conspiratorial tone, "I think I can get them all off by pleading self-defence."

"Really." My voice is flat.

"Really! A mysterious puppet master pulling their strings and forcing them to do his bidding … it's perfect."

"You've got no evidence of this person, even if he does exist."

"Yes, Bo, I do. I've got three gold bars and a handwritten note."

I pinch the bridge of my nose. Goddamnit.

I pull on some clothes and head out. Michael, having retrieved his discarded – and now rather rumpled – suit from the floor, has also dressed. Unfortunately for him there's now obvious evidence of Kimchi's attentions. Half of the suit jacket appears to be in shreds. Despite my anger at D'Argneau, I find it hard not to smirk.

"Laugh it up," he grimaces, adjusting the ragged cuffs. "What did he want?" His tone is casual but there's no denying the importance he's placing on the question.

"He was calling to tell me that he has three new clients." I take a deep breath. "Recently returned from Venezuela."

Michael's eyes fly to mine. "You mean…"

I nod. "Yes. The same ones who tried to kill Rogu3 and who attacked the Agathos Court."

"Why on earth did they return?" He's naturally flabbergasted. "They were safe in Venezuela. It doesn't make any sense."

Unable to tell him about X and his intervention for fear of reprisal, I hedge. "It does seem like a silly thing for them to have done."

Michael isn't easily fooled. "What aren't you telling me?"

"Nothing. There's nothing else."

A muscle twitches in his cheek. "You forget that I know you." He smiles slightly. "Inside and out."

I swallow. "D'Argneau thinks he can get them off by pleading self-defence."

He shakes his head. "That's not it, although that's bad enough on its own. There's something else, Bo."

"No," I lie, "there's not."

A faint snarl crosses his features. "After all this. After everything that just happened between us, you still don't trust me."

My eyes widen, alarmed. "I do!"

"Then what else is going on here?" he inquires.

"I..." Damn it. X will kill him if I so much as hint at his existence, let alone his interference. I falter.

Michael scowls. "I have to go," he says shortly. "I've got work to do."

I ball up my fists. Bloody hell. This isn't how it's supposed to go. "Can I call you later?"

His expression softens. "Do." He twists round and walks out, his wrecked suit flapping behind him.

Both Kimchi and I watch him go, equally mournful. I sigh loudly. "Brilliant. Just sodding brilliant." I look at the dog. "Come on," I say, "we've got to get to Forest Avenue. I'm about to find exactly what the hell has been going on."

Kimchi barks in response.

We jog down the stairs, passing by the door to New Order. I glance in, spotting Arzo and Dahlia sickeningly sitting together in the corner. Lars and the other new Family reps are in a huddle and my grandfather's door is open. With no sign of Connor or Matt, however, I decide not to waste any time and head straight out. Chance would be a fine thing.

"Bo!" There's no mistaking my grandfather's gruff tone. How on earth he managed to spot me from behind the wall, I have no idea. The man must have X-ray vision.

I jerk back. "I've got to go," I call back. "I've got things to do."

"Can you come here please?"

I mutter a curse under my breath and step into the office,

nodding out brief and terse acknowledgments to everyone there.

"I said," I repeat, walking into my grandfather's room, "that I've got things to do. They're important and I really don't want to waste any time."

"There's something else you need to do first." He gestures at a woman sitting in front of him.

I look over. Even though I've never met her before, I know instantly who she is. The apple doesn't fall far from the tree.

"Hello, Ms. Blackman," she says nervously, wiping her hand on her skirt and holding it out. "I'm Trudy Jones. Alistair's mum." She bites her lip. "Rogu3."

"I know who you are," I say softly. I take her hand and shaking it. Her grip is limp. "Is something wrong? Is Rogu3, I mean Alistair, okay?"

She looks to my grandfather for reassurance. "Don't worry, Mrs. Jones. She won't bite."

I shoot him a look at that comment but he just frowns at me. "I'm a new vampire," I tell her, "but I'm in control. I only drink from willing..." I almost say victims, "people," I finish.

She nods, although the trace of fear in her eyes doesn't entirely vanish. "Alistair speaks very highly of you. And of course I've seen you on television and in the papers. You're very brave."

"I'm not," I answer honestly. "What and we do for you?" She blinks several times and I realise that she's holding back tears. Taut with worry, I reach out and squeeze her shoulder. "What is it?"

"He's not doing very well," she bursts out. "He doesn't sleep at night. We took his computers away and tried to stop him from continuing with the ... stuff he'd been doing before." She seems unable to say the word 'hacking'. "He's been to counsellors. He won't come round though. He won't talk to us and he won't talk to his friends. His grades are dropping and I know he's playing truant."

My heart goes out to her. Dealing with teenagers isn't easy. Dealing with extraordinarily intelligent teenagers who've been through needless traumatic experiences must be even worse. "Is there something I can do?"

She takes a moment to compose herself. "Yes. Yes, you can come and talk to him."

I'm startled. "Me? I'm not sure I'm the best person."

"You are. You saved his life even though you are a…"

"Bloodguzzler?"

She nods.

"I'd been instructed to stay away," I remind her gently. Her husband had called New Order not long after Rogu3 got out of hospital. He'd made his feelings pretty clear.

"I know. I'm sorry. But now you're the Red Angel. You're a hero. You saved those people at the television studio. My husband's come around. And," she bites her lip again, "Alistair needs you."

I'm desperate to get to Forest Avenue. But this is Rogu3. I'd do just about anything for that kid. I nod. "I'll head over straight away."

CHAPTER 15
GOING ROGUE

There's something not quite right about entering Rogu3's house via the shiny front door and with his own mother leading the way. Despite his age, I'd always felt like we were equals. Coming in like this and sitting down on the spotless sofa with a cup of tea and a biscuit, sets me apart from him. It screams that I'm an adult and he's a mere child, instead of inept private detective and elite computer hacker.

"You gave her tea?" Rogu3's father inquires.

Trudy's hand flies to her mouth. "Oh, I'm so sorry. You probably don't drink tea." She flushes, fumbling with her own cup and setting it down on the table. A mixture of emotions flit across her face, then she pulls up her sleeve and awkwardly holds out her arm. "Here. Drink me."

I wince. "That's alright. Tea is fine." I take a sip to illustrate that very fact. "Mmm. It's delicious. Thank you."

We falter into an awkward silence, no-one quite meeting anyone else's eyes. It occurs to me how strange my life has become. From criminal activity to a job offer from a Kakos daemon to sitting here in suburbia and failing to make small talk.

Trudy stands up again, smoothing her hands down her dress. "I'll go and get Alistair."

I force out a smile and nod. Both her husband and I watch her leave. The instant the door closes behind her, he turns to me. There's a hard, angry slant to his mouth. "Just so you know, this wasn't my idea."

"Okay," I say quietly.

"I don't want him to get hurt. He's a good kid who's gotten mixed up with the wrong crowd." There's no mistaking which 'crowd' he's referring to.

"Okay."

"I mean," he balls up his fists, "what's a grown woman doing hanging around with a teenager anyway?"

I want to tell him that I wasn't hanging around Rogu3. That he's the best damn hacker in the city who's not the naïve little boy his father seems to think. Instead I bite my tongue and dip my head, acknowledging his words without giving him an answer.

"I don't care if you're a vampire," he continues, "if you do anything to harm a hair on his head ever again, I will kill you."

He obviously cares for Rogu3 a great deal. Rogu3 himself had been somewhat reticent on the subject of his parents but I'm sure the feeling is reciprocated. I think of my own father. There's something about parent-child relationships that can never be replicated, no matter how hard you try. The mutual need to protect each other from the harsh realities of the world, I suppose. A distant ache appears in my chest at the knowledge I'll never have any children of my own. Not now I'm a blood-guzzler.

I sigh. "I won't hurt him," I say in as clear a voice as I can manage. "I care for him a great deal." Then before Mr. Jones can get the wrong idea, I hold up my hand. "Like he's my own son. What happened before, at the school, that was all my fault. I should never have gotten him mixed up in my business."

"You're dam right you shouldn't have," he growls, although he does at least appear slightly mollified.

The living room door opens again and Rogu3's pale face appears. He looks thinner than before. It might just be because he's starting to lose the puppy fat of youth. I hope that's what it is anyway, and not as a result of any lingering trauma from being half killed, transformed into a vampire and abruptly brought back to human again. I want to hug him but I sense that might just throw his father over the edge. Instead, I give him a broad grin, attempting to convey how pleased I am to see him. I also sit on my hands.

"Hi Bo."

"Hi."

He runs a hand through his hair and glances at his dad who coughs loudly. "Whatever you have to say, I want to be present."

Rogu3 looks pissed off. "I'm not a child."

"Yes," his father says simply, "you are."

"Dad..."

Trudy appears behind Rogu3. I realise with a slight jolt that he's taller than she is. "Jonathan."

He throws her a look. "She's a bloodguzzler."

"She's the Red Angel."

"It doesn't change what she is."

Out of all the reactions I've had from members of the public since X's stupid stunt, I think Jonathan Jones's is the most honest. He may have softened enough towards me to permit this meeting to happen but he's not going to be swayed by celebrity. Not where his son is concerned. I respect that. "It's fine," I interrupt. "You can all stay."

He glares at his family. It's as if I've not even spoken. Rogu3 stares back at him. "Please, Dad. You can trust her. I promise."

His mouth tightens. They seem to exchange more unspoken communication. Eventually he hisses breath out through his teeth. "Fine. But," he adds, with another hard look in my direction, "we'll only be in the next room."

He strides out, with his wife right behind him. When the door shuts and Rogu3 and I are left alone, both us relax infinitesimally. "Your parents seem nice," I offer.

He snorts. "They're a pain in my fucking arse. They're probably putting glasses up to the kitchen wall to eavesdrop as we speak."

"Alistair! Don't swear!"

He puts his hands on hips, an almost comical expression of dismay on his face. "Bo, you did not just call me that."

"I'd have thought your hacking days were behind you."

He snorts and sits down opposite me. "They confiscated all my gear. Or so they think anyway. I've got back up. A mate of mine has an old garage where I stored a few things. Rogu3 isn't dead and buried. Not yet."

A glimmer of a smile touches my lips. "Maybe it's time to stop. It is illegal after all."

"I help people." He folds his arms and gives me a challenging stare. "Like you."

"I'm not sure if that's what I do," I say softly to myself. In a bid to chance the subject, I tilt up my chin and grin. "What's word of the week?"

"Redress."

I raise my eyebrows. "Alright."

"Last week it was reprisal. The week before it was retribution."

I look away. "I'm sensing a theme."

"That lawyer friend of yours is going to get them off, isn't he?"

"He's not my friend," I say. "But, yes, he might. He's very good at what he does."

Rogu3 is silent for a moment as he mulls this over. "Did you bring them here?"

I shake my head and button my lips. Sensing it's not a question I'm prepared to elaborate on, he switches tack. "You turned me into a vampire. Like you."

I twist my fingers in my lap. "Yes."

"And then you turned me back again."

"You can't tell anyone, Rogu3. You really can't."

"I've kept my mouth shut this far, haven't I? I can keep a bloody secret." He curses to himself, standing up and walking to the window. He stares out at the dark street. "Thank you." He turns his head to look at me and repeats his words. "Thank you, Bo."

Biting my lip, I mumble, "You're welcome. Your parents think you're struggling to," I pause, "cope with the aftermath and everything."

"Huh. It's only because I'm not sleeping. What do they expect? I've been awake during the night for the last three years because it was the best time to get my work done. They didn't used to care about that until I was on the evening news." He shrugs. "It's going to take some time to adjust."

I give him a hard look. "Are you sure that's all it is?"

He meets my eyes. "That and the burning rage I feel towards the pricks who tried to kill me." His voice is calm but there's a look in his eyes I've never quite seen before. Rogu3 senses my worry and changes the subject again. "You turned me back to human. Why don't you change yourself back again too?"

I tug at the lapels of my leather jacket. "It was a one time deal."

"It was for you," he says, realisation dawning. "Whatever you gave me was for you."

"And I'd use it to save your life a million times over. I wasn't even sure any more if I'd been going to use it on myself." I shrug, attempting to look complacent. "It's not so bad being a bloodguzzler."

He smiles faintly. "At least you get to kick some bad guys' butts."

I take a deep breath. "I'm going to get whoever did this to you," I tell him quietly. "I'm going after the person behind all this. I'll make sure they pay." I lay out everything I've done so far, leaving no detail uncovered.

Rogu3 blinks. "I have one."

I frown at him. "One what?"

"A time bubble orb. It's upstairs in my room."

My mouth drops open. "You're kidding me. Why would you have one of those?"

"I thought I could use it," he mumbles. "After I heard about them in the news. I managed to get hold of it before they," he jerks his head in the direction of the kitchen, "shut me down."

"I don't understand. Use it for what?"

Rogu3 just shrugs awkwardly.

I suddenly realise. "Oh. Alice." His eight year old neighbour who vanished. The reason we met in the first place.

"Yeah," he mumbles. "It didn't do any good. It wouldn't work because of all the people. Every time I tried to pick a time and go back, I just got bounced out."

"I'm sorry." I'd like to tell him that one day she'll be found – at least what's left of her anyway. Neither of us are that dumb though.

"If you can use it then it'll be worth it."

"How did you manage to avoid giving it up when they were all recalled?"

He rolls his eyes. "Please. This is me we're talking about."

He jumps up and runs out of the room. I hear him thumping loudly upstairs then, a beat later, thumping back down again. He comes back in, handing me over a box. I flip open the lid and stare down. The blue swirls of the orb dance around. I swallow. "Are you sure about this?"

Rogu3 nods, just as his father walks about in with a rather tentative, but relieved gait. I put the orb to one side, hoping he doesn't ask about it. He's more focused on his son though. "How are you?"

"Fine."

I clear my throat. "You're lucky your parents care about you so much." I throw Rogu3 a meaningful look. He almost manages to avoid rolling his eyes again. Almost.

I stand up, getting ready to leave, hugging the box to my side and sticking out my free hand. Jonathan Jones stares at it as if it might bite him. I'm about to withdraw it when he takes it and shakes. His grip is dry and firm.

"Your mother needs some help in the kitchen."

"Dad..."

"Now."

Rogu3 gives me a glance filled with teenage exasperation. I smile. "Look after yourself. Call my any time if you need anything." He nods. I narrow my eyes. "I mean it."

"I will. Thanks, Bo." He grins and lopes out.

His father watches me carefully. "What did he give you?"

Bugger. "This box?" I tell the truth. "It's a time bubble orb. He thought I could use it."

He sniffs. "I see." He continues to look at me. I wait, sensing he has something else he wishes to say. "I don't like you," he finally says. "I don't like vampires. It's unnatural to be what you are. Alistair trusts you though and I respect that."

I open my mouth to speak but he forestalls me. "Those three

that are in custody. Are they the ones responsible for what happened to him?"

I tilt my head back to meet his steady gaze. "They were acting under orders."

"From whom?"

"I don't know," I say softly. "But I'm going to find out."

He puts his hands in his pockets and nods. "When you do, kill them." His voice is quiet. "Kill them and keep my boy safe."

I stare at him mutely. "I'm not an executioner, Mr. Jones."

"No. But you are a vampire."

I search his face. He really does want me to do this. I put my hand in my pocket, finding my pebble. Its smooth hardness is comforting. Jones is incapable of that sort of action himself but he honestly believes that I can do it. Right now, I'm not sure either way. "I'll find them," I tell him finally, unable to go any further than that.

It's almost midnight by the time I rock up to Forest Avenue. Rogu3's present is safely tucked away under the seat of the motorbike. I turn off the engine and gaze up at the house. It's pretty modest in appearance. Large bay windows jut out from the front and the garden has been neatly tended. From behind heavy curtains I can just make out a chink of light. Someone at least is still awake. Not that I'd be prepared to wait yet another day anyway though.

I march up to the front door and ring the bell. Just to be sure, I knock loudly also. It's not long before a man appears, holding the door open a crack to peer out at me. His face is lined and weathered and his hair – whatever little there is left of it – is unabashedly grey. A tiny muscle jerks in his jaw. Then he nods to himself and opens the door wide.

"Please, Ms. Blackman. Come in."

I almost fall off the step in shock. Not that he knows who I am (bloody X) but that he has no qualms about inviting a vampire into his home. I could be here for any number of reasons but he doesn't even seem curious. My insides tighten. It can only be because he already knows.

I straighten my jacket and step in. A small part of me is expecting him to rush me. To take me down. Not that he'd manage, of course. He's old and he's human. He doesn't try anything, however; he simply directs me into a well appointed room to the side.

"I've been expecting you," he says.

I stare at him.

"Well," he amends, "expecting someone anyway. It was bound to happen sooner or later. Why not now with the Red Angel herself?" He laughs. "So be it." His voice subsides to a mutter. "So be it."

Feeling like I'm about twenty paces behind, I take a deep breath and try to work out how to play this. I'm just about to fake it and make it seem like I really do know exactly what's going on when my phone beeps, momentarily rescuing me. I give the man an apologetic smile and pull it out. It's a text from Connor with three addresses on it – the three remaining London based Checkers' Trustees. The second one is 12 Forest Avenue and in that instant I really do know.

"Is she dead?" he asks me, when I put the phone away again.

"Madeline?"

He nods.

I don't miss a beat. "Yes."

His shoulders drop fractionally but he's not shocked by the news. "I changed our name. I wiped out my past. And still he found me."

I watch him carefully. "Tobias Renfrew?"

"Who else?" he says sadly. He walks over to a large Welsh dresser and opens a drawer, taking out a photo and handing it to me. The edges are crinkled and the image is rather faded but there's no mistaking the familiar figure of Renfrew with his arm around a younger version of the man in front of me. Other beaming figures mill around. No doubt they're the remaining Checkers' Trustees.

"It wasn't my idea." He laughs shortly. "I know that's pathetic but it really wasn't. It was just easier to go along with everyone. We had good intentions, you know. We helped a lot of children. The Sixties weren't like now. There were a lot of women who got themselves into trouble. We dealt with the aftermath. Orphans the lot of them. We clothed them, sheltered them. Helped them."

I keep my expression bland. "Those women didn't get themselves into trouble. Men are involved in the act of creating babies."

He waves a distracted hand in the air. "Turn of phrase. Like I said, they were different times."

I don't have the will to debate gender politics with him. I focus on the matter in hand. "Tell me. Tell me what happened."

He moves to his left where a silver tray has been left out with a bottle of whiskey and a single glass. He pours himself a drink, sips it and closes his eyes in pleasure. Then he looks at me. "Would you like one?"

"Tell me," I repeat again.

He takes another sip. "Very well."

CHAPTER 16
FLASHBACK

Alan Deutscher, as he'd been known back then, had been on board with Checkers from the start. He hadn't initially fancied himself as one for charity work but he'd been full of ideals. When a favourite cousin of his found herself unmarried and unexpectedly pregnant as a result of her own summer of love, he began to appreciate how difficult things could be for women in that situation. With six like-minded acquaintances, they created Checkers. Essentially, it was a last resort. If you had a child and were unable – or unwilling – to bring it up yourself, they would do it for you. Unusually for that time, they were ethnically blind. It didn't matter whether a child were daemon, human, witch or any combination of the three. Checkers would take them in, no questions asked.

It was a grand premise and full of promise. The trouble was that no-one on the Board had any experience in how to run a charity. They had, Deutscher assured me, the very best of intentions. But they were several sandwiches, a dozen sausage rolls and a bottle of fizzy orange short of a picnic. Within six months of starting, their grandiose ideas were already faltering.

Part of the issue was their desire to permit any child of any origin through their doors. Nowadays, it wouldn't be such a big deal – in fact, there would be any number of big conglomerates, well meaning millionaires and open fundraising drives that would be keen to highlight such impartiality. Back then, it didn't work. The humans didn't want to be seen to be helping daemons, and vice-versa. The witches were even worse. Forget the issues they had with anyone else, their own black-white squabbles meant they wouldn't touch Checkers Children's Charity with a barge-pole. When Checkers' initial funding quickly dried up, it appeared as if they'd be forced to close their doors. In hindsight, it would have been better if they had.

It was a chance encounter with Tobias Renfrew that changed the charity's fortunes. Elizabeth De Mille, the trustee who'd met her demise at the wheel of her zippy red sports car, travelled in the most exclusive social circles. New money was admired and Renfrew's billions opened those same doors that De Mille enjoyed as a result of her family's name and stature. The way Deutscher told it, they'd wooed each other – her to gain financial benefit and him for sexual favours. However it happened, Renfrew generously agreed to become the charity's benefactor. I suppose it helped boost his reputation but there's no doubt that his own miserable childhood played a role in his decision. As months turned into years, Renfrew's largesse grew. The charity moved to larger premises. They gained a name for themselves. It was even said that children who'd benefited from being taken under their wing were well educated, well rounded individuals who would go far. The Trustees also enjoyed the benefits. They were vaunted across the country as being pioneers of a new, more liberal age. Invited to speak at dinner functions, open galas and rarely be required to foot any sort of restaurant or bar bill, they congratulated themselves heartily. Not only were they living the high life, they were doing it as a result of helping numerous impoverished orphans. They were virtually saints. OBEs were most definitely in the offing. And when Renfrew informed them that they were to be the sole beneficiaries of his will, they all agreed that it was only natural and fitting.

It took surprisingly little time for the cracks to begin to show. In less time than it would take the average boyband to rise to fame and disappear again, the bickering started. Funds began to be misappropriated. Unwise decisions were taken, from hosting overly lavish fundraisers that lost money rather than achieving the profit they were designed for to outfitting the orphans with a uniform with such a stiff and uncompromising fabric that half the children broke out in hives. Renfrew, growing tired of seeing his money frittered away, threatened to pull out if things did not improve. The Trustees held an emergency meeting then sent Deutscher himself to Renfrew to plead for another chance. It was for the children. Of course everything they did was all for them.

Unfortunately, while the billionaire took a few days to make his decision, the worst happened. Allegations of abuse sprang up against one of the teachers, a History tutor who'd been with the charity virtually since its inception. The boy making the claims was brought up in front of the Trustees in a meeting that occurred under the cover of darkness. It was imperative that he kept his mouth shut.

This one lad, however, was not prepared to back down. Having made the decision to tell all, he'd taken the plunge already and was not going to retract. Such bravery in the face of daunting adult opposition is impressive. Perhaps he would have one day become another Tobias Renfrew. We will never know.

Deutscher claimed it started with De Mille. Shaken by the boy's adamant refusal to bend to the Trustees' will, she grabbed his arm, sinking her red talons deep into his skin. He screamed, from as much shock no doubt as pain. Terrified that if he continued, their clandestine meeting would be uncovered, two of the other Trustees, Brownslow and Wiggins involved themselves, leaping into the fray in a bid to keep him quiet. The boy panicked and struggled. And in that struggle something went wrong.

Afterwards, all seven stood around his limp body. Recriminations were hurled. Brownslow, Wiggins and De Mille were responsible. They had to be turned over to the police. But then the remaining four were implicated also. If word got out – if even a whisper left the walls of that terrible room – Renfrew would not hesitate to distance himself. There wasn't any choice. They had to hide the evidence. Thus, bound now by a dark veil of guilt, pain and murder, there was no going back. Even though Renfrew was eventually persuaded by Deutscher to remain as benefactor, the bloody pact the seven of made that night created shadows amongst them all.

Three months later – and only five hours before Renfrew's ill-fated, infamous party was due to begin - the daemon billionaire broke the news to the Trustees. He'd met someone. He'd fallen in love. She was a human woman, the complete opposite to him. He was going to broadcast the news that very night and, Renfrew added with a jovial wink, was looking for some appropriate godparents.

The Trustees went into panic mode. He'd had women before – they all knew that. The possibility of a longterm relationship was, however, entirely different. De Mille herself encouraged them all to remember that such women far too often turned out to be nothing more than dirty gold diggers. If there was indeed a child or, god forbid, children, they could kiss goodbye to all those billions.

Deutscher told me he could not remember who it was

who'd first made the suggestion. Perhaps it had been him. Either way, once it was voiced aloud, the die was cast. They returned to Renfrew and asked to meet the woman of his dreams. They wanted to welcome her fully into the Checkers Charity family. The children were so excited, they said. Renfrew would know what it was like soon enough himself – once a child got an idea into their head, there was no forgetting it. They wouldn't rest until they met her. Arrangements were made and Miss Hope Havrington of Shrewsbury agreed to spend half an hour at the Checkers house in all her party finery. The little girls were going to love it.

Although Hope entered Checkers alone, she left an entire retinue waiting out the front. Tobias Renfrew was not about to let the light of his life travel alone. She had unfortunately insisted on meeting the children without the others. She didn't wish to intimidate them. She didn't, of course, meet a single child. She only met her death, courtesy of a hemlock spiked drink. Oh, the tragic symmetry of it all.

The moment the deed was done, guilt set in. A momentary madness had overtaken them all, Wiggins stated. De Mille agreed. They would never harm a child. They *helped* children. They consoled themselves with the fact that it could only have been scant weeks into gestation. Hope Havrington hadn't been showing at all. They would tell Renfrew with unfeigned dismay that she must have miscarried. Internal haemorrhaging as an unfortunate side effect. She had keeled over before they even knew what was happening.

In the midst of this discussion, they didn't hear either Hope's driver or her maid approach. It took only a moment or two of eavesdropping – and a single creaky floorboard – for all their plans to go awry. Left with three bodies, two of which betrayed signs of blunt force trauma, they had to switch tactics. They'd leave the corpses at Renfrew's mansion and the blame would land on the partygoers. There were lots of them – at least half of whom were no doubt involved in dodgy dealings. Someone else could be the scapegoat. The Trustees had children to look after.

The only way to transport the remains without being detected was to chop them up and sneak in through a side entrance. Even then they were still interrupted by two people – a vampire and a daemon – who had taken a wrong turn while searching for the way out. It wasn't their fault; however, there wasn't any choice.

They left the body parts in a rarely used bathroom, carefully arranging them in the middle of the floor. Each and every one of Trustees were sticky with blood. They needed somewhere as far away as possible from the scene to clean up. On their way to another wing, with the strains of Skeeter Davis and *The End of the World* floating up towards them, they were caught red-handed. Literally.

According to Deutschner, while most people believed Renfrew was still involved in at least some illegal activities, he had genuinely turned over a new leaf. He'd taken a vow to change his ways for good – and it was this vow the Trustees now had to count on. Wiggins blurted it out. He told Renfrew what they'd done. They'd killed. They'd murdered Hope and, along with her, Renfrew's own child. Tobias Renfrew, who'd seen more death with his own eyes than most other people and, thanks to his armament dealings, had been responsible for more death than anyone currently living in the United Kingdom, went into a state of shock. I guess when it's your own family, everything suddenly changes. He didn't cry, he didn't collapse, he didn't try to attack the Trustees. But he did go into a semi catatonic shutdown. Deutschner grabbed him and slapped his face, trying to revive him. It did little good, however. All their efforts did was smear him with their own bloody handprints

If the Trustees had felt things were bad before, it was nothing compared to what they thought now. They'd be found out for sure. The only recourse left to them was to pin the blame on Renfrew himself. Considering he'd been a equal opportunities employer, the deaths included a vampire, witches, humans and daemons. One of those groups would take revenge and kill him. They'd still get their money. He'd brought it on himself, they reasoned. He'd done plenty of things in the past that marked him as a villain. He deserved this.

They dressed him in a tuxedo they found hanging in his own closet, bundling up his now bloody clothes and throwing them into a fireplace to burn. Then they took him down to the party, frog-marching him all the way. If any party-goers saw the state he was in, they probably attributed it to too much wine. Then, while De Mille stood behind him and whispered in his ear to feed him his lines, they made him give a speech. Such was his shock that he repeated them verbatim. He spun a pretty tale for the crowd. De Mille was an artist, throwing in hints of people out to get him. His audience were rapt.

Her final denouement was to get Renfrew to admit to the murders right there on the stage, in front of hundreds. Such a public confession would always be upheld. Right after she told him what to say, however, Renfrew paused and fell silent. He seemed to shake himself. She repeated her words. He turned and gave her one long look. Then there was an almighty flash and he vanished. No-one ever saw him again.

"I WOULD LIKE to believe it was a momentary madness, just like Wiggins said," Deutschner tells me once he's finished his tale.

"But we were too greedy. We'd grown to care only about ourselves and we'd forgotten our lofty ambitions to only help orphaned children. We were fully culpable. We are fully culpable."

I can do little more than stare at him. I try to work my jaw but it seems like no words will come. Deutschner hands me his glass of whiskey, encouraging me to take a drink. When his fingers brush against mine, however, I flinch. He looks sad but he nods in understanding.

"I don't get it," I stutter. I shake my head several times as if to make sense of it all. I'm in a room with a cold-blooded multiple murderer and he's just confessed to everything. "Why are you telling me all this? No-one knew. No-one even suspected."

"Because," he says with an odd brightness in his eyes, "as I suspect Tobias already knew, in the end we all must atone for our sins." He barks out a short, sharp laugh. "Truth be told, I didn't think we'd ever get away with it. I thought we'd be found out almost immediately. I wanted us to be found out. Knowing what we'd done was too much. Once the blood lust had passed and the cold light of day was upon us..." his voice trails off. He licks his lips and straightens his shoulders. "It's such a relief to tell you now."

"So you have no idea what Renfrew did? How he disappeared or where he went?"

Deutschner shakes his head. "Not a clue. I knew he'd be back for his revenge sooner or later. I just didn't think it would take him this long. It would have been easier, you know, if he'd done it before. I've never forgotten. I've always expected him to show up on my doorstep one day."

"You think that's why he killed Madeline? You know there's an ear. We can check the DNA and see if it belongs – belonged – to her."

"It was her," he says simply, "I know it." He stands up and

walks over to the drinks tray, gazing down at it as if lost in thought. When he turns back around he's holding the whisky bottle. "To the sins of the father," he says to me, before chugging back several gulps.

I watch him, faintly sickened. "What happened to the charity?"

He shrugs. "It went bust, of course. None of us had any heart for it after everything had happened."

"And you weren't getting any money any time soon," I interject.

A ghost of a smile crosses his face. "No. We weren't."

"The children...?"

"They were taken care of. We found good homes for them all."

"Do you have a list of their names?" I ask. It's not beyond the realms of possibility that one of them decided to revive Checkers and use it to take their own revenge for what happened to Renfrew.

"They didn't know anything about what happened," he dismisses.

"They knew the boy you murdered. The child."

Deutschner winces. "Yes. But we told them all we'd found some distant relatives of his in Canada and that they'd agreed to take him in. Whatever is happening now is nothing to do with them."

I'm not convinced but I let it rest for now. I can get the list elsewhere. "Have you spoken to the other Trustees since?"

"I don't think any of us could face it. To look each other in the eyes and know exactly what we'd done..." he shivers. "I do know De Mille and Boyce are dead. Wiggins went to Australia. As if sunshine and kangaroos could erase our actions," he snorts. "Andrew McIntosh was on the news yesterday. His son has gone missing."

I think of the wide-eyed fear in the eyes of Creed and Wyatt's victim. "Was he a daemon?"

"Yes, Ms. Blackman, he was."

"So that leaves Brownslow." I pull out my phone and read the addresses again. He's the first one, living over in the East End.

Deutschner lifts up his head. "If I'd known Renfrew would take Madeline, I'd have put a stop to this long ago. If Brownslow has children, don't let them be hurt. What we did is not their fault." He puts down the whiskey. "I need to use the bathroom."

I watch him leave then sink back into my chair. My head is still reeling from everything he's said. I think I do need that damned drink after all. I stand up and walk over to the tray to grab the bottle. There's a drawer underneath it that's lying open by a few inches. I frown. It had definitely been closed before. I peer inside. When I see the tray of shiny bullets with a single one missing, I swear loudly and spin round, just in time to hear the shot.

CHAPTER 17

TIME WAITS FOR NO MAN

"Murder and mayhem just seem to follow you around, don't they, Ms. Blackman?"

Irritated, I stare at the Sergeant. "As do you, Nicholls. Besides, Alan Deutschner wasn't murdered. He committed suicide."

"Mm." She folds her arms. "Strange that such a celebrated heroine as yourself would allow something like that to happen."

"It wasn't my fault." I clench my fists. I should have known though. I should have managed to stop him.

"It wouldn't matter if it was though," she sneers. "You're a vampire."

I wonder how many times she's going to bring that little fact up. I should keep a damn tally. "Where's Foxworthy?" I ask instead.

"Why? So you can wrap him around your little finger even more?"

I gaze at her coolly. "I rather think he's a stronger man than that." I stand up to go.

"You can't just walk out of here."

223

I rub my forehead tiredly. "Except I can. Because as you've already pointed out, I'm a vampire. You can't hold me."

She hisses. I ignore her.

It's a relief to be back outside again. I suck in a breath of fresh air and hold it for a long moment in my lungs. My neck prickles and I know without turning who's behind me. "Isn't it rather dangerous for you to show up when so many police are around?"

X laughs, the sound pouring over me like liquid. "I don't walk around showing my true form to any old Tom, Dick or Harry."

This is probably supposed to be my cue to turn and face him. I don't bother. I already know what he looks like. And those damn writhing tattoos of his make feel faintly seasick. "What do you want, X?"

"Your little investigation is going well."

"A man just died," I say flatly.

"You know what I mean. A decades old mystery and little Bo Blackman is going to be the one to solve it."

"I'm no closer to finding Tobias Renfrew than the police are."

"Oh, come, come," he drawls. "You know that's not true." He moves up closer behind me until I can almost feel his heat. He leans into my ear and whispers. "It's not their fault they're incompetent. They have to abide by the law. You don't."

"If this is another job pitch, then I'm not interested."

"Unlimited funds. Unlimited resources. Just think what you could do."

"Find another stooge."

He laughs again. "That's why I like you. No-one has ever dared to talk to me like that. You can keep playing hard to get. Just know that I always get what I want though, Bo. Sooner or later."

"Well then, it's your lucky day. You can open yourself up to new experiences and discover what it's like to be refused." My words fall emptily into the street. X has already gone. I sigh and shove my hands in pockets. I tightly squeeze my little pebble and remember to breathe again. Then I pull out my phone and call Matt.

"Hey babe!"

I raise my eyebrows. "Babe?"

"Of course! You're my babe. I'm your guy."

"I think you're re-defining our relationship and taking it into fantasy land, Matt," I tell him.

He chuckles. "There's nothing wrong with a good fantasy. Are you avoiding the office?"

I think of Arzo and Dahlia and try not to stiffen. "No. I'm just busy. And I need some help. Call Connor and O'Shea too."

"They're already here." He lowers his voice melodramatically. "I think they like each other."

A flicker of a smile crosses my face. "I think they do."

"What do you need?"

"Brownslow," I say. "The Checkers' Trustee. The three of you need to get to his house now. Locate his family and keep them safe. Don't let them out of your sight."

Matt sobers up. "Are they in trouble?"

I bite my lip. "Yeah. I think they might be."

"Will you be there too?"

My eyes drift to the storage compartment under my motorbike seat. "No. I've got something else to check out first."

I'D BEEN HALF EXPECTING the Renfrew mansion to be covered in crime scene tape, or for security to at least have been beefed up. It seems even more silent upon my arrival than it had when I was here with O'Shea though. I park the bike, taking Rogu3's box with me, and walk over to the gift shop. The pane of glass has already been replaced. I crouch down at the door, examining the ground in front of it. There's no trace that anyone died here. I suppose commerce waits for no-one.

I stand back up again and peer inside. Foxworthy never did tell me whether they recovered any bullet fragments. Or the damn ear those bastards sawed off – not to mention the body. I suppose I should feel sad for Andrew McIntosh losing his son like that. I certainly feel bad for his son. But McIntosh was with Deutschner. They killed a lot of people for nothing more than the sake of some money and a highly regarded reputation.

I look around. I suppose I probably should try to keep my visit here inconspicuous. Somehow, in light of all the revelations of this night, I can't seem to muster up the energy to do it though. I gaze to my left and the path leading round towards the back of the house. Then I shrug to myself. The front door will be a lot sodding quicker. I march up to it, eye the lock and, without even drawing breath, kick it in. There's a loud splintering of wood. The security guard who I presume is still around here somewhere doesn't appear. I guess with all of Renfrew's money locked away, they couldn't afford to hire someone who wouldn't fall asleep on the job. Rather than worry about it, I simply push open the door and walk in. Five minutes later I'm standing back in front of the bathroom. I can still see Kimchi's scratches in the enamel of the bath. Whether anyone else has noticed them yet is unclear. I gaze inside, thinking over what Deutschner had told me about that terrible night. I shudder.

After Wiggins had told Renfrew what they'd all done, the billionaire had shut down. It might have been shock or overwhelming grief or a combination of both. However, when he'd been on that stage and giving his speech, he'd recovered enough to stop himself from repeating Elizabeth De Mille's lines. He'd done something to disappear. I didn't know much about the nature of daemon billionaires but I did know humans. And I knew myself. If I'd been about to vanish from the world, I'd want one last look at the person who was important to me. Michael's face floats in my mind. With effort, I push him away.

I'm betting that Renfrew came here. He wouldn't have had long, perhaps even just a minute or two before people came up searching for him. Every single person had been outside, eager to hear what he'd been saying. If I manage this accurately, I can set the time bubble to appear a few seconds after he did his disappearing act. If I get bounced out, then it's because Renfrew didn't travel far. He really did come here first to get one last look at poor Hope's dismembered body. If the time bubble orb works, then I reckon whatever happened was out of Renfrew's control.

I take a deep breath and open Rogu3's box, carefully lifting out the orb. It's heavier than I was expecting and the blue swirls create an eerie light in the darkened hallway. It might just be my imagination but I'm sure they react to my touch, spinning more quickly than before.

I stare at it. "It'd be really handy if you came with an instruction manual," I say to it. I turn it over in my hands, attempting to see whether there's any clue as to how to set it up. Its glassy surface is smooth but there's a faint buzz emanating from it that makes my fingers tingle. I lift it up and frown.

From out of nowhere, a hologrammed display appears, projecting upwards into the air. Date. Time. My heart rate picks up. I lick my lips and balance the orb in one hand, while my other reaches up. It's almost immediately apparent that it's like a sort of touch screen. The date section lights up when I touch it. I spin the numbers until I get the one that I want. The seventeenth of January, 1963. Then I move to the time, setting it for two minutes after Renfrew was reported to have blinked out of existence. The display vanishes to be replaced by a single word - Confirm? With my heart in mouth, I lightly touch it to agree.

My body jerks. It's an odd sensation, not entirely different to when a train or a bus comes to a halt. I lose my balance, tripping over my own feet. When I stand back up again and look around, I realise that everything's different. It's as if I'm suddenly viewing the world in muted tones. I blink several times. The neat barrier designed to hold back the tourists from entering the bathroom has gone. Unfortunately, the sight it's been replaced with is truly sickening. As my vision restores itself, bile rises in my mouth and I'm forced to look away. I might be a vampire but I've never seen so much blood. Considering Deutschner confirmed that this wasn't the scene of any of the murders, it's a testament to every single one of the Trustees' brutality that there's quite so much splattered around. Perhaps it's just as well Renfrew didn't apparently return here after all.

I take several steps, moving away from the bathroom. It's more of an instinctive reaction rather than a conscious one. I want to put as much distance between myself and the blood-bath as possible. I pinch the bridge of my nose and breath through my mouth. There's not the alluring scent I normally receive from fresh blood. This is just death.

My gaze falls on the painting hanging just behind me. It's the same pretty landscape I spotted a week ago — and five decades in the future. I try to use its picturesque scene to calm myself down. The tree and the golden fields stretching out behind the little farmhouse in the foreground suggest a far different scene to the one that's still seared into my brain. Then my mouth drops open. Oh God.

I stare at it again. My eyes search across the paint and I shake my head as if to clear my vision but there's no denying it.

The last time I saw this painting it had been signed at the bottom by Renfrew himself – and there had been a tiny figure sitting under the tree. Neither of them are present now.

I yank the painting off the wall and flip it over. There's nothing on the back other than the hook. I can hear blood drumming in my ears. Sodding hell.

Still gripping it, I start to move. Adrenalin pulses through my body. I half walk, half run. I need to get out of this bubble now and compare the modern version to this one. Maybe they're part of a series, I reason. They're not necessarily the same painting.

Something flickers up ahead. I slow down, trying to work out what it is. A blurred shape is coming towards me and it's moving fast. My brain struggles dimly to work out what's going on until I realise it's from the other side of the bubble. It's the first person coming to the scene. They're looking for Tobias Renfrew but they're not going to find him – and I'm about to be thrown out of the bubble. I feel my body jerk again, and there's the odd sensation of falling. As I twist to try to keep my balance, my eyes fall across an open doorway. Inside is a remarkable array of plush soft toys. I catch the edge of what is unmistakably a crib, just as my knees give way. This time the muted tones have given way to a harshness that makes my eyeballs ache. The door in front of me is now closed. I'm back in real time.

I stretch out and twist the doorknob. This clearly isn't a room that gets opened very often. The creak that sounds from the rusty hinges is quite extraordinary. There's also not a stick of furniture to be seen. I frown for a moment then spin round to go back to the painting. That's when I realise I'm no longer holding the original. I mentally slap myself on the forehead. Time cannot be changed; it's utterly, implacably immutable. That means that not only can I not alter the past, the same object can't exist twice. I studied it with enough desperation though. I pivot round and run, coming to a skidding halt in front of the 2015 version.

I touch the brushstrokes lightly with my fingertips. They look the same. The fields certainly look the same. The farmhouse has the same thatching and is casting the same shadows. I lift it off – more carefully this time – and turn it over. The back looks the same too. The only differences between this painting and the one I had in my hands scant moments ago is the signature and the little figure. I peer at it. It's difficult to tell because it's so small and indistinct but it looks like a man. He's definitely wearing black. I realise that I'm shaking. I know exactly where Tobias Renfrew is.

I sprint back down the hallway, the painting under my arm. The last thing I want to do is damage it so I'm taking considerable care. However, it feels like it's burning a hole against me. It runs through my head like a mantra: I've found Tobias Renfrew. I've found Tobias Renfrew.

Unfortunately the security guard appears to have woken up from wherever he was apparently dozing and come to investigate. If he's found the mess I made of the front door, then he'll have called the police. Even with Deutschner's confession, I don't want the first thing Tobias Renfrew sees when he's released from the confines of the paint to be the inside of a cell because they want to interrogate him as to exactly what happened that night. He deserves some time to acclimatise. I feel like I owe him that much at least. So when the guard shines his torch up in my direction, I take a running leap and vault over him. My shoes squeak on the polished floor as I veer round and reach the staircase leading down. I glance from the stairs to the banister and make a decision, jumping onto the smooth wooden rail and holding the painting above my head. I slide down, landing at the bottom with a little hope and a wide grin. Two seconds later I'm out the door.

~

THE MOMENT I pull up outside New Order, I jump off the bike and dash inside. Yanking my phone out my pocket, I dial Matt.

"Brownslow," I say, breathless and without so much as a hello, "do you have him?"

"No. I'm sorry, Bo. The police arrested him."

I curse. It was inevitable after what I'd relayed to Nicholls about Deutschner's confession. I had rather hoped they'd wait until morning though. After all, the crimes were committed over fifty years ago. He's an old man now; he's not going anywhere.

"His family?" I ask as I run past Drechlin's surgery and up the stairs to our offices.

"Two sons and one daughter. We've got eyes on them all."

"Good. Keep it that way. I'll be in touch soon."

"Bo, don't hang up. Your grandfather called about an hour ago and…"

I slam open the new Order door and run in, my feet coming to a faltering stop when I see who's there. I drop the phone.

"It's not even five o'clock in the morning," I say to my grandfather. He's standing in the middle of the room with Michael, Lord Gully, Lord Bancroft and Lord Stuart all seated around him. The only Family Head not present is Medici. The vampire Lords – and my grandfather – might have bland, impassive expressions but Arzo and Dahlia who are standing awkwardly to the side both look worried. Regardless of Dahlia, it's not a natural expression for the hulking Sanguine. I didn't even see him look worried when he was half dying on the blood soaked floor of Dire Straits.

"I've called everyone in," he tells me. "Although Matthew and Connor apparently have more important things to do than follow my orders."

I start. "Matt didn't..."

He throws me a warning look. "I only spoke to Connor." He leans down to the table next to him and picks up a cup of tea, sipping it.

I walk slowly over to my desk, placing the painting face down on top. He didn't just speak to Connor; he spoke to Matt too. And Matt always follows the last instruction he's been given, whether it supersedes the previous one or not. The enhancement spell that's warped his mind really is falling apart – except for some reason my grandfather doesn't want anyone to know about it. I absorb this information quietly. Matt's not the reason that four of the most powerful tribers in the country are sitting in our little office. I look at Michael. His dark eyes are raking over me, as if he's trying to ascertain where I've been up until now. I try to smile at him but he doesn't smile back.

"Let me guess," I say grimly. "Medici. The answering silence is all I need to confirm it. I grit my teeth. "What has he done?"

Michael stands up and moves beside me. The length of his body brushes against mine and, despite the severity of the situation, I still feel an involuntary flutter deep in my belly. He hands me a piece of paper. I scan through it, horror filling me as I do.

"He released this at midnight," Michael tells me. "He's breaking away from the other Families. He says he's going to hold the entire Medici clan accountable to human law but..."

"...But he's also going to open up recruitment to anyone who wants in." I shake my head. "He can't do this. *Your* law prevents him from it."

"Our law," Michael says quietly.

I gesture at him irritably. It was only a slip of the tongue.

"The four of you combined are easily stronger than him. Bring him down. You can probably even manage it before sunrise."

"That's exactly what I said!" Lord Gully splutters.

My grandfather holds up a grainy photograph. "And this is why it won't work."

I frown. "What is that?"

"One of my old colleagues at MI7 sent it over. It was taken this evening."

"Are those people?" I ask, squinting at the shapes.

He nods. "Vampires."

"That's more than five hundred!"

"MI7 estimate about two thousand."

I swallow hard. Each Family's numbers are capped at five hundred. It's been one of the immovable laws that's been upheld for centuries. "It doesn't make any sense. Medici is a traditionalist. He doesn't want to follow human law. He doesn't want to change the way the vampires do things. That's why he's so pissed off at us here at New Order. We're trying to change things and he doesn't like it."

"I can only imagine," Michael says, reaching for my hand and squeezing it, "that he's changed his mind. Maybe it's because he feels we've all ganged up on him for each having representatives here."

"Or he's tired of being one out of five. He wants all the power for himself," Bancroft comments.

"How are the others taking it? The government? The other humans? The other sodding tribers? They can't be pleased."

"It was only announced five hours ago," my grandfather says. "Most humans are asleep while the wheels of the government do not run that quickly." I roll my eyes. "They have, however, already sent some high ranking Members of Parliament to talk to him."

"And Medici's agreed to meet with them?" I'm incredulous. His disdain for humans is only matched by my disgust for him.

"They're in conference right now."

"And there's a rumour that the white witches want to parley too."

I gape. "You have to be kidding me."

Lord Stuart looks unhappy. "They feel sidelined by the black witches and the hybrids."

I draw in a shaky breath. 'There's going to be a queue all the way to the sodding Eiffel Tower once the rest of the world hears about the recruitment change. We need to move fast and move now. Either we get Medici to see sense or we'll have to take him out. We can't let him continue."

"You can't get involved, Bo."

I give Michael an astonished look. "Why the hell not? In fact, it makes sense for me to get involved. I'm the bloody Red Angel! People will listen if I make a statement. I can come out against him. It might help our cause."

"This has to be a matter for us." He points to the other three Family Heads who nod vigorously in agreement. "It's the only way it's going to work. A statement, even from you, isn't going to change his mind. We're the only ones who are going to be able to reach him. He'll respect us."

"He's not respected you very much by doing this, has he?" I can feel my anger rising.

"Bo," my grandfather interjects quietly, "Lord Montserrat is correct. You've already said yourself that he's a traditionalist. If anyone is likely to succeed, it'll be the four of them. There needs to be five Families for there to be balance. They can remind Lord Medici of that."

"Cooler heads need to prevail," Michael agrees.

I stare at him. "Are you suggesting I'm hotheaded?"

He takes on a pained expression. "No. But sometimes you do

act rashly. We can appeal to Medici if we plan things out before-hand and know exactly what we're going to say and how we're going to say it."

"So why did you all even come here?" I ask quietly. Michael glances at my grandfather. "Oh, I see," I say sarcastically, "you wanted to talk to *him*."

"And meet together. This is neutral ground. We all have a stake in New Order."

I look at the other three Lords. "Yeah, now you do," I scoff, pointing out that it took them a damn while to get involved.

Arzo picks the worst possible time to involve himself. "Bo, this isn't helping."

"Indeed. What you *can* do is help out by going on of those fake dates again," Lord Gully suggests, with a cold look in his eyes. "It'll help Montserrat appear as if he's in the right." He laughs. "Hell, why don't you go on dates with all of us?"

I keep my eyes fixed on Michael. "You told him about that?"

My grandfather clears his throat. "This isn't getting us anywhere. I asked them all to come here because there's actually an easy solution to all this that involves all four of them." There's an air of rigid finality to his voice.

I rip my eyes away from Michael. "What solution?"

He opens his mouth to speak but an odd expression comes into his eyes.

"Grandfather?" I prod.

He starts to choke, a small sound at first as if it's simply a frog caught in his throat. Then it gets louder and his face turns a strange shade of purple. I rush towards him. "What is it?" I ask in alarm. "What's wrong?"

His hands claw at his chest. I stare into his eyes – the pupils are wide and dilated. "Something's wrong!" I yell. "He's having some kind of attack! Call an ambulance!"

Arzo is already there on the phone. Michael takes his other

arm and together we lower him to the floor, angling his body into the recovery position. I don't understand. He'd been fine only a moment ago. It has to be the stress of the situation. I shouldn't have gotten involved.

"Water," I say. "Water will help." I reach up, fumbling for the tea cup he'd just been drinking from. I pause. I look from the cup to my grandfather and back again. Then I look at Dahlia.

"The ambulance will be here in five minutes," Arzo says.

Gully, Stuart and Bancroft exchange looks. "We should go," Stuart says. "If word gets out that we've been holding crisis talks, it won't help things." The three of them start to walk out. Michael says something to them but I don't hear what it is. I'm still fixated on Dahlia.

"You normally make him tea, don't you?"

"I have done once or twice. When I'm having a cup myself," she says, her brow wrinkling.

"Did you make him that?" I point to the cup, slowly standing up.

"I did actually. It's the same tea he normally drinks though. He couldn't be having a bad reaction to it." Her lips purse. "Unless the milk is off."

I sniff the dregs. It only smells of tea. "What did you put in it?"

Arzo steps in front of Dahlia. "Bo, I love you and emotions are running high, but you need to shut your mouth before I do something I regret."

I sidestep to my left so I can still see her. "It's the perfect timing, isn't it? The second Medici makes his move you throw us into disarray."

She flutters her eyelashes and her face grows pale. "Bo, I would never hurt your grandfather."

Michael growls. I glance down. My grandfather is still breathing. His face remains purple but I can see the throb of a pulse at his throat. He's not getting any better but neither is he getting any worse.

"Tell me what it is, Dahlia. Tell me what you gave him and I'll let you live."

Her hand goes to her mouth and she stares at me in horror.

"That's enough, Bo!"

"You can't go round accusing people of things," Michael interjects. "He's an old man. It's probably a heart attack."

I shake my head. "No. He might be an ornery bastard but he's as fit as a fiddle." I take another step towards Dahlia. "You did something."

Arzo's fist flies towards me. I duck in the nick of time and glare at him. The damage, however, is already done.

There's a strangled caterwaul from my grandfather's office. Michael points at both me and Arzo, his meaning very clear before he frowns and stands up, cautiously opening the door. His ginger monstrosity flies out, spitting and hissing at everyone. She takes guard over him, screeching in the spine-chilling way that only cats can manage to do. The door downstairs bangs open and the thud of paramedics' footsteps can be heard. My grandfather makes an ominous rattle and the rest of us stare at each other in malevolent silence.

CHAPTER 18

HOSPITAL BEDS AND BABY CRIBS

I sit slumped in a chair. The beeps emitting from the myriad of machines surrounding my grandfather's prone body are reassuring but, given that this is the intensive care ward, there regularly seems to be flurries of activity outside as small teams of doctors and nurses rush from emergency to emergency. Every time it happens my stomach gives a lurch. I take his hand and squeeze it. He doesn't respond.

"Ms. Blackman?"

I glance up to see a white coated doctor standing in the doorway. He gives me a professional smile. "We've had the preliminary lab tests back. We're not quite sure what's afflicting your grandfather at this stage. It's not a heart attack or a stroke and there's no evidence of internal haemorrhaging."

"Poison," I croak. "You need to test for poison."

He looks rather taken aback. "There's nothing so far to indicate..."

"Please."

He nods. "There are a lot of poisons out there. It might take some time."

I look back at my grandfather. "He's not going anywhere." The tightness in my chest grows. "Is he going to recover?"

"It's too early to say. He's certainly fighting. A lot of other people his age would have succumbed by now."

I smile faintly. "He's a tough old coot."

"From what I've heard of him, that's certainly true." He meets my eyes. "And from what I've heard of you, that's true for you as well."

I don't respond. Fat lot of good being the Red Angel is doing me now.

"You should go home and get some rest. He's comfortable for now and he's not going to wake up any time soon. You won't do him any good if you make yourself ill."

I don't move a muscle. Despite his words, the doctor seems unsurprised. "I'll be back in an hour or so to check on him then."

He leaves me in peace. I stare down at my grandfather's lined face and smooth a lock of his hair away from his forehead. The horrid purple hue has vanished from his skin but now he seems pale and wax-like. A single tear squeezes out, rolling down my cheek. "How did we get to this?" I whisper. "I'm so, so sorry."

There's a light knock on the door. Michael comes in, holding out a cup. "I decanted it from a vampette outside less than ten minutes ago," he says. "It's still not as good as drinking from the vein but it'll give you some nourishment at least."

I take it from him, gulping down the blood. It's still warm and slides easily down my throat. Michael watches me carefully.

When I'm finished, I place the cup to one side and squint up at him. "Why did you tell Lord Gully about the faked dates?"

He runs a hand through his hair and sighs. "It wasn't intended as some kind of betrayal, Bo, although I can see why you'd think that. At our last meeting we were simply batting around ideas for how to overcome our bad press. He wanted me to force you to return to being fully part of the Montserrat Family. He kept pushing it and I got angry and blurted it out."

My eyes narrow. "You mean you were being rash? Well, I guess that makes two of us, then." I don't bother concealing the bitter hurt in my tone.

"I'm sorry about that." When I look away, he persists. "I really am. You have to remember that I'm responsible for the lives of five hundred vampires though. I have to work with the other Heads and I have to ensure that Medici is taken care of. I can't afford screw this up. It's not about you. It's about what's going to work to ensure peace."

I bite my lip and gesture down at my grandfather. "Is this what you'd call peace?"

"You have no proof your grandfather's collapse has anything to do with Medici or Dahlia." He looks at me heavily. "I don't particularly like her either but she deserves the benefit of the doubt."

"You know what she's done in the past! What she did to Arzo and the way her and her damn husband conducted them-selves! She's more than capable of this."

"Perhaps. But I think her forced recruitment has made her turn over a new leaf."

"And you're all about second chances, aren't you?" I spit. "You and your band of de-criminalised vampires."

"Arzo trusts her."

"Arzo is blinded by his dick." It's harsh and not entirely true but I don't take it back. I tilt up my chin. "I want to talk to her."

Michael shakes his head. "I don't think that's a very good idea."

"I don't care what you think. I want to talk to her alone."

"Arzo won't permit it."

"Sodding hell! Since when was he in charge?"

"Bo..."

I stand up. "No. Don't you dare 'Bo' me. Since the moment I came into the office tonight you've treated me like a bloody teenager. You really think you can sort the Medici mess out without me? Then, fine. Go ahead. But you cannot stop me from finding out who has hurt my own fucking grandfather. If he dies..." I draw in a shaky breath, "if he dies then I won't be responsible for my actions. Once I'm done, you and Arzo can forgive me and give me a second chance. You both clearly like that kind of thing."

He gazes at me impassively. "I'm not the enemy."

Another tear escapes but I furiously dash it away. "I know that!"

He reaches out towards me and pulls me into a tight hug. For a moment, I don't respond but then I'm unable to help myself. My arms clutch at him.

"It'll be alright, Bo," he whispers.

"You don't know that," I mumble back. "You really don't."

I STAY by my grandfather's bedside until dark falls once more. His condition is stable and the doctor assured me he's going to be unconscious for at least another twelve hours. I make it clear that they're not to let anyone else in to see him unless I approve of them first. If it's an unusual request, then he doesn't comment. I guess my reputation as someone who deals daily in danger helps me out there.

I give my phone number to virtually every medical professional I see, telling each of them in no uncertain terms that they're to call me if there's the slightest change in his condition. Michael left hours ago. Gully, Bancroft, Stuart and himself still have to work out the best way to approach Medici. I tell myself to keep an open mind and that perhaps they'll manage to win him round. Considering how far Medici has taken things – and how publicly – I'm not convinced. There'll be a lot of vampiric blood shed if it doesn't work out though so I'm keeping my fingers tightly crossed. It doesn't help when I overhear a conversation between two distraught family members who are arguing over whether to take their loved one straight to the Medici complex to have him turned. As tempted as I am to get involved, I manage to bite my tongue. With my grandfather at death's door, part of me can understand the sentiment even if it twists my stomach. I wonder if Medici has any real clue about just what a can of worms he's opened by offering blanket recruitment.

The only good thing about Medici's actions is that, when I leave the hospital, there are only a few journalists hanging around to get a statement. I've obviously been surpassed in the news stakes. I mumble something generic about the hospital doing everything they can before marching off, leaving them to shout empty questions after me as to what I think of Medici's move.

New Order, when I return, is as silent as the grave. All the Stuart, Gully and Bancroft reps have vanished. They've probably called back home to deal with the upcoming Medici confrontation. The teacup my grandfather had been drinking from has also gone. I frown at the space where it had been and go instead to Dahlia's desk, pulling open drawer after drawer. There's an incredible array of make-up but nothing incriminating. She's too smart to leave anything lying around though. I gnaw on my cheek. I have a fairly good idea where she is right now. I could go and knock down Arzo's door and demand to speak to her. I take my white pebble out of my pocket and lay it on her desk instead, staring at it. I'm going to need proof first. I just have no idea how to get it.

I'm still gazing into space and working through various scenarios in my head when I hear the familiar voices of O'Shea and Connor float up the stairs. There's a loud bark and, a few heartbeats later, Kimchi appears, his lead trailing behind him. He leaps up onto my lap, squishing me with his weight and subjects me to several delighted slobbery licks. I ignore his doggy breath and let him have his way. It's actually rather comforting.

"Hi Bo."

I peer round Kimchi. Both Connor and O'Shea look uncomfortable. "I hope you don't mind. We weren't sure when you'd be back so we took Kimchi out for a run. We managed to persuade all of the Brownslow kids to get together. Not that they're really kids any more. They're all in their forties. Matt's babysitting for now so we can keep an eye on them in shifts."

"Thank you. I appreciate it."

"How's Mr. Blackman?"

I shrug, willing myself not to cry again. "Stable for now." I scoot the dog off and stand up, idly brushing the hairs from my clothes.

"We heard what happened with Dahlia."

O'Shea nods grimly. "Just say the word, Bo, and we'll be right with you. We can go after her now. I'm ready. I was born ready."

I offer him a half smile. "No-one believes it was her."

"You believe. That's enough for me."

"Thank you," I say quietly. "But I need to get some evidence. With everything that Medici's doing right now, I'm not sure if there's a way to get it."

"You'll think of something. You're the Red Angel." For once his tone is serious rather than playful. I give him a grateful look.

"The hospital's going to call me if anything happens. But I can't just sit around here and do nothing, even if I can't think of a way to force Dahlia into telling the truth. I need to do something else."

"Whatever you need."

I walk over to my own desk. Renfrew's painting is still there, undisturbed. That's something at least. I flip it over and show it to the pair of them.

O'Shea's brow furrows. "That looks familiar."

"It's from Renfrew's mansion. I need you to take it to Merlin. Don't let it out of your sight."

Connor cocks his head, obviously confused. "Merlin?"

"I'll explain later," O'Shea says. Connor gives him a soft smile. I watch for a moment as the pair of them gaze into each other's eyes. The connection they're feeling is unmistakable. I bite my lip and look away.

"What are you going to be doing, Bo?"

"I'm going to track down a certain army colonel." I have a theory.

I WAIT for Arbuckle in the same copse of trees where we first met. She knew I was here last time so I'm counting on the same again. I make little effort to conceal my presence. I want her to come.

When she does arrive, it's only the sound of a snapped twig that alerts me to her approach. "You move quietly for a human," I say.

She steps forward. The moonlight filters down through the trees, lighting up one side of her face. Her hair is still tightly wound into a bun. I'm starting to wonder whether she ever unties it.

"I've had a lot of training," she says calmly. "I didn't always spend my days hanging around bases dealing with trivial matters."

"You're one of those soldiers who prefers the glory of war?"

Her strange eyes harden. "There's no glory to be had in death, Ms. Blackman."

"Then why do so many seek it?"

She doesn't answer. In fact, there's only the faintest trace of tightening around her mouth that tells me she even heard my question. I lift up a single shoulder. Her views on the politics of killing aren't really why I'm here. Not entirely anyway.

"I was at a house last night," I tell her. "One single occupant. A man called Alan Deutschner. He and I had a chat then he put a bullet in his brain."

Arbuckle's expression barely wavers. "He must have felt he'd done something very wrong to merit suicide."

"He was indeed very sorry for his actions. As awful as they'd been."

She meets my eyes. "How did you know?"

Yahtzee. I let out the breath I hadn't realised I'd been holding. "You wear coloured contact lenses. You're not as human as you want everyone to think. I'd not understood why you wanted to hide your daemon side but now I think I do."

"I'm only half daemon."

"Your father's side," I say quietly. "Does the army know that?"

"Let's be clear, Ms. Blackman. I am not ashamed of that part of me. The army knows what I am. Mandatory blood testing sees to that. But when people see human they don't think to make other ... connections."

"Like family resemblances?" I ask. "Do they test your DNA when they test your blood?"

"I think we both know the answer to that is no."

"Because you followed in your father's footsteps and joined the army too."

Arbuckle adjusts her cuffs. "I like to think I've been more ... committed than he was."

I nod my head. "You didn't come back to New Order. You stormed in with your tales of my illegal activity and, when I pointed out the errors in the photo, you left again in a hurry. You were going to investigate it." I lean forward. "What did you discover?"

"I don't answer to you."

I smile humourlessly. "No. You don't. Which is why it also never made sense that you showed me the special classified file in the first place. Or that it even exists. People generally aren't good at keeping secrets, Colonel. Sooner or later there's always a whistleblower. Even if the reasons for keeping Tobias Renfrew's death to yourselves made sense, it's impossible that someone wouldn't have leaked it by now."

"The military isn't like the general public," she sneers. "We take our duty seriously."

"So do MI7. And they knew nothing about it."

"They're not as competent as they'd like to think."

"Actually," I say quietly, thinking once more of my grandfather, "they are. You doctored that photo yourself, didn't you? A bit of Photoshop to throw anyone who came calling off the scent. You really did plan things out very carefully. One might almost say with military precision."

She folds her arms, pacing first to her right then to her left. "The photo wasn't for someone like you," she says finally.

"It was for the people you hired, right? In case they got curious and thought there could be more in it for them?"

For a moment, I think she's not going to answer. Then she takes in a deep breath and reluctantly nods. "I wanted to keep them under control. They're mercenaries. Their bottom line is money. I paid them enough initially to draw them in and make them think there was a lot more. And that I knew exactly where it was."

"Because you had access to secret military files. Not because you are Tobias Renfrew's legitimate heir."

"If they knew that, then don't you think they'd have treated me rather differently?" she inquires. "I'd have become their toy instead of the other way around." Her face shadows. "Maybe that would have been best."

"Tobias Renfrew's fortune is locked away. Where did you get the gold from?"

"My nanny had access to some funds he'd kept hidden away. She didn't use them for herself. She was a good woman who gave up her life to look after me. I was only ten months old when my parents were murdered, after all." Something inside me twinges at her words but I don't let my expression betray my thoughts. Arbuckle continues. "She died four months ago."

"Right before Madeline Gregory was murdered," I say in sudden understanding. "You waited until your nanny was dead before you took your revenge."

Arbuckle closes her eyes for a moment. "She wouldn't have liked it. She thought the past should stay in the past. And she wanted to keep me safe."

So much for that then. "I've learnt quite a lot about revenge since I became a vampire," I tell her. "The ins and outs of it. The way it can consume people and make them act out of charac-ter." Dahlia's face flashes into my mind. "I do understand it, however. I understand how it can become such a driving force. Hurting the Trustees makes sense. They destroyed the life you could have had. Chopping off their children's ears and piercing them with a ruby also makes sense. You wanted to give them a sign and make them think that Tobias Renfrew was after them. It would have scared them shitless." I purse my lips. "There's an odd symmetry to that last action that's almost artistic. It should scare me that I think that. I clear my throat. "What I don't understand, Colonel, is why you'd want the children dead. Their parents certainly. But their kids? They'd done nothing wrong."

Arbuckle stares at me. "That's not what you really want to know, is it? You want to know why I had the Agathos Court bombed. Why I had a school attacked. Why you had to rescue a teenage boy from certain death."

I tighten my jaw. "Okay," I say. "You're right. That is what I want to know."

She backs up, leaning against the trunk of a nearby tree. For the first time her shoulders slump and she rubs a tired hand across her forehead. It might be the only honest emotion I've seen from her.

"Oh." I exhale loudly. "You didn't want that."

"It's my fault though," she says simply. "I dangled the carrot of my father's money in front of their eyes and that's all they saw. I told them he'd hidden away lots of gold and that it was theirs if they did what I wanted. And I wanted the Trustees scared. I wanted them to know that someone knew what they'd done. They'd live out the rest of their lives in terror. Their children could lose an ear for that. It wouldn't kill them. I didn't want those Trustees to know it was coming though. I had special envelopes made up. The kind people leave their cash in for donations. Checkers Children's Charity. Hah!" she scoffs. "I wanted their reaction when they opened up that envelope and saw that ear to be one of not only absolute fear but also complete shock. So I told the mercs that if any of the Trustees caught wind of what was going on before it happened, they'd get nothing. It didn't occur to me that they'd kill the Trustees' children to make doubly certain of secrecy."

And then when O'Shea inadvertently discovered the first

ear in the pocket of a one-night stand and stole it, all hell broke loose, I think to myself. The mercs were prepared to do anything to get their hands on Renfrew's hidden fortune. "Money," I say disgustedly. "That's what it boils down to. The Trustees killed your mother because they wanted your father's money. The mercs you hired tried to kill everyone because they wanted it too." I eye her suspiciously. "Why did you hire D'Argneau to get Creed and Wyatt off?"

Arbuckle shrugs. "The others were already dead or in Venezuela. I really don't understand why they came back from there. Still after more of my father's fortune, I suppose." I keep quiet at her words. "Creed and Wyatt, however, had managed to stay anonymous. They weren't going to quit. Not when they thought they could get all the money for themselves. I hired that lawyer because I knew he was good. He'd get them set free and then I could take care of them."

"By killing them."

"They weren't going to stop," she says, trying to explain, an odd pleading expression crossing her face. "Sooner or later they were going to do something that no barrister would be able to free them from. They would give up my name in exchange for time off their sentence and I'd end up being punished. And I really hadn't wanted anyone to die. Not when I started this anyway."

I think about this. "Bullshit," I finally answer. "If you'd said that to the mercs and made it clear there was more money in it for them if they didn't actually murder anyone, then they'd have stuck to that. I know you only hired Creed and Wyatt after the others failed so spectacularly. They weren't part of the original plan and they still committed murder. Even if you can't admit it to yourself, it's what you really wanted."

Arbuckle is silent for a long moment. "Maybe all of us are

lying to ourselves. We all want the people who hurt us to suffer."

I grip my pebble. "Most people don't act on those kind of thoughts though."

She regards me steadily. "You know, I misjudged you, Ms. Blackman. I thought when I sent you the gold, you'd back off."

"Money doesn't drive me."

"You could have used it to buy your little daemon friend a new car. I saw it you know. Out by the warehouse."

"You were there, weren't you? You met up with Creed and Wyatt before the police arrived and you took McIntosh's body and his ear."

For a brief second, there's a tiny smile playing around her lips. "I didn't want it to happen but there's still something satisfying about knowing that as far as Andrew McIntosh is concerned, his son is probably dead. He can't be sure though. He'll always have a bit of doubt. His son will always be missing. Just like my father."

"His ear?"

She shrugs. "I stuck it in the post. It's not ideal and someone else might get suspicious and open it before it gets to him. Under the circumstances, however, it's the best I could manage."

"All this for two people who you never really knew, even if they were your parents." I shake my head.

Arbuckle gives me a steady look. Her eyes are clear and guilt-free. "And the life I could have had."

"Does it make you feel better?" I ask, curiosity getting the better of me. "Hurting the Trustees, I mean. Is revenge sweet?"

She smiles. "Despite the path those idiot mercenaries took, it actually is. That's why I'm sorry I have to do this now."

I raise up an eyebrow. "Do what?"

Arbuckle reaches behind her back and calmly takes out a

gun, pointing it in my direction. "Kill you. You really shouldn't have involved yourself."

"I was involved when my friend was almost killed."

"But he wasn't. He survived and he'll get over it. My mother didn't. My father didn't."

"Except," I say, smiling back at her, "your father did survive."

Her smile falters ever so slightly. Then she sets her jaw. "Nice try. He's dead."

"No," I tell her. "He's not." I let her see the truth reflected in my face.

Confusion clouds her face. Then she sets her jaw. "He loved me. If he were alive, he'd have found me. I know that much."

"He thought you were dead, Colonel. Deutschner and the others thought your mother was pregnant. They hadn't realised she'd already given birth. When they killed her, they thought they were killing you too. A tiny foetus not even big enough to be visible. When Renfrew confronted them, they told him they'd killed Hope Havrington and her baby along with her. He believed them because they believed it. The only reason I knew you even existed is because I found a time orb after all. I made a bubble and used it at his mansion. I saw your nursery and your crib. No-one buys baby stuff and kits out a room when you're not even showing signs of pregnancy. It tempts fate."

Arbuckle blinks rapidly. "None of that means he's alive. He'd have made himself known to someone by now. It's been over fifty years for goodness sake!"

"Kill me and you'll never know." I shrug. "Your choice."

CHAPTER 19

LOOKING INTO THE ABYSS

It's little over an hour later when Arbuckle and I arrive outside the gates of the Black Market. I'm not ashamed to admit that I'm relieved to see that it's free this time of any dodgy black witches who might be hanging around at the front.

"If you're playing me for a fool, Blackman, I'll shoot you where I stand."

I give the Colonel an exasperated look. Considering that's what she'd been going to do anyway, I can't see why I should be scared of the threat now when I wasn't before. It's not an absolute given but I reckon I have a fairly good chance of avoiding being shot. I'm stronger and faster than she thinks.

"I'm telling you the truth. Come on. It's this way."

I lead her inside, weaving in and out of the stalls. We pass the creepy woman with her creepier snow globes. We ignore the purred sales pitches about spells and faked goods. I stroll along the narrow aisles as if I don't have a care in the world. Arbuckle marches like she's on sodding parade.

I find Merlin's embroidered tent quickly enough. Out of politeness, I step aside and gesture to Arbuckle to go ahead of me. She curls her lip, however, as if to indicate that she's not that much of a fool. I shrug and go in first. Sitting round a hubbly bubbly pipe are O'Shea, Connor and Merlin. I can't see the painting.

"Ms. Blackman!" Merlin coos. "Good to see you again. And who's your friend?"

O'Shea jumps to his feet when he spots Arbuckle, alarm across his features. "What's she doing here? We're not doing anything illegal this time! The army has no jurisdiction here!"

"Shh," I tell him. "It's okay. I'd like you to meet Tobias Renfrew's daughter."

Every single one of them looks shocked. Even Merlin's mouth drops open. He recovers quickly though, putting on a charming smile and holding out his hand. "Ms Renfrew. What a delight!"

Arbuckle eyes him as if he's a snake. When he doesn't react to her animosity, however, she begins to soften, disarmed no doubt by his brilliant grin. Sociopath or not, the man knows how to schmooze. "Call me Hope," she mutters.

I start slightly at her first name, although I should have guessed. Noting my reaction, she turns to me. "I'd have been called Tobias if I were a boy. My nanny changed my surname to keep me hidden but I'm proud to have my mother's name." There's a defiant tilt to her chin as if she's daring me to disagree.

I watch her as she nods in greeting to O'Shea and shakes hands with Connor. For all that she's done, I can't really think of her as an evil person. I understand how much the desire for revenge must have burned inside her. Her own secret desires aside, I think she probably did just hire the wrong people. Someone else with more honest intentions might have helped steer her onto a different path. She could still have gotten her revenge but it wouldn't have involved the death of innocents or out-and-out terrorism. Or even the severing of various ears.

"So," Arbuckle says, looking around the interior, "where exactly is my father then?"

Merlin lifts both his hands in the air with an overly dramatic flourish. "It's so obvious! I can't believe no-one noticed until now." He shakes his head. "Honestly!"

Arbuckle draws herself up, her demeanour returning to its typically glacial nature. "It's not obvious to me."

Merlin glances at me with a large, demonstrative wink. "Can I keep it? It'll go nicely with my other piece."

I fold my arms. "No. Bring the damn thing out." I narrow my eyes at Arbuckle. "You need to give me your gun first." I might think I have this situation under control but there's no telling what Arbuckle will do when she discovers the truth.

She frowns at me, obviously unwilling to let go of her weapon. When I harden my gaze, she seems to give in though, placing the gun on a nearby shelf. She still keeps her body angled so that I can't get to it without going through her first.

Both O'Shea and Connor are frowning at me. It takes O'Shea a moment, his gaze drifting to the painting still up on Merlin's wall, then to my face. It's pretty damn obvious when it hits him because his expression becomes almost comical shock. "No!"

I nod. "Yes."

Connor kicks him. "What?"

"The painting. Tobias Renfrew is in the fucking painting."

Arbuckle stiffens. "What the hell do you mean?"

Merlin reaches down behind the table and brings it up. "Here," he says. "Meet your father."

Even though I already knew the truth, I join the others in staring at it. His back is still turned. Unlike the figures in Merlin's other painting, who are staring out as if pleading for someone to help them, Renfrew doesn't seem to care.

"He must have done it to himself," I murmur. "Without

Hope and their child, he couldn't see any point in continuing. He trapped himself inside it."

Merlin purses his lips. "It's a theory," he says cheerfully.

"Daddy?" Arbuckle whispers in small, childish voice. I give her a surprised look. Across her face, disbelief is combined with desperate desire. She can't believe the little painted figure is him but she doesn't want to believe it's not.

"I don't get it," Connor says. "If things were that bad for him, then why didn't he just top himself? It'd be far less painful in the long run."

"Maybe he wanted to punish himself," I suggest. "He's the one who got involved with Checkers in the first place. Perhaps he thought it was his fault and he deserved to suffer."

"And he just happened to have that spell hanging around where he could get to it in a hurry?"

I drop my voice. "Maybe he had it on him because he was planning to use it on someone else."

O'Shea nods. "You're right. They changed his clothes, didn't they? The Trustees. They put him into an old tuxedo. The spell could have been in the pocket. He'd been going to use it on some other poor devil and changed his mind. And he never got around to getting rid of it."

We all look at Renfrew's back again. "Talk about your chickens coming home to roost," Connor says.

"Shut up!" Arbuckle shouts. "Just shut up! My father was not a bad man!"

"He was involved in the black market arms trade," I point out.

"Fuck you!" she spits. "What would you know about it?"

I'm tempted to tell her that I know his daughter has also incited terrorist activity. Instead, however, I keep my mouth wisely shut.

She snaps her hands out, grabbing Merlin by his collar and

yanking him forward until his face is inches away from hers. "How do we get him out? What do we do?"

The witch is not in the slightest bit fazed by Arbuckle's aggressive attitude. He raises his eyebrows at me. I take three steps back, almost tripping over a small wooden chest. I reach into my pocket and take out the pebble. I stare at it for a moment, then put it away again.

"Bo," O'Shea begins, dismay written all over his face.

"It's fine," I tell him. "it's absolutely fine. There's no doubt that Tobias Renfrew was responsible for a large number of criminal acts in his day, regardless of what the good Colonel wants to believe. He's been imprisoned for them. Maybe he deserved it."

Arbuckle spins round and punches me in the side of my head. I could have ducked but it seemed fairer to give her a chance to have her shot. At least she'll have that to think about when she's imprisoned also. There's an odd crunching sound. I think my cheekbone has fractured. She certainly packs a wallop.

I shake my head to rid myself of the searing pain and meet O'Shea's eyes. He tightens his lips and gives me an almost imperceptible nod. We both know it wasn't Tobias Renfrew I'd been talking about.

Merlin claps his hands together. He's probably glad that he wasn't the one on the receiving end of Arbuckle's fist. "As it just so happens," he beams with unbridled glee, "I do have a spell that's meant to release such captives." He holds up his index finger in caution. "I can't guarantee that it will work though."

I put my hand to my cheek and wince. Then I stare mean-ingfully at Arbuckle. If she does this, it has to be of her own free will. "Not every spell works," I say, while O'Shea sucks in a breath. "And some of them even have some very nasty side-effects."

She gives me a scornful look. "You just don't want him to be freed. It's been well over fifty years! He'll be an old man. He's not going to hurt a soul." She lifts up her chin and addresses Merlin. "Do it."

"It tends to work better when someone close to the subject performs the spell," he says amiably. He withdraws a wrapped scroll from his robe and passes it over. "Just read the words."

There's something sickening about the gleeful anticipation in his expression. I bite my bottom lip. I promised Rogu3 I'd punish the person ultimately responsible for the attack on him. Arbuckle's actions have caused a lot of deaths. She deserves to pay for them. Doubt gnaws at me though. Maybe she just doesn't deserve to pay for them like this. "Actually," I interject, "you shouldn't do this. The thing is..."

Arbuckle twists round and hits me again. This time I wasn't expecting it. She connects with my already broken cheekbone and I reel backwards. Both O'Shea and Connor dash to me while Arbuckle fumbles with the scroll, unwrapping it. She starts to chant.

"No!" I protest. "Don't..."

There's a flash of light and a strange crack as if of thunder. It's too late. She's already gone.

"Where the hell did she go?" Connor asks, utterly bewildered.

Merlin, O'Shea and I turn to the painting. There, next to the door of the little farmhouse, is a small uniformed figure. I squeeze my eyes shut.

"That's not ... but that can't be ... but ..." he stammers.

Nobody responds.

"You all knew this was going to happen." His voice is filled with disbelief.

I open my eyes and stare helplessly at him.

"Bo, you did that deliberately? How could you?"

I almost can't bear to see the pained disappointment in his expression. He looks at O'Shea. "You knew too?"

"Connor…" O'Shea puts a hand out to touch his shoulder but he yanks himself back.

"Is that we do now?" he yells. "We take revenge on people? What happened to due process?"

"She did it, Connor. She hired the mercenaries that attacked the Court and Rogu3. She's responsible for the deaths of the Trustees' children. She would have tried to kill me if I hadn't brought her here."

"That doesn't make it right!"

I avoid his horror-filled gaze. My phone beeps. Worried that it might be the hospital, I pull it out and read the message for a moment. Then I hold it out to Connor. "There," I say quietly. "The three bastards who hid themselves in Venezuela have just been released. Charges are still going ahead but even though they've already fled once, they've been granted bail. Harry D'Argneau did his job."

"That doesn't mean that she'd have gotten off," he says, wrapping his arms around himself and backing away as if fearful of what we'll do.

O'Shea tries again. "Connor, she knew there might be side effects. She knew…"

He whirls away. "That's bullshit and you know it! I thought you'd turned over a new leaf, Dev. I thought things were going to be different."

O'Shea opens his mouth to answer but it's too much for Connor. He throws up his hands in the air and pushes past me, shoving the folds of the tent's draped exit to one side as he departs.

"Now that," says Merlin, "is why I prefer canvas to solid wood." He shudders. "It's just so loud when people get annoyed and start slamming doors."

O'Shea and I give him mutual looks of loathing. The daemon turns to me, a pleading expression in his eyes.

"Go," I tell him. "Go after him." He virtually sprints out in Connor's wake.

Merlin knits his fingers together. "Are you sure I can't tempt you to sell me this?" He strokes the edge of the painting with one finger. "I'll give you a good price."

I pick it up. "No."

"What are you going to do with it?"

I consider. I should pass it over to Rogu3 but I don't want to infect him with its negativity. I'll simply let him know that the matter has been taken care of. "I'll put it back where it belongs," I say. At least Tobias and Hope will be at home as well as together.

Then I grab Arbuckle's gun from where she left it, tuck it under my waistband at my back, and walk out.

I'm just at the gates to the Black Market when my phone rings. It's Michael. Assuming he's calling to inform me of D'Argneau's deeds, I answer it.

"Hey," I say. "I already know. D'Argneau himself sent me a text."

"What?" He sounds baffled.

"Rogu3's attackers have been released on bail."

There's a moment of silence. "That's not why I'm calling."

Dread taps on my spine. I curl my fingers tighter round the phone and inhale. "Then what? My grandfather?" My voice rises to a screech. "Is it my grandfather?"

He sighs. "I'm just outside the hospital. They wouldn't let me call from your grandfather's room."

My mouth works. I try to find the words. "What?" It's barely audible.

"He's taken a turn for the worse."

"He's dying?" Sharp pain far worse than anything I'm feeling in my cheek wrenches at my heart. My knees buckle underneath me.

Michael doesn't answer my question directly. That almost makes it more ghastly. "Bo," he says softly, "he's slipped into a coma. His prognosis is ... not good."

Seconds stretch out. The night air feels as if it's closing in around me. I can't move. I can barely even breathe.

"Bo? Where are you? I'll come and pick you up."

"I'm going to kill her," I whisper.

"Pardon?"

I grit my teeth and raise my voice. "I said, I'm going to kill her."

"The lab results still aren't through. You don't know that it was her."

But I do know. I'm not sure how but I can feel it deep inside me. Dahlia poisoned him. Now she's going to pay.

"Thank you for telling me," I say dully.

"Bo, wait! Tell me where you are!"

I drop the phone and crunch it under my heel. Michael's voice can still be heard for half a second, a disembodied sound that's frantic and pleading. When the phone is finally silent, I get back up to my feet. Despite the leaps and bounds our relationship has made, it cuts me to the bone that he won't trust my instincts. I don't need him though. I can do this all on my own. I wobble unsteadily for a moment before I manage to gain control over my balance. I stumble forward, not even completely sure where I'm going. To get my bike, I suppose, and drive round to Arzo's place. With unfocused, unseeing eyes, I veer left and collide with another figure.

"I'm so sorry! So sorry! So sorry!"

I pull back, giving myself a shake. Unable to speak, I simply frown at the woman. Her smile is over-bright and her pupils are wide. She's definitely on something. Ecstasy or coke or whatever. Uncaring, I brush past her. It won't take me long to get to Dahlia once I'm driving.

Then I halt in my tracks. Slowly, I turn round and stare. The woman is wearing high heels and a short dress. It's hardly the sort of attire that's appropriate for somewhere as dodgy as the Black Market. I think of the characters within. If she's wearing that, then she's asking for trouble. She looks more like she's off out clubbing than anything else. She trips over nothing, her arms stretching out in amazingly perpendicular fashion to stop herself from falling. When she straightens back up, she glances over her shoulder.

"Hey, aren't you the Red Angel?"

I raise up a hand in acknowledgment. She beams. "I love vampires! And I love you! You're so heroic!" Her smile vanishes into a pout. "I wish I was that brave."

It's a struggle but I find my voice. "Where are you going?"

She brightens again. "To a party! D'ya wanna come?"

"Do you have friends there?"

"Lots and lots and lots."

"What's your name?

"Ellie." She frowns. "Actually, it's not. It's Fiona. But they call me Ellie." She winks at me. "It's short for El Cebo."

"That's Spanish for bait," I say sadly.

Fiona seems surprised. "Is it?"

"It is. Thanks for the invite. I love parties."

"The more the merrier!"

"Great," I tell her. I still don't smile though. "That's great."

CHAPTER 20

ON THE EDGE

The 'party' is more like an illegal underground rave than cocktails and canapés. It's located in an old warehouse not too far away from the Market. It's clear that the building has seen better days. Old posters advertising forgotten bands hang bedraggled from the exterior walls. Any windows that there are look either grubby or smashed in. It's a far cry from the nightclub where Bergman met his end.

There are about twenty people outside waiting to get in although, from the thump of music that I swear is reverberating through my heart, I can't imagine why they'd want to. Fiona, unsurprisingly walks right up to the front.

"Hey yay," she calls out.

I catch her arm just before she stumbles again. Both bouncers give me dark, unimpressed looks. "I'm with her," I tell them.

"No, you're not. I know who you are. There's no way you're with her."

I mull this over then shrug and lean over, standing on my tiptoes so my I can get closer to both of their box-shaped skulls. "If you know who I am," I murmur, "then you'll know that it's a really bad idea to piss me off. To borrow a line, you wouldn't like me when I'm angry."

They throw each other doubtful glances.

"Oh, come on, boys," I purr, "if I can take out a Kakos daemon, do you really think that the two of you are going to cause my any bother?"

The burlier one to my left looks over my head to the next person waiting. "Do you have an invitation," he asks?

I grimace unpleasantly and walk in behind Fiona. That was just too sodding easy.

Inside is rammed. I'm taken aback at the amount of people writhing around. Strobe lights arc over their heads and there's the distinct aroma of stale pot in the air. At least the music, if that's what it can be called, doesn't appear to be any louder inside than it was outside. Realising that Fiona is already heading off to the far side, I quickly dash after her, squeezing my way between the dancers. None of them even register my presence; they're more concerned with what's tripping inside in their own heads than who's tripping over them.

The one good thing about all of this is that Fiona doesn't appear quite as drugged up as the woman who'd died in the alley does. I guess the guys who'd been manipulating Bergman haven't quite tired of her yet. Whatever's in her system isn't lethal. Not tonight anyway. She swings her hips in time to the beat and raises her hands above her head, swaying them alongside a hundred others. It's only when she reaches a small set of stairs leading up to a low lying balcony that she drops them.

There's another bouncer guarding the staircase. He moves to let her past, then returns to his original position. I watch her wobble up then stand in front of him and gave him a little wave. He frowns at me in confusion, as if he's sure he's seen me somewhere before but he just can't place where. I grin and put my hands on his shoulders. He's a bit of brute and it's not particularly comfortable for someone of my height. It's going to be less comfortable for him, however. The moment his eyes widen as he finally realises who I am, I knee him in the groin. He doubles over and I smash down onto his solar plexus. He collapses. I dust off my palms and wander up.

It's barely been a few seconds but Fiona is already wrapped around a vampire. He's wearing the red of the Medici Family and, although I don't recognise him, I'm tempted to leave him to the consequences. It wouldn't be fair on her though. An alert had gone out after what had happened with Bergman but with Medici's position out in the cold, it's possible they didn't receive it.

I lift up the corners of my mouth in the vague semblance of a smile as the two human guys from the alleyway – the very ones responsible for Bergman Stuart's death – turn to me and gape. The nearest one recovers the fastest, throwing his glass in my direction. I dodge it with ease. Waste of a good drink.

"We meet again," I say.

They leap to their feet. Tweedledum reaches inside his suit jacket and takes out a stake. The Medici vampire pulls his fangs away from Fiona, sending a spray of her blood across the table. "What the hell are you doing with one of those?" he asks.

Everyone ignores him. Tweedledee lunges for me. I grab his arm and pull it behind his back, spinning him just in time for Tweedledum's stake to end up lodged in his shoulder. He screams. Several members of the dancing crowd below hear him and scream back in delight, assuming it's all part of the fun. I snatch his collar and fling him into the nearest wall. He slumps down in an ungainly heap. One down.

Tweedledee, now apparently weaponless, is utterly terri-fied. He points to me with a shaky finger. "Kill her," he says to the Medici vamp. "Kill her now."

The bloodguzzler eyes me. He's obviously older than I am –

and therefore a damn sight more powerful. I've got reputation on my side, which might aid my cause. I'd rather not get into with him if I can help it though.

"I'm not here for you," I shout. "I just want him."

He stands up, wavering ever so slightly. Of course. The drugs in Fiona's system are already affecting him. Perhaps this will be easier than I thought.

He flicks a glance at Tweedledee. "Sorry, mate. She's off limits. Orders of the boss."

My nose wrinkles. Why would Medici want me unharmed? Before I can ask the guzzler, however, he pushes past me and stumbles down the stairs, disappearing into the crowd. I could go after him but he's not the reason for this diversion. I turn my attention back to the human.

"I guess you're all on your own," I comment lightly. "Unless you want Fiona here to be your bodyguard."

His brow furrows. "Who?"

"He calls me Ellie," she reminds me helpfully.

Oh yes. Because she's the bait. I step towards him. "People say a lot about the vampires, you know. That they only care about their own Families and will throw anyone else to the dogs. You, however, will use your own kind to get what you want."

"I ... I ... don't know what you mean," he stammers.

"Yes, you do." I lick my lips and allow my fangs to lengthen. He flinches. "She's drugged so you could drug the vampire. It wasn't the smartest move to make. Bloodguzzlers don't tend to be particularly amiable creatures when someone threatens them."

"Fuck you!"

I raise my eyebrows. "Is that the best you can do? Really?" I sigh and tut. Then I whirl round, pick up the chair to my left and spin again, slamming it against his head. His jaw goes slack and he collapses. "Swearing is so uncouth," I tell his prostate form.

Fiona stares at me. She doesn't look particularly afraid, no doubt as a result of her drug-induced haze. She's still very aware of what's going on though. "Are you going to kill me?" she asks.

I shake my head. "No. I'm going to ask you for a favour."

She gives me a puzzled frown while I turn my attention back to the two unconscious humans. I suppose I should call Foxworthy. It would be the right thing to do.

I take out my phone and find the number I need. When someone answers, I speak with unhurried brusqueness. "This is the Red Angel. Put me through to Lord Stuart."

There's a fuzzy silence, followed by a click. Excellent.

Stuart's voice fills the line. "What's going on?" Even with his booming tones, however, it's difficult to hear him. I stick one finger in my ear to block out the worst of the thumping music.

"I'm at a warehouse near the Black Market," I tell him. I prod Tweedledee with my toe. "I have two people here who would hate to make your acquaintance."

"Who?" he growls.

"Do you remember Bergman?"

Lord Stuart hisses. "Give me your exact location."

"I want something in return."

"Name it."

"Make sure Arzo is occupied and bring his girlfriend to the New Order office," I instruct. "Immediately."

"Arzo? The wheelchair Sanguine?"

"That's the one."

"Done," he snaps.

I give him the exact address then hang up. I glance at Fiona. "You're a vampette?"

"Uh huh."

"Those men gave you drugs," I tell her. "They'd probably have ended up killing you sooner or later."

From her expression, I reckon my words have penetrated her drugged brain. "Maybe being a vampette isn't for you," I say gently. "But before you think about giving it up, I'd like you to help me out with someone else. Another vampire." I hold up my hands in a gesture of friendliness. "You don't have to though. If you want to leave I won't stop you, I promise."

She wobbles up to her feet. There's still a smear of blood at her throat and the two puncture wounds from the Medici vamp are very visible. I think she's going to refuse but she tilts up her chin and meets my eyes. "Okay."

"You're sure?"

She bites her lip and nods.

I acknowledge her agreement but I don't smile. "Come on then," I say, holding out my hand. "I hope you don't mind motorbikes."

I LET Kimchi out when we get back. He's excited to see me but he sniffs cautiously at Fiona then keeps his distance from her. Sometimes he's a smarter dog than he lets on. She perches on a nearby desk.

"Are we waiting for someone?"

I start to nod, just as the door opens. Dahlia's head appears, flanked by two Stuart vampires. "Thank you," I tell them politely. "You may go now."

They exchange looks. I'm not entirely sure what orders Lord Stuart has given them but, happily for me, they've decided to do as I ask. They both give me small bows and hastily depart.

I focus on Dahlia. She's perfectly made-up, not a hair out of place and not a blemish showing. I can only imagine that the little black dress she's wearing was for Arzo's benefit. It's certainly not for mine.

I take a deep breath. "I'm sorry for bringing you all the way out here."

"They wanted Arzo first." She meets my eyes. "He's already at the hospital though. He's been there for hours." What she leaves unspoken is, of course, the question of why I'm not there too.

"Mm," I murmur non-committedly. "I'll see him there later. I thought it was important to do this first though."

Kimchi growls, making Fiona jump. I shush him.

"Who's that?" Dahlia asks, addressing only me.

"A peace offering."

She jerks as if in surprise. "For what?"

"For accusing you of poisoning my grandfather." I keep my voice level and calm. "It wasn't fair of me. You've been trying really hard to get on with me and I threw all your efforts back in your face. I was ... hurting. And panicked." I undo my ponytail and run my hand through my hair. "I don't know what I'm going to do without him."

She steps over to me and puts her hand on my arm. I manage not to flinch but it's sodding hard. "He might pull through. Even if he doesn't, you'll be surprised at where you can draw strength from. You'll cope."

"Thank you. You're being very gracious."

Fiona drops the paperweight she'd been idly toying with. It smashes to the ground, splintering everywhere. Oblivious to my conversation with Dahlia, she looks at me guiltily. "Oops."

Dahlia frowns. "Is she alright?"

"She's been drinking," I say smoothly. "I bet you've not tried drinking from someone with alcohol in their system. It gives you a hell of a buzz."

"That's why you brought her here?"

I shrug. "She was keen to come along. She's a friend of mine and I thought you might be hungry."

Fiona provides us with a happy smile. "I'm a vampette," she announces.

"You didn't have to do that, Bo."

"I know," I answer. "But I wanted to."

I hold my breath as Dahlia steps over to her. "Nice skin," she comments, talking directly to Fiona for the first time.

Fiona smiles dreamily, stretching out her neck. Dahlia doesn't waste another moment. Her eyes meet mine as she sinks her teeth into her flesh. She drinks hungrily. I watch her, ready to stop her if I think she's taking too much. She pulls away long before that though, dabbing at her mouth. "She certainly has an interesting taste," Dahlia muses. "Almost like wine."

If I'd felt any guilt about what I was doing, it vanishes with Dahlia's apparent insistence on treating Fiona like she's nothing more than an object. Even after guzzling her blood, she still won't acknowledge her as another person. It's simply rude. I make a point of finding a napkin and passing it over for Fiona to press against her neck. She smiles at me gratefully.

The office door bangs open and Matt appears. His hair is ruffled and he appears remarkably irritated. "Bloody hell, Bo!" he exclaims when he spots me. "You could have told me you didn't need me to watch those people any more!"

I belatedly realise that he's referring to the Brownslows. Either Connor or O'Shea must have given him the all clear. "Sorry."

He grumbles under his breath although his expression lightens when sees Fiona. "Hello. Who are you?"

Fiona simply smiles again and offers him her neck. He starts forward but I clear my throat. "Actually, she's already lost quite a lot of blood tonight. Dahlia was her last. It's probably better to leave her be for now."

Matt's bottom lip juts out. "I've been with that freaking family and their non-stop chatter for hours. I'm hungry."

I try to soothe him. "Maybe you should head back to the mansion then and pick up a vampette there. In fact, you could drop Fiona off on your way."

"I live in Wandsworth," she tells us, attempting to be helpful.

I wince. That's miles away from the Montserrat mansion where Matt stays. He looks at me incredulously. "You have to be kidding me."

"Go."

He struggles with the order. I can see it written all across his face. There's enough still lingering from the old enhancement spell to make him do my bidding, however I reckon that before the week is out, he'll be a completely changed man. Good for him.

Dahlia's nose wrinkles as Matt and Fiona both leave. "She still had a lot of blood left in her."

"If he took any more from her, she'd have been feeling weak for days. It's better this way."

She raises up one shoulder. "I guess you're the expert. You've been a vampire for longer than I have."

I try to laugh. "Not much longer. How are you feeling anyway? Are you alright?"

"I'm fine. Worried about your grandfather, of course."

"Of course."

She licks her lips. "I'm also really thirsty. It must be the alcohol effect. Some water will help."

I don't want her to start diluting the drugs before they even begin to work. "Before you do," I stall, "I wanted to see how things were going with Arzo. I care a lot about him, you know."

"I do." She nods. "He cares a lot about you too."

She stands up to walk through to the tiny kitchen. I get up and bar her way, attempting to not be too obvious about it. "Is he really mad?" I ask. "You know, because I accused you of … that stuff."

"He'll get over it. He's like that. It's so easy to twist him round your finger. He might be Sanguine but his spine's not any stronger than it was when I knew him as a human." She blinks, as if surprised at her own words.

"So you think he's weak?" I prod, my stomach tightening as it becomes more obvious that the drugs are already starting to work.

"Yes." She slurs the word. "Like most men."

"Is Medici weak?"

There's a flash of fear across her face. "No. He's not." She shakes her head emphatically. "He's definitely not weak at all." At least we agree on something. I'm about to ask her another question, in order to test just how far gone she is, when she speaks again. "He's going to make me strong too. He promised."

My body tenses. "Medici is going to make you strong?"

She nods.

"Why is he going to make you strong, Dahlia?"

"Because I've done everything he asked."

"Did he ask you to hurt my grandfather?"

"No."

Damn it.

She's not finished though. "He asked me to murder him."

I stop breathing. Even though I'd believed it deep in my core, it still stuns me to hear her say it out loud.

"So you poisoned him?"

"I did." She looks at me anxiously. "He is going to die, isn't he? Lord Medici won't be happy if he lives."

I launch myself at her, wrapping my hands around her

throat. "I knew it!" I spit. 'I knew you'd done it all along. You've playing every single one of us!"

Her eyes bulge and she scrabbles at my fingers. There's a croaking sound as she tries to gulp for air. I tighten my grip. Tears squeeze out from her eyes and her legs start to thrash around. I stare into her reddening face. I want to see her die.

Kimchi whines. He pads up next to me and licks my arm. It's a tentative movement rather his usual exuberant slobber. I rip my eyes away from Dahlia to check on him. He whines again.

"Go away, Kimchi!" I order.

He lifts one paw and places it on my knee.

"Kimchi…" I curse and release Dahlia. She crawls backwards, hugging herself and staring at me in horror.

"Why?" she whispers, barely able to speak. "Why would you do that?"

I pass a hand across my forehead. "If you have to ask that," I say tiredly, "then you're not as smart as I thought you were." I stand up. "Come on, Kimchi. Let's get out of here." He barks, nudging me with his wet nose. "You're a good dog," I tell him. I leave Dahlia where she is and walk out, my shoulders slumped and my body heavy.

Kimchi and I shuffle down the street. He keeps throwing me anxious looks, as if he's afraid I'm going to run back and finish the job. Instead I just fondle his ears. There's a faint rain falling, cooling the night even further. Washing away all our sins. When we reach the small park several streets away, I let him off the lead. For a moment he doesn't move. He stays by my side. I give him a gentle push and his tail thumps. He takes off racing round after invisible rabbits.

I reach into my pocket and pull out my little white pebble. I examine it. It's a silly thing really. I lift it up and clutch it against my chest. Another tear leaks out. Then another and another. I sit myself down a nearby swing and gently rock myself up and down. The familiar, child-like movement helps. When I finally think I have control of myself again, I tuck the pebble carefully away.

"You're alright, Bo," I say to myself. "You're still alright." Barely.

Kimchi lopes up. His tongue lolls out in what I can only imagine is some kind of doggy relief. "Let's go back," I say. "I need to get to the hospital and I'm pretty sure they're not going to let you in." I stroke his coat. "Even if you do eat all my clothes and all my furniture, you're pretty much the best dog in the world." He barks again and I hush him, placing a finger to my mouth. "Normal people are sleeping. Let's be considerate." I smile at him, probably the first genuine one that I've given for hours. Then the pair of us leave for home.

CHAPTER 21
THE END

Before we even turn the corner into our street, I know something is wrong. I can't put my finger on it exactly, but there's an uncomfortable prickle dancing down my spine. Kimchi growls. I press myself against the grime covered wall and peer round.

There are two figures standing in the middle of the street, gesticulating angrily at each other. Dahlia and her Lord.

The fact that Medici has taken it upon himself to blow her cover by appearing like this can only mean thing. I'm not going to let that happen. If I'm not going to kill her, then no-one else is either.

I loop Kimchi's lead round a nearby lamp post. He whines, his large brown eyes looking at me with hurt.

"Sorry, buster," I whisper. "I don't want you to get hurt." I pat his head and emerge out, foregoing the pavement for strolling down the centre of the road. Dahlia continues to wave her arms around in the air but Medici twists round to watch my approach.

"The Red Angel," he says, as soon as I'm close enough.

"Have you come to rescue this poor little flower?" He raises a single thin eyebrow at me.

"You're not welcome here."

He throws back his head and laughs. "This is a public place. You can't stop me from walking down the street, Ms. Blackman."

"Bo!" Dahlia shrieks. "You have to do something! He's going to hurt me!"

We both ignore her. "Last chance, Medici. Get your bony arse out of here."

He runs his tongue across his gleaming white fangs. "Or what?"

"Just leave."

He takes a step towards me, obvious amusement lighting his expression. "No."

I rush him, head down and fists out. He's too fast though. The only thing I manage to head butt is air.

Medici tsks. "You brought down a Kakos daemon. I'd have thought you'd be faster."

I growl and try again, using the bonnet of a car as traction to leap off. This time I have more success, scissoring my legs round his neck. He grabs onto my calves and turns his head, his teeth sinking into my thigh. I howl and he throws me off.

Rolling back to my feet, I confront him once more. "Do you really think you're going to get away with all of this?" I ask. "With opening up recruitment? Breaking away from the other Families?"

"My dear Bo. I already have."

I swipe out a punch, catching the edge of his jaw. He reels back.

"Everyone's against you, Medici. All four Families. They'll stop you dead in your tracks."

He makes a show of looking up and down the street. "I don't see any of them here."

I kick out, aiming for his chest. He grabs my foot and twists, causing me to crash back down to the hard tarmac again. Leaning over me, he gives me a curious look. "How did you do it?" he inquires. "How did you kill that daemon? You're as weak as a kitten."

I snarl and snatch his lapels in both hands, rising up and slamming my forehead against his. He curses and falls back, stumbling.

I leap to my feet. "I'm just getting warmed up."

Medici sighs and straightens up. He inspects his fingernails. "You must have gotten lucky," he decides. "Because the reality is that you're still nothing more than a wimpy little fledgling." A slow smile spreads across his face. "Imagine the look on your darling Michael's face when he learns that I've ripped your head clean off your shoulders."

"I'd like to see you try," I spit.

He shrugs and drops his hand. "Very well then."

Before I can even blink, he smashes out a punch, connecting with my already shattered and only just slightly healing cheekbone. I scream in agony. Then he takes my shoulders, spins me round and pulls me back against him, holding my head in both hands. "The sad thing," he whispers in my ear, "is that you won't be around to see it."

I gulp in a breath. "And here was me thinking that you rather liked me. After all, you did tell your Medici goons to leave me alone."

He laughs. "That was when I thought that stupid woman was going to be of some use." He tilts my head up towards Dahlia who is barely able to stand up. She's clutching onto a postbox and staring at us wide-eyed. "Unfortunately, she's as much of a waste of space as you are."

I take advantage of the moment and drop to my knees, bringing Medici down with me and forcing him onto his back. A second later, I pinion his torso with my legs and snarl down. "Not quite so much a waste of space now, am I?"

I don't have much time. For all my fine words, there's no denying that Medici is far, far stronger than I am. The only way I can win this is by surprising him. Before he can free himself, I feint with my right hand. With my left I pull out Arbuckle's gun from where it's stuffed in the back of my waistband. I squeeze the trigger just as Dahlia flings herself at me and throws me off. The shot goes wide.

"What the fuck are you doing?" I yell. "He's going to kill you! I'm trying to help!"

Her knees wobble and she collapses in a heap. Her face is white and she stares helplessly at me. I curse to myself. She really is loyal to Medici.

He starts to laugh again, getting to his feet. He throws his arms out. "You see? Everyone loves me."

I shoot again but I've missed my chance. In a blur of movement, Medici launches at me, grabbing my wrist and forcing me to drop the weapon. In fluid movement he picks it up and presses the barrel against my forehead. "Such a shame," he coos.

I grit my teeth. "Do it."

Medici shrugs. "Alright."

I squeeze my eyes shut. There's a deafening crack as the gun goes off again. There's no pain, however – other than the continued throb in my cheek. Oblivion doesn't come either. I open my eyes again. Medici grins and waves the gun over to the side. I track it with my gaze. Shit in a hell basket. Dahlia is lying flat on her stomach, with only her head twisted to the side. Her eyes are wide and unseeing.

"You know," Medici comments, "most vampires can escape

gunshots easily enough. You fledglings, however..." he shakes his head. "You're just not fast enough."

"Why?" I gasp. "Why kill her?"

His eyes narrow. "She failed me." He reaches into his jacket pocket and takes out a handkerchief, methodically wiping it down. Then he takes my hand and places my index finger against the trigger. I try to pull it so I can still shoot him, but his grip is too strong. "I was going to kill you too," he says. "I really was. But now I think it'll be more fun to see you try to wriggle your way out when the rest of your little New Order buddies think you murdered her in cold blood." His lips curl into a nasty smile. "I need some light-hearted relief." He throws the gun to the side. I look at it helplessly. It's too far away for me to reach.

"If you let me go, you know I'll come after you again!" I shout, trying to goad him into making another mistake. It's literally all I have left.

"And I'll beat you again," he says. "Because I will always be stronger than you."

"They won't believe I killed her!" I say desperately. "I'm not a murderer."

"You and I both know that's not true."

I stare into his eyes. For a brief fearful moment it strikes me that perhaps Medici understands me better than almost anyone else in the world.

He laughs again, his eyes focusing on something in the distance. "It seems I'm not the only person who's after your blood, Ms. Blackman. I'd like to stick around but I have things to do. I'll leave you to him."

Medici moves so fast, leaving the street in an instant, that I barely have time to do more than gape after him. Then I slowly turn round to see who else has decided to show up. It's even worse than I imagined. It's the black witch from the Black Market. And he's not alone.

"You really are a popular lady," he crows, holding Connor's helpless body out in front of him. "I'm glad now that I was patient when I saw you again at the Market. It's much more fun this way. First I get to grab your snivelling little friend running out in a blind panic, then I get to watch you get your face smashed in by another bloodguzzler."

The puddles reflect the silver moonlight, giving off an eerie light that adds to the dangerous atmosphere. I take a step towards the witch.

"Let him go," I call out in a clear and steady voice that belies everything that's just happened.

His grip on Connor's throat merely tightens. "I don't think I will, Ms. Blackman."

"He's got nothing to do with you."

The witch laughs. There's a maniacal edge to it that sends a ripple of fear through me. I'm starting to think that I'm not going to be able to reason with him. "And Eric Kent had nothing to do with you?"

I shake my head, confused. "Who?"

"You've already forgotten?" he hisses. "Your arrogance knows no bounds."

I bite my lip. "The black witch you were threatening," I say, remembering the trembling witch who'd been cowering at his feet in front of the Black Market all those nights ago. He can't mean anyone else.

"I wasn't threatening him. He was part of my coven and I was showing him the discipline he required to stay in line. Then you got involved and fucked everything up. Do you realise how weak you made me look?"

"You involved me," I yell. "You called *me* out."

"You were supposed to turn tail and walk away. You think you're so special because you're the flavour of the moment. The Red Angel," he scoffs. "The darling of the country. Our bloodguzzling saviour. Well, I'm going to give the public something else to think about," he snarls.

There's a sickening sensation in my stomach as I realise what he's about to do. Connor's face turns to mine, his freckles standing out in stark relief against his pale skin and his blues eyes filled with panic and fear. "I'm sorry, Bo," he whispers. "I'm so so sorry."

I stare at the witch. "If you do this, I will kill you. I will rip you from limb to limb."

He cocks his head, his dark tattoo pulsating in his cheek. "Bring it on." Then he snaps Connor's throat.

I let out an inarticulate scream and rush forward. The witch drops Connor's limp body and raises up his palms. A stream of dark magic flashes out towards me. I drop to the ground to avoid it, rolling out of the way and springing back to my feet. I barrel towards the witch, knocking into him and slamming his body backwards. He lets out a harsh cackle.

I grab a tuft of his hair and pull it upwards before thrusting down as hard as I can, knocking the back of his head against the ground. He grunts in pain but he's still very much conscious. He jerks his forehead upwards, headbutting me. I fall back, little lights dancing in front of my eyes. Another jet of magic launches out from his fingertips, this time crashing into my shoulder. The pain is searing. My arm turns to ice, falling useless and limp by my side. I can feel the cold spell spreading downwards, coursing through my veins. It won't be long before it reaches my heart.

The look on the witch's face is one of smug self-satisfaction. "You're not all that," he spits.

He's right – I'm really not. I let Dahlia die. I let Connor die. I let Medici walk away without so much as a limp. But I'm not entirely useless. I let myself drop to my knees.

"I'm going to end you," the witch tells me with a smile.

"No," I say sadly, "you're not." I reach down to where the discarded gun lies. In one swift movement, I raise up the barrel and fire. There's no-one around this time to knock off my aim.

The force of the recoil sends me flying and I land sprawled on my back. Struggling, I prop myself up on one elbow. The witch is on his knees, his hands clasped to his heart. He seems stupefied. A tiny bubble of blood appears on his lips. "You shot me," he gasps. "That's so ... human." His eyes roll back in his head and he collapses.

Barely able to stand up, I half stumble, half crawl over to him and check his pulse. He's gone. I lurch towards Connor's body and cup his face in my hands. There aren't any words though. There's nothing that's going to make this any better. Connor's dead.

I'M NOT sure how long I lie there for, one arm wrapped over Connor's chest. Some instinct tells me I should be keeping him company. I can't leave him like this. The ice of the witch's spell has affected my entire left side, attacking my system like a stroke. I don't care. I just stay there, uselessly clutching Connor as if I can make him return from the grave. Somehow I'm not surprised when a shadow appears, blocking the bright moon from my view, and X's face swims down towards me.

"What kind of a world do we live in, Bo, where innocent children are slaughtered in the street?"

I don't answer him.

He gently takes my arm and hauls me upwards. I realise Kimchi is by his side, watching me with anxious eyes.

"Well?" X inquires.

I don't speak. I don't even nod. He already knows my answer.

"You won't regret it," he tells me.

I muster up just enough energy to reach back inside my pocket once more. I squeeze the stone hard and feel the pain of unshed tears build in my chest. Then I take it out and let it drop. It clatters to the ground, bouncing a few times before resting next to the witch's head. I don't bother turning my head to look at it; I simply allow X to help me stumble away. I don't even look back when I hear the squeal of tyres and another car pull up. A door opens and Michael's voice yells out my name. It's all far too late though. At least Connor will be taken care of though.

EPILOGUE

The three men are sitting at a small table in the corner. The stools are too small for their bodies and they all are forced to hunch over to pick up their drinks. The sight might be comical to some but I'm not smiling. I watch them in the mirror. They're so busy congratulating themselves that they don't even notice me. Idiots. I might be wearing a baseball cap and dark glasses to hide but it's a weak disguise. They really should be paying more attention.

I sip my Coke and wait.

When they eventually stagger up to their feet and leave, their table a mess of empty glasses and crisp packets, I drain my drink and leave. It's late enough that the street outside is empty. Not that I particularly care either way. This is happening whether there are witnesses or not.

I walk behind them, listening to their boisterous chatter.

"The money must be somewhere. We just need to be patient."

"Yeah. I'm looking forward to a few daemon billions."

I reach out and tap the nearest one on the back. His head

turns. I grab his hair and sink my teeth into his throat. Blood spatters out as I rupture his jugular. He collapses.

The other two come at me from both sides. I leap up and somersault, landing away from them. The first one trips over his buddy's body. The second one recovers more quickly, spinning round to come at me again. I adjust my cuffs and two springloaded daggers burst out. It takes one swipe to slit his throat. Then I step over to the last one. It's the chatty one who spilled the beans in the first place. I take off my cap and shake out my hair, then carefully remove my glasses and place them in my pocket. He blinks up at me.

"It's you."

I gaze down at him. "Hi there."

"You don't want to do this. You didn't want to hurt us before. Why now?"

I continue to watch him, cocking my head to one side as if I'm taking his question seriously. Eventually I shrug. "I changed my mind." I bend down and do what needs to be done. It doesn't take long.

About the Author

After teaching English literature in the UK, Japan and Malaysia, Helen Harper left behind the world of education following the worldwide success of her Blood Destiny series of books. She is a professional member of the Alliance of Independent Authors and writes full time, thanking her lucky stars every day that's she lucky enough to do so!

Helen has always been a book lover, devouring science fiction and fantasy tales when she was a child growing up in Scotland.

She currently lives in Edinburgh in the UK with far too many cats – not to mention the dragons, fairies, demons, wizards and vampires that seem to keep appearing from nowhere.